A Secret War

JACKIE SHARP

Book Cover by V.H Nicholson

Edited by The Word Emporium.

First edition 2024

ISBN 978-1-9992578-5-9 (Paperback)

ISBN 978-1-9992578-7-3 (Hardback)

ISBN 978-1-9992578-6-6 (Electronic)

An Irish Blessing

May the road rise to meet you
May the wind be at your back
May the sun shine warm upon your face,
The rains fall soft upon your fields,
And until we meet again,
May God hold you in the palm of His hand.

Contents

Prologue

DUBLIN. NOVEMBER 20, 1920

It was raining. Not the usual damp drizzle that hung in the air and seeped into the fabric of daily life in Dublin, especially in November, but cold hard shards of rain, which stung Maggie's cheeks as she ran so fast her lungs burned.

Fear propelled her along, keeping her upright as her boots splashed through puddles and her skirt dragged in the mud. It was early and dark, but she could navigate the muddy track from the cluster of stone cottages to the cobbled streets of Dublin with her eyes closed. One of those stone cottages had been her home since she was six years old, and she'd walked the track with Aunt Peg thousands of times, and then, when Uncle Ryan had insisted she earn her keep, she'd cycled that way to work, six days a week, and once again on Sunday to attend Mass.

She dared not slow down or look back. Every second she expected to hear a shot ring out, to feel the pain of a bullet strike her, and it was only after she'd been running for a while, that she realised she was probably out of range, even for Sean's rifle.

She'd seen the rifle propped up in the kitchen. Sean would not hesitate to use it, even though Maggie was kin. Kin didn't matter to Sean anymore, just The Cause. Not that Sean needed a reason to use that rifle. A bolt-action Lee-Enfield, stolen from the British, right from under their bloody noses, Sean proclaimed. He had a pistol too. She couldn't remember what kind it was, but this one had been smuggled in from America, or so Sean said.

The pistol had been on the kitchen table this morning.

Maggie had seen both weapons—Sean's prize possessions—from the glow of the kerosene lamp which had been burning all night because both Maggie and her Auntie Peg hadn't stopped to extinguish the flame before they fled upstairs in terror to wait for Uncle Ryan and Sean to pass out from the drink, after what Sean had done to poor Mrs Doherty..

This morning, Maggie had concentrated on avoiding the creaky floor-boards as she edged around the table. She didn't want to wake Uncle Ryan, who was sleeping off the booze from the night before, his head on the table and his arms hanging loosely beside him.

But Maggie had to look at the pistol. She and Aunt Peg had huddled in Maggie's bed and finally dozed off when the shouting stopped the previous night. Then, when Maggie woke, for the first dream-like seconds between sleep and waking, she believed she must have imagined it all, the memories of the previous night almost too disturbing to think about. But one look at the terror still etched on her sleeping Aunt's face, and the chair she'd jammed under the door handle, in the hope it would keep them safe, she knew everything she'd witnessed and everything she'd heard was all real. And she had to leave now if she was to prevent more killing, even if she could only save one man.

The pistol, smeared with blood and tissue from poor, murdered Mrs Doherty, discarded on the kitchen table with empty bottles was further evidence that this was no dream. Although this had made Maggie sick to her stomach with fear, she had known she only had one chance to get out of there.

Sean was an early riser. Although she'd heard his snoring as she crept down the stairs, she knew this morning especially, he would not be late.

Maggie's pace slowed slightly. The rain blinded her and her breath was coming in raspy gasps. She'd glanced at her bicycle as she was leaving the house, propped up against the gate, but discarded that thought immediately. The squeaking from the unoiled chain was too much of a risk. And if Uncle Ryan and Sean noticed the bicycle, they might not check to see if she was still there. It might give her a few more minutes.

Eventually, they would know. And they would come hunting for her. She used her terror to keep her moving.

Soon it would be time for Sunday morning Mass. She had to hurry. The plan would go into effect just as the righteous filed into church. As hymns soared into the rafters, as the priest gave the blessing, the slaughter would happen. Sean was always loose-lipped after a few whiskys, and last night, pumped full of anger and bloodlust and alcohol, roaring about ridding Ireland of traitors and oppressors, Maggie had stood trembling in the bedroom as the details of the murders planned for this morning came tumbling out of Sean's mouth, in between drunken rants and revolutionary songs.

While everyone was at Mass, praying for God to absolve them of their sins, blood would spill like a crimson river.

With that image in her mind, Maggie wiped the rain off her face, lifted her skirt higher, and forced her legs to move as fast as they could.

The streets of Dublin city were still quiet as Maggie staggered slightly on the slippery cobbles, as she tried to move quickly through the narrow streets until she arrived at the boarding house on Mountjoy Street.

The door was propped open. Maggie hesitated before pushing it and stepping into the musty hallway. Did a tenant leave the door unlocked last night? Or was this part of the plan? Sean's men were all over the city, sometimes in the shadows, sometimes the buskers stomping their feet in time to their accordions or fiddles. Nobody knew who was watching.

Too late now, Maggie said to herself. Right up until she stepped through the door, she could have changed her mind. She could have turned south towards the River Liffey and then to the church on Arran Quay. And now she was here at the boarding house... what if he didn't believe her? Why would he? She was just the maid, paid to pick up after him and clean his room. And what a sight she must be now; her hair plastered to her head from the rain and covered in mud. What if he laughed at her, or worse, called the DMP, the British police force?

But she'd promised Aunt Peggy. Poor Auntie Peggy, who had taken her in; the only time she'd stood her ground to her brutal husband in order to care for her only sibling's daughter after she died in childbirth, leaving Maggie all alone in the world.

Maggie closed her eyes for a moment and covered her mouth to stop her sobs escaping as her mind flashed back to the night before. Sean dragging Mrs Doherty into the street from the cottage next door by her wispy grey hair, her screaming and crying as her skinny white legs and bare feet turned blue with cold as Sean bellowed his accusations of treachery in her face. Then the scene slowed as Maggie and Aunt Peggy, forced to watch from their front door by Uncle Ryan, opened their mouths to scream as Sean raised his pistol, held it against Mrs Doherty's temple, and pulled the trigger.

The image was all too much, and Maggie had tried to close her eyes. "Don't you look away," Uncle Ryan spat, as Sean's face blurred into a red mass from the splatter of blood and Mrs Doherty's lifeless body dropped into the mud. "Don't you look away," he yelled again. "You take heed of what we do to traitors."

Maggie held Aunt Peggy in her arms for the last time, and the frail woman made her promise to leave and never come back.

"Go n-éirí an bóthar leat, a stór," were the last words Aunt Peg said to her before Maggie made her escape.

May the road rise to meet you, my darling.

And here she was. There was no going back now. Maggie went through the door and bolted it behind her.

She ran up the flight of stairs and pounded on the first door she came to.

She listened for movement, heard none, and then pounded again.

This time, she heard footsteps, and then the door jerked open. "What the hell..." the man said, sounding surprised. 'Maggie? What on earth..."

"Mr Delaney," Maggie replied, her voice stronger than she expected. "You have to leave now. They're coming for you."

Chapter 1

PATTERSON ROAD, PLUMSTEAD, 1944.

Fat drops of rain fell from an ominous sky and splashed down Maggie's cheek as she struggled with a sheet. She cursed under her breath as a gust of wind pulled the heavy damp cotton away from her, and the corner dragged in the dirt.

She gathered up the sheet and stuffed it in the basket, hoping she could rinse off the mud, rather than wash it all over again. It was the wrong weather to hang washing outside, but this February day had started with a blue sky and a lukewarm winter sun, which deceived Maggie into thinking it might be an early start to spring—a relief after the long grind of winter, and a respite from the heavy gloom which had hung over London since Hitler resumed his bombing campaign.

Radio broadcasts had declared the Fuhrer's latest attacks were failures with "minimal damage", but that was little compensation for the people of London who hadn't yet recovered from the Blitz. When Maggie went to the Woolwich market, she noticed passersby kept their heads down and hurried about their business, not seeming to want to linger on the streets or socialise with their neighbours.

Maggie felt the same. She was waking early these days. When she eased out of bed in the mornings, her joints ached. She was a young woman, only in her forties, but the weight of constant worry had etched lines on her face and hunched her shoulders.

The sun was short-lived, and Maggie hurried out of her house to gather her sheets before the skies opened for another downpour, and now she fumbled with the pegs as the sky darkened.

Maggie wished Birdie was there to help, but her daughter was working at the Woolwich Arsenal. When she thought of her daughter, Maggie's breath caught in her chest. She was so proud of her beautiful Bernadette, but she wished she could keep her safe at home, not have her working ten-hour shifts in the munitions factory, which surely must be a target high on the Luftwaffe's list.

Maggie wished she could move herself and all her family to the country, away from the shriek of sirens in the night, and the stench of burning during the day. Her twin boys could play outside. They could have a garden instead of this grimy patch of dirt, just big enough for an Anderson shelter and her washing line.

When war had been declared all those years ago, before George was called up, they had discussed it.

"This will all be over before we know it," he'd said confidently. "Before Christmas, they're saying."

That was five Christmases ago.

The four of them—her, Birdie and the twins—had muddled through, living for George's occasional letters from the front line, until a few months ago when their lives had been turned upside down.

Before Christmas, one of the young women on Birdie's shift had been murdered. Birdie herself had been in danger but had escaped being hurt. It had left Maggie and her daughter shaken, but Birdie insisted on going back to work as soon as she could. Maggie understood her independent streak, and they needed the money, but every day Maggie was on edge until she heard Birdie's footsteps coming up the street, and then the key turning in the lock before she called out, "Ma, I'm home. Put the kettle on!"

It wasn't only the worry of Birdie working at the factory. Maggie missed Birdie's company and help with the twins. The boys were nearly eleven and a handful. They needed their father at their age, she thought. They'd been so young when George left to fight in the war that she wondered if they remembered him at all.

Thank the Lord for Mr Larkham, her elderly neighbour, who often invited the boys to tinker in his shed, and showed them how to use his woodworking tools.

"Don't you mind, Mrs Carroll. I like having them," he'd say, waving off her concerns about the boys disturbing him. "Gives me something to do with my time."

There were some benefits of staying on Patterson Road, Maggie thought as she picked up her basket of damp washing.

Maggie saw a movement in the corner of her eye and turned to see her other neighbour, Mrs Grenfield, gathering her own washing off the clothesline. Maggie nodded in her direction, but as usual, Mrs Grenfield pursed her lips so tightly that her mouth looked like a bright red slash across her thin face. That woman was the exact opposite of Mr Larkham.

Maggie shook her head and returned to her task. It didn't matter how white her laundry was, or how often she scrubbed the front step, her neighbour had made her mind up about Maggie and her three children and that was that. Maggie tried not to care, but she did.

Shirley Grenfield had looked Maggie up and down when Maggie knocked on her door eight years ago. Maggie had Birdie with her and the twins, and they were all dressed neat and tidy, ready to make a good impression on their new neighbours.

"I see," Mrs Grenfield replied without smiling as Maggie explained they had just moved in next door. Her face had tightened the second she heard Maggie's soft Irish brogue, and her glance drifted to Maggie's left hand. She sniffed when she saw the wedding ring, as if surprised that Maggie was a married woman, and therefore "respectable", but could not help allowing her bigotry to show.

"Well," Mrs Grenfield had said, enunciating her words slowly, as if addressing a small child. "I suppose some Irish families are clean." And with that, her front door banged shut.

"Bloody old cow," Birdie had said loudly enough for the entire street to hear, and certainly the lady on the other side of the door.

"Enough of that!" Maggie glared at her daughter. "We don't need to be making enemies. We'll keep ourselves to ourselves and eventually, she'll come round."

Although privately, Maggie agreed with Birdie.

Mrs Grenfield had never come round, even after Maggie delivered soup when she heard the old spinster was sick, or when she instructed the twins to shovel snow away from the front step when they had a grim winter in '42.

"Some people don't like Irish folk," Maggie explained to the boys, who didn't understand why other boys at school would shout 'cowards' at them and run away.

Some people, she told her wide-eyed, red-haired sons, are upset that Ireland isn't with Britain and Allies against Hitler.

"But we are Irish, and we don't like Hitler," James said, the confusion showing on his face.

"Yes, son, I know. We just need not bother ourselves about silly people," Maggie said, rubbing her fingers through his curls as she smiled down at him.

Maggie was used to the bigotry and let it go, but it hurt to see her boys upset.

Maggie carried her washing basket into the warm kitchen. She rubbed at the muddy corner of the sheet and hung it in front of the fire over the wooden clothes horse.

Soon the windows were coated with condensation, and the room filled with the scent of lye taking Maggie back to her childhood. She had vague memories of a large room hung with dripping sheets, the smell of laundry mixed with sweat. She was running in and out of the washing, skipping puddles on a stone floor, and playing hide and seek.

In her mind's eye, she saw the figure of a large red-faced woman, with fat shoulders and muscular forearms wringing and twisting the sheets to get the last drop of moisture from them. She heard the laughter and easy chatter of another woman in an accent, not a soft Dublin sing-song, but a fast jumble of words, with a questioning lilt at the end of each sentence. Even now, Maggie strained to hear what was being said. Was one of those faceless women from her memories her mother?

Maggie remembered the feeling of freedom and playfulness and she darted in between the sheets. But the vision faded, and she remembered being afraid. There was a figure behind her. A man, she thought. The chatter died down, and the laughter was replaced with something else... what was it? An argument? She couldn't remember. As hard as she focused, the memory slipped away. The next thing she recalled with clarity, she wasn't in the room anymore. She was standing alone in a cobbled street, crying. And then she looked up to see a face come close to hers. "Maggie," a man's voice said, "don't cry..." and then it was all gone.

Maggie pushed those thoughts away. That was a long time ago, and now she had to make the most of her life here in England. Even if she was, at best, tolerated as an outsider, and, at worst, despised as a dirty peasant. She thought about her son's confusion and wished she could help him understand why things were the way they were.

But how could she explain that George, his English father, wasn't welcome in Ireland, and she wasn't welcome in England? The War of Independence in Ireland, followed by a bloody civil war that lasted for another two years, had forced many Irish people to emigrate to England hoping to find a way out of poverty. Maggie was one of them. She could never return to Dublin. She'd chosen her path a long time ago. Ireland was in her past, she kept telling herself, as much as she missed her homeland. She must make an effort to blend into her new home for the sake of her children. But England and the Allies were angry about the Republic's strict neutrality in the War, and public opinion of the Irish was at an all-time low. An Irish accent was enough to be shorted rations at the Butchers' or left to the last for coal deliveries. And to have the door closed in her face by her neighbour.

Maggie was grateful for the few people on Patterson Road who were friendly. As well as Mr Larkham, there were the Bernsteins who lived at number nine, one of the terraced houses on the opposite side of Patterson Road. Mrs Bernstein always smiled and nodded when she passed Maggie or Birdie on the street. Mr Bernstein was a quiet man. He sat huddled in his chair, looking blankly out the window most days. Maggie always waved at him when she walked to the shops. Some days she was rewarded and the old man raised a hand. The other women in the street whispered about the Bernsteins being Jews. There was talk about a son and daughter missing somewhere in Europe. Maggie sighed when she thought of the curtain-twitching and rumours spread over the garden fences. If the stories were true, those poor people had endured enough without finger-pointing and gossip. Maggie felt an affinity with the Bernsteins. They would always be outsiders too.

Mrs Bernstein was retired now, but she had been a dressmaker by trade. As Maggie sat in her kitchen after folding more laundry, she thought back to one Sunday morning last autumn when Mrs Bernstein had gestured from her front door to Birdie and Maggie, as they walked home from Mass.

"Come in, dear. Come in, come in," she'd called to Birdie.

Maggie nodded, giving permission, and Birdie went in, shy at first.

"Come, Bernadette, I have some things you might like."

Mrs Bernstein always called Birdie by her full name. Birdie looked anxiously at her mother. Maggie was very firm about not accepting charity—we are better off than most, she always said—but Maggie squeezed Birdie's arm, silently telling her it was all right to follow.

The elegantly dressed Mrs Bernstein and Birdie went upstairs and Maggie stood in the hallway and waited. She looked around curiously. The house was a mirror image of their own, a tiny terrace affair on three floors. From the hallway, a staircase went straight up to three bedrooms. Above that would be an attic room. Downstairs, a kitchen, dining room, and the living room looking out to the street. Maggie always kept the front room for Sunday and special occasions. She, Birdie, and the twins spent most of their lives in the kitchen, keeping warm by the AGA. It was easier for the privy, too.

Maggie wondered if the Bernsteins had an inside privy. She'd seen one before and wished they could afford it. They'd moved to Patterson Road because it was cheap. Nobody wanted to live there because it was close to the Woolwich Arsenal. George was worried when the war started, but Birdie was a munitions worker at the Arsenal now and getting decent pay, which they sorely needed. Until the beginning of this year, everyone had been certain the worst of the bombing was over. Plumstead High Street still had piles of rubble where shops used to be, after the blitz of '41, but then there had been a year or so of quiet. Everyone had hoped that Hitler was on the back foot now. Maggie paid close attention to the news, listening to the radio broadcasts every night. The German blockade of Leningrad was over. The Red Army defeated the Germans, so surely the Allied forces could get the upper hand this year. But then the bombing started again. Everyone was so weary of this war.

As Maggie had stood in the hallway of the neighbours house that Sunday morning, she'd watched Mr Bernstein in the front room. He'd moved from his chair by the window and shuffled over to a gramophone. Gently he placed a needle on the vinyl disc and an Italian aria filled the room. Maggie didn't think she'd ever heard anything so beautiful. She stood, mesmerised by the music. Mr Bernstein turned and nodded at Maggie, his face filled with sadness. As Maggie nodded back, she saw the tears glisten on his cheeks before he moved slowly back to his chair.

"Look, Ma!" Birdie had broken the spell when she rushed down the stairs, her arms full of dresses. "Look, Mrs Bernstein says I can have them. They were her daughters. She thinks we are the same size. Maybe I'm a bit taller, but she says she'll show me how to let the hems down..." Birdie was breathless and excited, and Maggie smiled at her daughter.

"Well, now, that's very kind of Mrs Bernstein, I'm sure. They all look grand darlin'," she said softly, before turning to Mrs Bernstein.

"Are you sure?" Maggie asked. Birdie, too busy exclaiming over the silk, must have missed the sorrow in the older lady's face, but Maggie didn't.

"A beautiful girl must have beautiful clothes, Mrs Carroll," she had said.

As they had walked home, Maggie had stolen a look backwards and saw Mrs Bernstein watching them walk away, until finally, she had closed the door.

Sitting at her kitchen table now, Maggie felt sad for the elderly couple and grateful for their kindness. Then she shook herself from her reverie.

She must get on. The twins would be home from school, and then Birdie, from her shift at the Arsenal. It was getting dark outside.

There was a knock at the front door, and Maggie hurried to answer, a knot of anxiety forming in her stomach. She rarely got visitors. These days, a knock at the door could mean bad news. The worst news. As she opened the door, she took a deep breath.

Chapter 2

PATTERSON ROAD, PLUMSTEAD.

"Father?" Maggie said, relieved and startled. "I'm sorry. I wasn't expecting you."

A priest stood outside the door, a look of concern on his face.

"Oh, I'm sorry to bother you, Mrs Carroll. I'm Father Brennan. I'm new in the parish, taking over from poor Father Thomas while he recovers from his illness. I thought I'd come to introduce myself and see if I can be of service," he said, smiling. Maggie thought he didn't look much older than her boys. He had a young, freckled face and red hair. She realised she was staring at him as her anxiety subsided.

"Oh, Father, I'm sorry. What am I thinking? Do come in."

Maggie ushered him into the living room, relieved she had lit a fire earlier in the day to get the damp out of the air.

He smiled his thanks at an offer of tea and waited in the living room while Maggie fussed in the kitchen to find her best china. When the tea was ready, she carried it through on a tray and poured them both a cup.

They sat in silence as they both sipped the steaming brew.

How did he know her name, Maggie wondered. She wasn't close to Father Thomas, and it had been a long time since she'd been to Mass. As if he were reading her mind, Father Brennan smiled and said, "Mrs Carroll, you'll excuse my intrusion, but I saw the reports of all that nasty business with your daughter, Bernadette in the newspapers and I've been meaning to ask if she needs any help or spiritual guidance after her ordeal? I'll be happy to pray with her."

For the first time, Maggie noticed the priest was carrying a leather attaché case. He opened it, pulled out an old newspaper, and handed it to her.

"When I saw that, Mrs Carroll, I thought, what a terrible thing to happen to a family, and I must offer my support. I'm just sorry it took so long to visit."

Maggie remembered the reporters coming round after the murderer was caught. She hadn't wanted the attention, but the murders had been front page news, and Birdie's story of escape had caught people's attention. Birdie had smiled as the camera flashed.

Maggie had not been in the picture. She had wanted to put the whole terrifying incident behind them. Before Christmas, the local community had been on edge after two young women were murdered. The police were stumped. The victims seemed to be picked at random, and young women were frightened to walk the streets alone. Then Phyllis Heaton had been killed, a supervisor at the Woolwich Arsenal and one of Birdie's friends.

Birdie had been one of the last people to see Phyllis alive, so Maggie wasn't surprised when the police wanted to interview her daughter. But Maggie hadn't been prepared for her past to come visiting at the same time.

Detective Chief Inspector Robert Delaney had knocked on Maggie's door and came back into her life after over twenty years. Maggie's emotions were still in turmoil. She'd closed the door on her life in Ireland when she'd met George. But when she stared at Robert Delaney, a man whose life she'd saved many years ago, it had all come rushing back.

Delaney had asked for Maggie's help again, and because she wanted to keep her daughter safe, she agreed to look at the case. It had been her who had finally made the connection between the victims, which helped Delaney solve the case, but not before Birdie was abducted by Connor Byrne, an Irishman who befriended Birdie at work, and the killer. Thankfully, Maggie and Delaney had got to Birdie in time to save her, and Byrne was sentenced to hang.

He'd been targeting women who had access to war time classified information and had picked Birdie because she worked in a specialist department in the Arsenal. He'd been working for an enemy intelligence group, supplying them with secrets, and even though he'd been offered a deal to save his life, he refused to speak about his co-conspirators.

Birdie fully recovered from her ordeal, and Maggie had wanted to put the incident behind them, but the reporters had pestered them. In the end, Delaney had agreed to give them a brief interview and allow them to take a picture of him and Birdie, with the understanding that the reporters would leave Birdie and her family alone. Maggie had been grateful but still couldn't shake her feelings of unease at the attention. Mrs Bernstein had hurried over after she'd read the article to see if Birdie was alright, and even Mrs Grenfield had asked after her.

Now Father Brennan was bringing it all up again, but Maggie smiled at him and said, "That's very kind of you, Father. Bernadette is grand, and she is back at work now."

"And yourself, Mrs Carroll? I understand you were instrumental in catching the murderer?"

Maggie felt her chest tighten. Had the newspapers reported that? She didn't remember.

"Oh, Father, all I did was tell the police all I knew. I am sure I didn't help that much. I am just relieved the man is behind bars now."

"That's good news indeed. Is that your husband?" Father Brennan asked, changing the subject and pointing at a photograph of George on the mantelpiece. He must have noticed the British uniform, Maggie thought as she confirmed that it was, but he chose not to dig for any more information about George, and Maggie chose not to offer any.

"And you, Mrs Carroll, where are you from? Is that a Dublin accent?"

Maggie smiled. She'd told this story many times.

"Father, I'm not from Dublin," she told him. "I was born in Belfast, but my mother died in childbirth, along with my baby sister, so I was sent to relatives in Black Rock. That's where I grew up."

It was mostly true.

"Ahh." Father Brennan nodded. "I wasn't certain of the accent, but that explains it. Such a blessing, to have a loving family able to take you in, in your hour of need."

He paused, as if waiting for a response. Maggie forced her mouth to smile as her mind flashed back to a vision of her uncle's fists raining down on her aunt's huddled body after she'd accidentally dripped hot tea on his lap.

She nodded her head in fake agreement. "I was very lucky, Father," she said before she took another sip of her tea.

Maggie waited for the inevitable question, and it wasn't long in coming after another brief silence.

"I haven't seen you at Mass since I took over from Father Thomas."

It wasn't couched as a question, but Maggie heard the hint of accusation in his voice, even though the young priest smiled as he spoke.

"You're right, Father. It has been a while. I'll be sure to be there next Sunday." She didn't mean to lie to a priest, but there it was.

"That's grand, Mrs Carroll. We need the comfort of the Lord in such dark times."

Maggie nodded in agreement and then they chatted about the war and the weather until Maggie heard the commotion of her sons arriving home from school.

"Well now, Mrs Carroll, I'll not take up any more of your time. Thank you for the tea, and I trust I'll see you on Sunday?" He continued to keep his eyes on Maggie, as she answered, "You surely will, Father, and thank you for visiting."

She saw him out and stood at the door as she watched Father Brennan walk down the street, disappearing into the fading light. He explained his visit, she supposed but something felt off. There was no reason to feel suspicious, she chided herself. Maggie went to Mass sporadically, and although she knew some of the regular congregation, she wasn't close to anyone. She felt her stomach tighten again, just a little, but pushed the feeling aside. Was she overreacting? Had the trauma of nearly losing her daughter made her question everyone?

"Just a priest doing his job," she said to herself. "Looking after his flock." She shook off her paranoia and turned her attention to the boys.

Birdie arrived home just before the blackout. They sat as they usually did, around the kitchen table. James and Patrick were chattering about school and Birdie told stories about the girls at work, while Maggie smiled and nodded, allowing the warmth of family camaraderie to blot out the nagging anxiety still lingering in the back of her mind.

Maggie chased them off to bed before the nine o'clock news came on the radio. The boys argued a little, just to push Maggie's buttons, but ran, laughing, up the stairs as she pretended to chase them with a broom. Birdie had to get up early for her shift, and she liked to read a little before she turned in, so she followed the twins shortly after. She kissed Maggie's cheek.

"Is there something the matter, Ma?" she asked, before she left the kitchen.

Maggie hesitated, not wanting to worry her daughter, especially over something so silly.

"Come on, Ma, you can tell me," Birdie urged.

"Oh, it's nothing really," Maggie said and then told Birdie about Father Brennan's visit.

"Maybe he was just worried about us?" Birdie said, and then, with a mischievous gleam in her eye, she wagged a finger at Maggie. "You had better go to Mass more regularly, and say your confession. I think you're feeling guilty."

Maggie laughed. "Off to bed with you, young lady."

And then Maggie was alone again, her hands clasped around a cup of tea, and her thoughts on the young priest, still wondering why his visit had unsettled her.

Chapter 3

LEINSTER GARDENS, LONDON.

Damp mist clung to Patrick Dowd's face, and he bent his head as he hurried on foot through the dark streets. The temperature was plummeting, and he wished he had a warmer jacket, but he'd have drawn attention to himself if he'd taken the time to bundle up. He'd waited as long as he could, finally leaving the others drinking and playing cards to ease the tension that had been building for days now.

He'd waved his hand and grunted when they called on him to join them at the table, feigning tiredness. He'd noticed Liam glancing in his direction a few times before he left the room, and he hoped the boy would keep his mouth shut. Liam had been having doubts and was stupid enough to voice them.

He'd grabbed Liam's head with both hands and drawn the boy close.

"You listen ta me, lad. You are committed to tha' cause, you understand? There is no other way. And you never, I say never question orders again."

When Liam didn't answer or meet his eye, he'd tightened his grip, until finally the boy had said, "Aye. I understand."

Patrick had replayed that exchange in his mind. Liam was not a threat, he was sure. The boy was just affected by the tension and the waiting, like all of them.

The orders had come down, but only two of the team had received the full briefing. All he and the rest of them knew was a date and time. He hadn't dared ask questions, and held his breath when another lad, young and naïve, just like Liam, had piped up, "What's the target, boss?"

"You'll know when ye need ta," came the curt answer, and that had been that.

It didn't matter. He'd done the best he could, and a date and time were better than nothing. The target would be high profile, he was sure. Somewhere that would cause the most carnage, the most mayhem, and the most fear. If he kept his head down and his ears open, he might get a clue in the next day or so.

McClary, second in command of the group, was prone to drinking too much and loosening his tongue. He'd keep close, hoping he would let something slip.

The streets were quiet enough for him to hear the slap of his footsteps against the pavement echo around him. It was unsettling and Patrick pushed on, anxious to get this task done. The pub he'd chosen was a known haunt to the rest of them, and it was a risk, but anywhere else would mean he'd have to walk further and would be gone longer. And if he was spotted, he reasoned, he could always say he just slipped out for a quiet drink.

The only light was the faint glow of the occasional street lamp, which was dimmed and shielded to comply with the blackout. It was too late for trams to be running, so there wasn't even the buzz of the electric wire above him, and yet the city air seemed to crackle around him.

London had been on high alert for a month since Hitler had unleashed his retribution bombing campaign against the capital city. Night after night, Londoners had woken to the whine and rumble of Hitler's bombers and then ran for their lives as the distinctive whistling sound of the bombs hurtling towards their targets stopped for a terrifying moment of silence before the blast.

The nighttime shadows had been lit up by the orange glow of fires, the quietness shattered by sirens and screams. The mist and low clouds trapped the smell of acrid smoke, and Patrick wheezed a little as he increased his pace.

Maybe it would have been easier to do this in the middle of a raid, he thought. But he didn't have a choice. This may be the last time he could get away, and who knows how long it would be before orders came and the campaign was set in motion. It would all be out of his control then.

For the second time, he paused and swung around, straining to listen for rustling or catch a glimpse of a moving shadow, but there was nothing. He wasn't being followed; he was sure.

He pulled up his collar and hurried on, being careful to keep to the shadows. One thing was for sure: he was finished with this. It was too dangerous, and the money wasn't worth it. He wanted to go home. He wanted to smell air that wasn't tainted with the stench of this crumbling, doomed city.

Blackout curtains kept the pub in near darkness, but as Patrick got nearer, slivers of light were visible from a crack under the door, while the general hum of conversation and the odd chink of glass could be heard from the near-deserted street. It was still early and the air raid wardens wouldn't be out doing their rounds for a while yet. Patrick needed to get this over and get back to the other quickly. He didn't want to risk being stopped and questioned.

He knew the pub wouldn't be busy. It was a Monday evening. It wasn't ideal, he knew. On the busy nights, he was invisible in the crowd, the barman barely glancing up as he served beer to the soldiers from the Woolwich barracks, and American Airmen on leave from the nearby base.

He hesitated outside the pub door, conflicted.

This wasn't a good idea. If he went back now, he could slide in and nobody would be any the wiser. This was an important meet-up that he had arranged, but maybe it was time to think of himself.

"You in or out, lad?" a brusque voice said behind him.

"Sorry," he mumbled and went to step aside, but the impatient pub patron pushed forward and opened the door. Before he knew it, he was propelled inside.

"Door!" the barman shouted, and Patrick hastily slammed the pub door behind him.

So much for keeping a low profile.

He glanced around. He was probably worrying for no reason. The barman was busy serving the man who'd pushed in behind him. There were a few other patrons sitting on bar stools and a couple in a booth, their heads together. Nobody took any notice of him.

He waited at the bar and ordered a pint when the barman came over. He grunted his thanks, took his pint to a booth, and slid into the corner. He took his cap off and placed it on the table in front of him, making sure he could see the door.

Patrick sat with his hand around his beer for five minutes before the door opened again. He felt the blast of cold air before the door swung shut. He watched a man walk to the bar and disappear from his sight line so he could only overhear as he greeted the barman cheerily, like an old friend. Not him then.

He'd never met his handler face to face. They had passed messages, always left in different places.

This was dangerous for both of them. But it was the last time, he told himself. Give up the information, go back to the safe house as if nothing was wrong, get arrested like the rest of them, just like they had arranged. And then, when it was safe, back to Ireland. Not Dublin. No, he'd hide himself on the West Coast somewhere. It was easy to get lost out there.

A commotion at the bar cut into his thoughts. He cursed to himself and focused on his surroundings. This was no time for daydreaming.

He relaxed when he saw it was a woman. She was swaying slightly, trying to light a cigarette. Her dark hair was piled on top of her head, but strands hung down as if she'd been caught in a windstorm. It was hard to tell how old she was. Her lips were bright crimson. Hard to get lipstick in the war, he thought. Unless she was overly friendly with the Americans.

"Gin and tonic, please, love," the woman said to the barman when she'd finally lit her cigarette. She took a long drag and looked around the pub as she exhaled, while the barman poured the drink and glowered at her.

"That'll be enough for you," he said, "Drink that and be on your way,"

"Oh, don't be like that." She winked at the barman and giggled, "The night's only just started."

Patrick slid down in his seat a little. The last thing he needed was attention from this woman. How much longer? He needed to get out of here.

"Oh, who have we here?" Another giggle.

She was standing beside his booth now. He looked up briefly, caught her eye, and quickly looked down again.

"C'mon, handsome, buy a lady a drink," she slurred.

"You've got one," he muttered, nodding at the gin and tonic in her hand.

She laughed and then stumbled, spilling the liquid on the table. "Not anymore."

She thrust her hand into the neckline of her dress and pulled out a handkerchief. "Never mind, handsome, I'll clean it up."

She bent forward to wipe up her spilled drink, as he grabbed his cap before it got wet.

"It's fine, leave it..." he said, but she put a finger to her lips.

"When and where," she whispered. "Quickly."

"W-what?" he stuttered, confused. This was not the plan. The handler was supposed to come in and ask directions. That would be the signal for Patrick to leave. Then they would bump into each other outside the pub and Patrick would slip the handler the information he had scrawled on a scrap of paper in his inside pocket.

The woman didn't move.

"Your information. I need it now, quickly." Her voice was steady; no hint of the slur.

This was all wrong, but what could he do? He fished in his pocket and handed over the paper. She grabbed it and shoved it into her cleavage.

"I don't know where. Just the day," he said, and she winked before she straightened up.

"Alright, alright, that's enough." The barman towered over them, scowling. "Time for you to leave." He grabbed the woman's elbow. He was a large man, with fleshy jowls and a sweaty face. The woman slid her hand from his chest to the barman's stomach, which strained against his shirt.

"Ooh, you like to play rough," she cooed.

"I'll pay rough alright if you don't move yerself," the barman grunted as he pulled her away from the booth.

Patrick watched as he shoved the woman towards the door, opened it, and pushed her outside as she protested. As the door swung shut, he heard her cackle of laughter fade away.

He drained his beer and pulled his cap down on his head, ready for the cold night. He slid out of the booth and made for the door.

"Hold on there, sir."

The barman stood in front of him.

Patrick froze but tried not to let his panic show on his face.

"Sorry about that." The barman jerked his head toward the door.

Patrick shrugged.

"Nay bother," he replied. "I'll be off now." He stepped to one side to pass the large framed man.

The barman put a heavy hand on his shoulder. Instantly, Patrick's heart beat faster.

"Another drink, sir?" the barman asked. "On the 'ouse. To make up for the trouble."

Patrick stared at him and knew instantly he'd been set up.

The barman pushed him towards the bar. He felt the weight on his shoulder increase as the heavier man forced him into a seat.

"Now you wait there." The barman grinned and winked at him.

The door to the pub swung open again. This time, two men pushed the same woman through the doorway. One, Patrick knew. McClary. The other was a stranger to him.

The woman was sulky now. "I wanna gin and tonic," she pouted, "and then I want my money."

"Sit down, girl," the stranger said. "I'll see you right." Then he and McClary walked up to the bar. Patrick's eyes flickered towards the door. His only chance would be to run.

The stranger's voice was soft with a Dublin lilt, a contrast to the harshness of McClary's northern accent.

"Patrick, lad," the stranger said, a hint of amusement in his tone. "Did you think we'd not find out?"

Patrick opened his mouth to protest, to plead, to say anything that might stop what was to come next, but the stranger put his finger to his lips.

"Shhhh, say nothing, lad. We know. Barman, get this man a drink. A round of whisky for all of us."

The barman poured whisky into three glasses and put them in front of the three men.

"May the road rise to meet you," the stranger said; a line from an Irish blessing which Patrick had heard many times before in his homeland.

Patrick put his hand around the glass of whisky, as the two other men said in unison, "Éirinn go brách."

It was his only chance. Patrick hurled the glass of whisky in McClary's face and made a dash for the door. He pulled it open and made it outside.

The last two things he heard as he darted into the darkness were the two men laughing and McClary saying, "He'll not get far."

Chapter 4

FULHAM, LONDON.

Detective Chief Inspector Robert Delaney was dreaming someone was banging hard on his front door. He groaned and turned over, muttering in his sleep, but the sound continued.

"Who the hell is that? Don't worry, dear..." he said groggily to the empty space beside him, as he realised the noise was real, and someone was indeed knocking at his front door.

"Damn." When would he ever get used to being alone in the bed?

Robert was fully alert now. "Alright, alright, I'm coming," he grumbled.

The Detective Chief Inspector swung his legs out of the bed and shivered in the night's chill. It must be freezing outside, he supposed. A glint of moonlight around his blackout curtains illuminated the clock on his bedside table.

1.00 am.

He hoped to get a full night's sleep. The bombing raids had sent him to his shelter too many times in the last weeks, even though he lived in a quiet street in Fulham, nowhere near Hitler's targets. And then there was the long hours at work, attempting to do his job and stop criminals taking advantage of the nervous and vulnerable population of London with a skeleton staff, and half of Scotland Yard in rubble when the Embankment took a direct hit. The Parliament buildings took the brunt of it, but it made a damn mess and it was bloody inconvenient. All he wanted was a decent night's sleep.

He sighed and pulled on a robe before hurrying down the stairs to the front door, just as the knocking resumed for the third time.

"Sorry to wake you, sir,"

A nervous-looking constable with a ruddy face rocked from leg to leg. Billows of white steam rose from the black Wolsey parked behind him.

"What is it, Constable Hunter?"

"A body, sir."

Robert Delaney glared at him and opened his mouth to say something, but Constable Hunter had presumably expected his response, because he quickly continued, "Definitely a murder, sir. Not a bombing victim. I already went to look for myself before I woke you up."

Delaney sighed and felt ashamed for his initial reaction.

"Oh no. Come in Constable." He gestured for him to step inside, so he could turn on a lamp. The blackout was strictly enforced these days. Not only that, Delaney felt sorry for the constable. He remembered night duty in the middle of winter.

"Close the door, Constable. Where are we going?"

The constable pulled out his notebook and told him the address. "Leinster Gardens, sir. Just off the Bayswater Road"

"And what do we know about the victim?"

"A male victim, sir. I don't have many details, but it seemed he was beaten to death. Dr Holberg is on his way. "

"Right. Wait here, son. I'll be a minute."

Robert Delaney ran upstairs to his bedroom and dressed quickly.

He paused for a moment before leaving the bedroom and looked at the empty bed. The covers were pulled back and the indentation of his body still visible on one side, the other undisturbed.

Elizabeth had always woken up when he'd been called away in the middle of the night, and he'd always said the same thing, "Try to go back to sleep, darling. I doubt I'll be home until morning," before dropping a kiss on Elizabeth Delaney's forehead. She'd been his wife since he'd been a young constable, like the one waiting for him downstairs, and had never complained about his long hours at work and interrupted nights. He missed her terribly.

The Wolsey was already rumbling when the Detective Chief Inspector emerged into the night air.

"Ready, sir?"

Robert Delaney nodded, and Constable Hunter drove as he shared the details he had. They were headed to the Leinster Arms, a pub in Leinster Gardens. There had been an illegal after-hours lock-in, when a drunk participant had stumbled out the back door and found a dead man in the alley.

Robert listened closely to the constable. There was a uniformed officer already on the scene waiting for them. The unfortunate customer had sobered up quickly when he found the body and had pulled himself together enough to go back into the pub and call the nearest police station.

The night sergeant had followed procedure and had made the call to Scotland Yard, where Detective Constable Hunter was also on night duty. He'd already been out to check on the body and make sure an officer was there to preserve the crime scene. He'd known that DCI Delaney would want to know about this immediately.

Constable Hunter had been on the job for a year, after recuperating from wounds sustained in the ill-fated Dieppe Raid the year before, including the loss of his foot. The Wolsey he was driving had been specially modified with hand controls. Delaney rated the young constable highly.

Apart from his courage and determination to serve his country despite his injuries, he was intelligent and quick to learn.

As the Detective Chief Inspector listened to Billy recount the night's events, he was reminded of his own son. Robert Delaney Jr. was a RAF pilot, stationed who knew where, doing his duty for the country. He hadn't heard from him for months, and Robert knew his wife had lain awake most nights, worrying about her only son before she had died herself. Their only child, Robert thought with a pang. He hoped he would see his son soon.

Delaney set aside his private thoughts.

"I don't mind admitting, sir," Billy was saying. "It affected me, seeing that poor bugger lying there. I've seen my share of dead bodies, but there is still something about…" He trailed off, and even in the dark, Delaney could see the young man flush with embarrassment.

"There's something about a cold, ruthless murder," he finished for the constable. "I know, son. I know."

Leinster Gardens was dark and silent when they arrived. The Wolsey rumbled over the cobbles and tram tracks and stopped in front of the Leinster Arms. The two-storey building was in darkness, except for a chink of light under the main entrance.

Billy parked the car.

"This way, sir," he said as walked to the front entrance and pounded on the door.

"Open up, it's the police."

The door opened a crack, and a large fleshy face appeared in the shadows.

Wordlessly, a man opened the door wide enough for Delaney and Constable Hunter to enter.

Through the gloom and haze of residual smoke from earlier in the evening, Robert saw a thin man with black slicked-backed hair sitting at a table. His hands were shaking as he sucked on a cigarette, and a tumbler of brown liquid, Robert assumed was whisky, sat in front of him.

"For the shock," the other man said, apparently watching Delaney's gaze.

Delaney nodded. He didn't care about the after-hours drinking or the illegal alcohol. He'd already noticed empty bottles on the bar, no doubt, black market booze.

"And you are?" he asked.

"Bill Knowles," the large man answered. "I'm the owner of this establishment. And this 'ere is Charlie Sutton. 'E's the one who found the bo... the deceased."

His tone was matter-of-fact, but Robert could see the corners of his mouth twitch as if he were trying to keep himself under control.

Delaney was silent for a moment, waiting. Sure enough, Knowles felt uncomfortable and spoke again.

"Now look 'ere, I don't want no trouble. I run a respectable establishment." He shifted his considerable weight from foot to foot, and Delaney didn't bother to point out the evidence in front of him that showed Knowles' establishment wasn't respectable at all.

Constable Hunter had already pulled out his notebook and was scribbling notes.

"Take their statements, Constable while it's all fresh in their minds. And get a list of all the customers this evening."

"Sir, that's a lot of people..." Bill Knowles started to protest, but Delaney ignored him.

"Where's the body?" he asked.

Knowles raised his chin toward a door at the end of the bar.

"One of your lot is already out there."

Once outside in the darkness again, Delaney could make out a figure crouched over what looked like a pile of clothing dumped in the alleyway behind the pub. As he got nearer, he saw it was Dr Joseph Holberg, head of forensic pathology at the Police Laboratory, leaning over the body.

"This is a nasty one I'm afraid, Detective Chief Inspector," Dr Holberg said, with no preamble as he glanced over his shoulder. "Evidence of torture, broken hands, beaten face, and cause of death, a single gunshot at the back of his head."

"A professional job, then?" Delaney asked.

"Hard to say at the moment," Holberg replied. "All I can tell you is that this man suffered."

"Any identification?"

The professor shook his head. "None that I can find." He shifted his position so a dim glow from a lamp illuminated the body, and he gestured for Delaney to move closer.

"Quite the beating." Delaney swallowed down the bile that rose in his throat as he gazed at the bloody mess where the man's face had once been.

"Brutal," Holberg agreed. "I estimate this man to be in his early thirties. His hands are rough, so he may be a labourer, or more likely a munitions worker."

"Maybe Irish?" Delaney questioned. Most young men of the victim's age were at war or worked at a reserved occupation, doing all those essential jobs to keep the country functioning. But there was also a community of Irishmen who came to London looking for work. There were hostile feelings towards the Irish, because of their neutral position in the war, and the hostility had often resulted in violence. But this man's injuries were more than the result of a drunken brawl. As Dr Holberg had noted, this man had been tortured. This had taken time.

"Did he die here?"

Holberg hesitated. "Not sure. I'll need to do a thorough examination when I've got some light. Hard to imagine he was beaten and shot without someone hearing or seeing something."

"Unless they did," Delaney said grimly, "and were too afraid to say anything, or call it in." He thought back to Knowles and made a mental note to subject the shifty man to some vigorous questioning.

"Can't blame them." Holberg straightened up. "This was a vicious attack. Some brass nerve, though," he said, "killing this poor chap here, or even dumping the body, even in the blackout, they risked being noticed."

Delaney sighed. "Maybe whoever did this was sending a message? Doesn't look like the killer even bothered to cover him up. They wanted him to be found."

He thought back to the empty bottles in the pub. The criminal gangs in London who organised the black market had grown more bold and vicious since the war began. Maybe this poor man had crossed them.

Delaney and Dr Holberg stood up.

"There must have been more than one person involved," Dr Holberg continued. "Someone must have held him while he was being tortured. Maybe two or three."

Delaney nodded. "You're right." He wanted the full report before he started concocting theories though. It was too easy to get caught up in an early hypothesis and become blinkered.

"Damn blackout," Holberg muttered. "Makes everything harder. I'll wait for the wagon and get the body to the morgue. Then I'll be able to tell you more tomorrow. I mean later today... I say, did you hear that?"

Delaney had heard it. A low-throated rumble getting louder. He looked up just as the night clouds parted and in the moonlight saw an ominous shadow grow bigger. He grabbed Dr Holberg's arm as a loud whistling sound got louder and then stopped. In the momentary silence, he cried out, "Get down, man. It's another bloody raid!"

Chapter 5

PATTERSON ROAD, PLUMSTEAD.

Maggie took a sip of her tea and made a face. It was cold. She must have dozed off because the kitchen had chilled and the gas lamp flickered down low. Time for bed. But although she was tired, she didn't feel like climbing the stairs just yet. Instead, she wandered around the house, tugging on blackout curtains to straighten them, wondering why she felt so distracted. She felt as if there were a dark cloud of doom above her.

Maggie walked into the living room and picked up a photograph of George in his uniform. She rubbed a finger over it, wishing he were here. She stood for a few minutes, replaying the visit from Father Brennan in her mind. Was it his visit that had unsettled her? She turned slightly from chair to chair, recalling his questions and her answers. Was it her imagination, or was he a bit too curious about her background? Why was he singling her out for a visit?

Maggie closed her eyes and breathed in and then out. Paranoia. She couldn't let it overwhelm her.

She trod carefully up the stairs. She knew every creak and groan in this old house. The nights she lay awake, missing the warmth of George's body beside her, she catalogued each noise and movement in her head. She could hear when the twins were restless, muttering in their sleep. She knew the crunch of Mrs Grenfield's footsteps when she crept outside to indulge in a secret cigarette. When Maggie's bedroom window was open, she sometimes caught a waft of the illicit smoke. She didn't mind. It made her haughty neighbour a little more human.

Tonight, she didn't rush to close the blackout curtains and light the lamp in her tiny room at the top of the house. Instead, she sat on the bed in the dark, looking out at the night sky. When George was home, they had the bigger bedroom on the second floor. But after a year of him being away, Maggie gave it up to Birdie and took the smaller attic room.

It was stuffy in the summer, but Maggie didn't mind. She loved the view over the terraced roofs. The dark shadows of buildings silent and brooding in the blackout.

Maggie shivered a little. Tonight, she longed to see twinkling city lights again. As she sat facing the window, the clouds parted and the February night sky was clear and crisp. Moonlight illuminated the shabby bedroom.

Maggie stood up and looked out.

Far in the distance, she thought she saw birds flying, silhouetted against the moon. Maggie watched as they flew nearer. Faster. In a V shape. It didn't look quite right to Maggie. In an instant, she knew it wasn't birds.

In one movement, she was across the bedroom floor and taking the stairs two at a time.

"Birdie! Birdie!" she screamed. "Wake the boys! Down to the cellar! Now!"

Birdie burst out of her bedroom. "Ma! I don't hear…"

"Planes. Not ours, I'm certain. It's another bombing raid. Grab the boys," Maggie shouted. There was no mistaking the danger.

"What about the shelter?" Birdie called over her shoulder.

"No time." Maggie ran to the ground floor and grabbed the bag of blankets and their gas masks, which she kept under the stairs for emergencies like this.

Birdie hurried down, the boys close behind, white-faced and bleary-eyed.

"Quick," Maggie said… and then a loud drone of an engine drowned her voice out.

She pushed Birdie towards the cellar door, handing her a gas mask, and as quickly as she could with trembling fingers, she fastened the gas masks on Patrick and James and ushered them down the steps too. She pulled her own mask on, and followed, pulling the door shut behind her.

At the same moment as the door slammed shut, an explosion deafened her. The ground seemed to shake and lift under her, and Maggie fell forward down the steps. Her face slammed into hard concrete and she thought she heard Birdie scream. She tried to pull herself up, but the pain in her head and violent tremors meant she couldn't get her balance.

The house is falling in, Maggie thought. We're being buried alive. Oh Lord, this is it. Please spare the children, she prayed.

The rumbling and thunder of falling masonry deafened Maggie. Then a lull, leaving her with just the ringing in her ears.

It was pitch black now. Maggie crawled on the floor, frantically feeling for her children.

"We're here… we're here…" she thought she heard Birdie say, but before she could reply, there was another thunderous roar and Maggie was thrown onto her side once again and she felt a trickle of warm liquid down her cheek.

"Like the rain this morning," she thought, as her world went dark and silent.

Chapter 6

SCOTLAND YARD, LONDON.

"Close one last night, sir,"

Delaney looked up to see Constable Billy Hunter standing in the doorway. He gestured for the young man to come into the office.

"It was, Constable," he answered, taking off his reading glasses and rubbing his eyes. "Hitler is not giving up yet, I suppose. They didn't hit any significant targets, I hear."

"Tell that to those poor sods in Plumstead," Billy Hunter said, his face solemn.

"Indeed. Any word on casualties?"

Constable Hunter shook his head. "Not yet, sir. But one street took a direct hit. Not one house standing. I suppose they must have been targeting the Arsenal."

Delaney recalled feeling the earth shake as the bomb hit a few miles away, in the direction of the munitions factory. The bomb was slightly off target—thank goodness—but it was no compensation for the citizens buried in the blast.

"Let's hope they had time to get to shelters."

"Yes, sir. Mrs Berkley lives nearby, but there was no damage in her street."

"That's good news, at least."

They were silent for a moment, knowing it was unlikely that many had escaped with their lives.

"What can I do for you, Constable?" Delaney asked.

"Oh, sorry, sir. Chief Superintendent Whaldon has requested to see you immediately. About the murder."

Delaney sat back, surprised. "He has?"

"Yes, sir. He said to say it was urgent and not to... er, dilly dally, sir."

"Right. Well, do you have those statements?" Delaney shuffled papers on his desk. "From the barman and the chap who found the body?"

"Yes, sir, right here."

"Good man. See if you can get some preliminaries from Dr Holberg, would you?"

"Right, sir."

Delaney stood up and straightened his tie. He was glad he'd taken the time to go home and freshen up after the events of the previous night. He and Dr Holberg had remained crouched in the alley until the sirens had sounded the all clear. Then they'd headed back into the pub. They'd found Constable Hunter and their two witnesses huddled under a bench.

"All clear, Constable," Delaney had said, sounding far calmer than he felt, before despatching Hunter to see if he could help the rescue teams.

Hours later, Dr Holberg had rounded up some transportation for the dead victim, and Delaney had taken the opportunity to get home on a tram. He'd hurriedly shaved and changed before arriving at his office.

For the last two hours, he'd been typing up his report on his rickety typewriter while he waited for Dr Holberg's report. His secretary, Mrs Berkley, usually did all his typing, but at the beginning of a case, he did his own. It helped him to make sense of the crime. This time, though, he made little sense of anything. Apart from taking statements from the witnesses, he had made no progress at all, and now he had to explain this to Chief Superintendent Whaldon.

Delaney stood facing the closed office door and took a deep breath. Inside, he could hear the clack, clack, clack of a typewriter, and he wondered if Whaldon also did his own typing. Everyone did everything these days; the force was so short staffed. Delaney knocked three firm raps on the solid oak door.

"Come," a deep voice called out. Delaney grasped the door handle, twisted it, and pushed open the door.

Charles Whaldon was a living legend in Scotland Yard. He'd joined the force in the early twenties and worked his way up the ranks, joining Scotland Yard in 1929. He was known to be plain-speaking and did not tolerate foolishness, but officers who'd worked under his command told stories of kindness and encouragement from their mentor. Whaldon had been instrumental in cracking a number of tough cases and had won awards for his bravery. He'd never asked any of his subordinates to do anything he wasn't prepared to take on himself. He could be a little pompous, though, in Delaney's mind.

Delaney held out his hand to shake the superintendent's. "How are you, sir?"

"Good, good Thanks for coming by Bob," the tall man said as if Delaney had any choice in the matter.

"Yes, sir. My pleasure." Delaney couldn't help grinning back at Whaldon, who seemed relaxed, puffing on his pipe.

"Damn paperwork never ends, does it, Bob? Sit, sit." Whaldon gestured at a chair, while he perched on the edge of his wide desk.

The office was smaller than Delaney remembered, but it might have been the wide desk and the walls lined with bookcases that made the space appear cramped. Delaney could see academic volumes on all subjects, from anatomy to firearms.

"Now, I won't keep you long. I understand you've had quite the night," Whaldon said, reaching behind him and grabbing a packet of cigarettes. He offered them to Delaney, who shook his head.

"Good man, it's a bad habit. I'm trying to stick to my pipe," Whaldon said. "Now, this dead body you found last night..."

"Yes, sir, here's my report." Delaney held out his file. "I'm afraid I don't have much for you yet. We're waiting on Dr Holberg's report, but given the bomb last night, I don't know if he'll have time..."

"I have his report here," Whaldon said cheerfully. "Holberg updated me an hour ago. We have a firm ID for your man. Patrick Dowd, thirty-five years old, only known address a boarding house in Leinster Gardens, formerly from Belfast."

Delaney didn't know what to say. Whaldon must have seen the surprise and irritation on his face, because he continued, "I asked Holberg to keep me up to date. He's sending his preliminary report over to you as we speak."

"Right, sir. No problem at all." Delaney tried to keep his voice neutral. If Whaldon had wanted the case, why hadn't he just taken it off his desk?

"Bob, I know you're wondering why I'm interfering. So let me explain. You were here in '39?" Whaldon read his thoughts.

"Yes, sir, I was."

"Well, you'll remember that miserable squabble we were having with the Irish, while we were wondering what Hitler would do next?"

"I do, sir."

Delaney recalled the explosions which had rocked London, just as war broke out. Homemade bombs, planted by Irish extremists, killed innocent people, blew apart pillar boxes and mail vans, and most notably, destroyed the left-luggage offices at Tottenham Court Road and Leicester Square railway stations.

Delaney remembered something else. "Didn't you diffuse one of those bombs, sir? In Piccadilly Circus?"

Whaldon nodded. "Only one of 'em, unfortunately. There were six explosions that night, and twenty people injured. Nasty business."

Whaldon waved his hand, as if to dispel the memory, although Delaney knew the man had saved many lives by courageously hacking off the pencil fuses from sticks of gelignite. Whaldon had been awarded the King's Medal for Gallantry in 1940, by His Majesty at Buckingham Palace.

Whaldon was still talking. "Most of those bastards either hung or will be behind bars for the rest of their lives. But it's not over, Bob. We have intelligence that the Republican Army is actively recruiting and planning another campaign. And, of course, there are the loose ends from the murders before Christmas. All connected, we believe."

"Bloody hell... Sorry, sir," Delaney blurted out. "Was Patrick Dowd one of them? And who killed him?"

"Patrick Dowd was an informant. We think the head man got wind he had a traitor in his midst and Patrick blew his cover somehow. We don't know why Dowd was at the pub, and how they got on to him. But the man was tortured before he was shot. We've seen that before," Whaldon said gravely. "And Dowd's handler says the man was getting nervous."

"Was he meeting his handler that night?" Delaney asked.

"He hadn't made contact in a while. But going to the pub was out of the ordinary for him. He usually stayed at the boarding house unless he was working. He and his handler had a drop site for messages near there. The theory is that Dowd left a message—maybe asking for a meet—and was spotted. Then the message was probably removed, so his handler was in the dark, and Dowd walked into a trap."

Delaney shook his head. "Poor chap. So what do we do now, sir?" he asked. "Hand this over to MI5?" He felt a guilty sense of relief, picturing the pile of files on his desk.

"No such luck, ol' boy. No, MI5 want our help on this one. Dowd was the only informant they had, so he needs to be replaced. And we need to be seen investigating the murder as per usual, so as not to raise suspicion."

Whaldon leaned forward and looked Delaney in the eye. "I need my best men on this, Bob. We'll only have a small team, and it'll be... well, a bit unorthodox."

Delaney was confused. "You mean the murder case? Of course, sir."

Whaldon shook his head. "Not just the murder, Bob. Homeland Security is stretched thin. We are on a special assignment, and we need to work quickly. Before Dowd died, he gave our operative some information. I can't tell you much until you've been briefed and given clearance. But I can tell you we are up against a nasty bunch who will take advantage of our country's vulnerability."

Delaney's relief evaporated. "Of course. But they will be waiting for that. Unless we get an eyewitness or other solid evidence, if this was a professional job, we'll be unlikely to crack it. And as for the special assignment, sir, I'm flattered, but I have a heavy caseload."

Whaldon paused for a second before continuing, ignoring Delaney's protest. "We know the group has friends in London. Operatives who are helping them. This murder will have made them all nervous. When we bring the group down, we need to make sure we get everyone. All the traitors. Now, you'll get a full briefing soon, but I need to ask you about something else."

"Right, sir." Delaney's head was spinning, but Whaldon was still talking

"The murders before Christmas. You did an excellent job. We suspect Connor Byrne, the murderer, might be part of all this..." He waved his hand around in the air. "But he's not talking. He'd rather dance at the end of a rope than help us out and save his life. But with your experience in these kinds of operations, I think we can handle it. We must handle it. But I know we are short of manpower, so I have an idea."

Whaldon reached across his desk and picked up a file. As he handed it to Delaney, he said, "This operative impressed me. Tell me everything you know about her, going back to your time in the military. If you can, of course."

Delaney recognised the name on the file immediately. He also knew now why Whaldon wanted him for this special assignment. Nearly twenty-five years ago, the British Army Intelligence Centre had recruited him in Ireland to be part of a special plainclothes unit made up of demobilised ex-army officers and some active-duty officers to conduct clandestine operations against the IRA.

In January 1920, after training with Special Branch, the agents were shipped to Dublin, one by one, including Delaney, with one mission—to infiltrate and disrupt the Irish Republican Army.

Delaney lived in a boarding house at Mountjoy Street in Dublin and took a job as an office clerk. In the evenings, the agents would slip out of their accommodations and meet up at the Cafe Cairo to share intelligence.

It was dangerous work. The IRA had eyes and ears everywhere. Ultimately, they were one step ahead of the Cairo Gang, as Delaney's unit called themselves.

Delaney's hand shook a little as he recalled the fateful day in November 1920. The IRA had apparently been watching them for months, and through their network of diligent spies, they had identified all the agents.

There had been a bang at the door early on a Sunday morning. Delaney had been in bed. He'd pulled on some trousers and a shirt, and shouted, "Coming," thinking it was his landlady.

Maggie McVeigh had been standing outside, gasping for breath as if she'd been running.

"You need to go now," she'd said urgently. "They're coming for you."

Delaney had stared at her, not comprehending at first, followed by a suspicion for a second that he was being led into a trap. The fear on Maggie's face persuaded him otherwise, and he did what she told him.

"We need to leave now," she'd urged, and they both hurried down the back stairs of the boarding house. They had almost been too late. The mob of assassins arrived a minute later, and one of them spied Delaney down an alleyway. He took a shot, and a bullet clipped Delaney's leg, but he and Maggie got away. He'd escaped Bloody Sunday as that day became known and owed his life to Maggie McVeigh, but fourteen agents lost their lives.

Absentmindedly, Delaney's hand now moved to his calf to rub the scar from the bullet wound; a permanent reminder of his close escape.

"How did you turn her?" Whaldon's voice broke into Delaney's thoughts and pulled him back to the present. "How did she end up working for us?"

"I didn't turn her, sir," Delaney said. "Her own family did that."

When he'd met Maggie, she was employed as a maid to clean the rooms in his boarding house.

"Her uncle was a brute," he said. "Her cousin, Sean, was worse."

He paused for a minute, remembering the first time he'd ever spoken to Maggie McVeigh.

Maggie had been crying when he found her in his room. She was crouched in the corner, her arms wrapped around her knees and her face buried in her skirt, muffling her sobs. She'd kept her head down, but Delaney had seen the purple bruising on her face, and the welts on her arms.

She'd leapt up when she noticed him.

"I'm so sorry, sir," she'd mumbled, and had made a move to leave the room. Delaney had stopped her, and after some coaxing, Maggie had told him about her abusive family.

"Maggie knew I was part of the Cairo Gang," Delaney told Whaldon. "Her Uncle Ryan and Sean were foot soldiers for the IRA. Sean wanted to be higher up. He was always trying to impress the leaders, I think. He had a network of informers and he forced women and girls to spy for The Cause. One of them was Maggie, who he threatened and beat regularly. Maggie was never a believer. She was just trying to survive."

Delaney thought back to that day when Maggie had opened up to him.

"She wasn't crying for herself," he said. "She had several jobs as a maid, and one of them was in a household of a British army officer. Maggie helped care for his wife and baby. Sean had hatched a plan to plant a bomb in the house. It would have killed the woman and her child, but Sean didn't care. He wanted to make a name for himself. Maggie was beside herself. She didn't know what to do but knew she had to save them somehow. So she took an enormous risk and told me about the plan."

"Did you stop it?" Whaldon asked.

"No. But we tipped off the officer and moved his wife and child. The house was damaged but nobody was hurt. But after that, Maggie essentially was working for our side."

Delaney struggled to find the words to describe the chaos and confusion of his time in Dublin.

"It was hard back then to know whether we were being fed disinformation. Maggie passed on tidbits when she could, but she had to be careful. The IRA had great power, they were disciplined and fanatical. We were completely under-prepared. But they made mistakes, and one of them was relying on brutes like Sean McVeigh. He was a loose cannon."

Whaldon nodded. "Untrained and undisciplined, a lot of 'em."

Delaney nodded. "Sean McVeigh was definitely undisciplined. He loved violence. And ironically, it was because of what he did the night before Bloody Sunday that I escaped."

"What happened?"

"There was an elderly neighbour Maggie was fond of," Delaney told Whaldon. "Sean came home drunk on Saturday night and accused the old lady of being a spy. He dragged her into the street and shot her in the head. Maggie witnessed it. Then Sean and his father carried on drinking and shouted about killing all the Cairo Gang the next day. Maggie and her aunt locked themselves in the bedroom, but they heard everything. Maggie escaped in the early hours of the morning and ran all the way into the city to warn me. It was a close call, but Maggie and I got out of there. The others weren't so lucky."

Delaney stopped, the words stuck at the back of his throat. After all these years, his emotions were still raw whenever he thought of his comrades who were slaughtered that day.

Whaldon nodded slowly in understanding.

"What happened to McVeigh, after Bloody Sunday?" he asked.

"She helped me escape to the outskirts of Dublin. There was a safe house there." Delaney said, "Maggie could never go back home. Sean would have killed her. So the boys at the Intelligence Service spirited her away, and then I heard she was recruited by the Igoe Gang later. They were better equipped than us. After that, she must have left Ireland. Last December was the first time I had seen her in over twenty years."

Whaldon pointed to the file. "You're right about the Igoe gang. She worked undercover for them. It was dangerous work."

Delaney agreed. The Igoe gang was famous in the intelligence world. They were made up of special agents pulled from all over Ireland who managed to penetrate the IRA. "They took the fight to the IRA. They succeeded where we didn't."

"According to her file, Maggie McVeigh was an asset," Whaldon said, puffing on his pipe. "When she got to England, she made her way from Liverpool to London and met George Carroll. She got married and stayed out of sight until you found her again."

Delaney flipped through the file and then looked up.

"Special Branch kept an eye on her? All these years?"

Whaldon nodded. "They keep files on everyone, ol' boy. Anyone who brushed up against an operation, anyway. Your Maggie McVeigh caused a ripple when she helped you out with those murder cases last year."

"But that was circumstance, sir. Her daughter was in danger. Are you telling me she's some kind of sleeper agent?"

"No, no, nothing like that. But she was useful, as I recall?"

Delaney nodded. "Yes, of course."

"Here's the situation, Bob. We need another informant. Someone who can go undercover and take over from Dowd. The thing is, those boys will be on high alert now, so whoever it is needs to be skilled and experienced. I think Maggie McVeigh can do it."

Delaney fell silent for a moment and thought of the woman who'd saved his life all those years ago, and then reappeared to help him all over again with his case. Even if Maggie had been out of the spy game for all these years, she still had a brilliant mind. Why not ask her?

"It couldn't hurt to ask for her help, sir," he said eventually. "But she has children now. And a husband who might not—"

"That's up to you, Bob. Find out what she needs. We can look after her family. Special Branch takes care of their own, Bob. You know that."

"I do, sir."

"Good man, call her in, and we'll get the briefing set up. You can read this too."

Whaldon stood up and went back behind his desk. He pulled a thicker file out of his drawer and handed it to Delaney.

"It's as much as I can give you before the briefing. Let me know when McVeigh is on board. Then you'll get your instructions."

Then, with a quick nod of dismissal, Whaldon sat down and resumed his typing.

Delaney stopped at his secretary's desk on the way back to his office.

Mrs Berkley looked up from her typing. She sat upright in front of the typewriter on her neat desk. Her grey hair was pulled back into a sensible bun, and she had a serious expression on her face. Mrs Berkley rarely smiled or laughed, but Delaney knew her well enough to know she had a dry sense of humour. She was completely unflappable, and Delaney couldn't remember a time when she hadn't been his secretary. In all those years, she had never been late or been absent for any reason, except when her mother died. Even during the Blitz, she arrived at work on time. She had marched purposefully around rubble and workmen along the Embankment and had ignored all orders from police officers to refrain from entering Scotland Yard.

"It's imperative we do our job, Detective Chief Inspector," she'd said when he had found her dusting her desk and sweeping the floor of fallen plaster from the vibrations of the bombing, "We can't let that terrible man, Hitler, interfere with our important work."

Mrs Berkley's husband had died of TB many years ago, and they had no children. She was devoted to her work, and Delaney relied on Mrs Berkley more than he cared to admit.

"Mrs Berkley, a close call last night, I hear? The bombs fell close to you?"

"A couple of miles from my house, sir. No damage at all for me and my neighbours. But some poor souls were not so lucky."

"Quite so."

"What can I do for you, Detective Chief Inspector?" Mrs Berkley asked briskly, after a moment. She was not the emotional type, Delaney knew.

"Do you remember Mrs Carroll? She helped us out with the murder cases before Christmas."

"Of course I do, Detective Inspector."

Mrs Berkley had initially disapproved of Maggie, Delaney remembered. But Maggie had correctly interpreted Mrs Berkley's attitude as a motherly protection for her widowed employer and had been patient and taken no offense.

When Mrs Berkley had seen what an asset Maggie had been to the murder case, she was soon delivering cups of tea in the good china, a sign of utmost respect from the older woman.

Mrs Berkley peered at Delaney over her horn-rimmed glasses. "Would you like me to contact her for you?"

"Yes, please. Ask her if she is available for a meeting at my office tomorrow morning, would you? 9.00 am."

"Yes, sir."

"I am going to Dr Holberg's office, Mrs Berkley. I won't be back until after six, so I'll see you tomorrow."

"Very good, Detective Chief Inspector."

Chapter 7

PATTERSON ROAD, PLUMSTEAD.

Maggie heard a scrabbling sound, her heart racing as her mind conjured up images of rats or mice invading their dark, cramped shelter. She hated mice, their tiny feet skittering across the floor, their beady eyes glinting in the shadows. The sound seemed to come from far away, echoing through the thick, oppressive darkness around her.

Something brushed against her cheek, and Maggie jerked her head, a wave of panic washing over her. Not mice in her bed, she thought, her stomach churning with horror and disgust.

"Ma?" Birdie's voice was low and near, tinged with fear and concern.

"Ma? Thank God, are you okay?"

With a monumental effort, Maggie forced her eyes open, blinking against the overwhelming darkness that engulfed them. She couldn't focus, her mind fuzzy and disoriented. Had she fallen asleep downstairs again? The cold, hard concrete beneath her body suggested otherwise.

Maggie parted her lips to answer Birdie, but to her surprise, her voice came out as a hoarse croak. "Birdie?"

"Ma, are you okay? You fell and hit your head." Birdie's voice trembled, the telltale sign of recent tears.

Maggie stretched out her hands, her fingers brushing against the rough, unforgiving surface of the cellar floor. Slowly, the memories trickled back—the piercing wail of the sirens, the earth-shattering explosions, the house shuddering as if it might collapse at any moment. They must have been bombed, she realised, her heart constricting with fear.

A sudden, terrible thought struck her, and Maggie bolted upright, ignoring the searing pain that lanced through her skull. "Birdie, the boys..."

"We're here, Mum..." Two small, tremulous voices spoke in unison from the darkness, and Maggie felt a rush of relief so profound, it nearly brought tears to her eyes.

Gingerly, she eased herself into a sitting position, taking stock of her body. Her arms and legs seemed to be intact, but when she ran a hand over her head, she felt the sticky, matted texture of blood in her hair and a tender spot that made her flinch when she touched it. But apart from that, she appeared to be in one piece.

As her eyes adjusted to the gloom, Maggie could make out the huddled shapes of the twins and Birdie sitting beside them on the floor. "Boys, I'm just grand," she said, forcing a note of calm into her voice. "Just a bump on the head. Now, Birdie, can you remember where I put those candles?"

Maggie rose to her feet, fighting back a wave of nausea as the room swam. She shuffled forward, her hands outstretched until her fingers brushed against the familiar contours of the old wooden cabinet. She tugged open the drawer, her heart leaping with joy as she found the candles and matches nestled inside.

Soon, the soft, flickering glow of two candles illuminated the cellar, casting eerie shadows on the walls. Maggie's relief was short-lived, however, as she surveyed the damage. Most of the cellar's sturdy walls and ceiling had withstood the blast, but a pile of bricks and mortar now blocked the steps, and a jagged crack ran along the outer wall, the concrete bulging ominously.

"Ma… what are we—" Birdie's voice was high and thin with anxiety, but Maggie hushed her, not wanting to frighten the boys.

"Well now," she said, injecting a false note of brightness into her tone. "We have got ourselves into a bit of a pickle. But no matter, let's get ourselves organised and we'll make a plan. Birdie, you take one candle and see what we have on those shelves over there, and I'll take the other one and see if I can get to the door."

Maggie crept forward, testing her weight on the rubble with every step. The last thing she wanted was to cause a shift that might bring the wall down on top of them. On her hands and knees, she crawled towards the cellar door, half-hidden by debris. If she could just get it open, even a crack…

She reached for the handle, her heart pounding as she gave it a tentative turn and pushed. Nothing. The door remained stubbornly in place, unyielding against her efforts. Maggie gathered her strength and threw her entire body against it, sending tremors of pain up her spine and into her head, but still, it refused to budge.

Despair welled up inside her, hot and bitter. What would George say? She was supposed to protect the children, to keep them safe, and now they were trapped, entombed in this dark, suffocating space. Tears burned at the back of her eyes, and she sank down onto the rubble, her head throbbing with renewed pain.

"Ma, come down!" Birdie called softly from behind her. "We'll be alright, we just have to wait. Someone will find us soon."

Maggie rubbed at her eyes, drawing in a shaky breath. "You're right, darlin'. I'm coming down now."

As she made her way back to the others, Birdie reached out to rub her arm, her touch gentle and reassuring. "You saved us, Ma," she whispered, her voice cracking with emotion. "If we had tried to get to the shelter..." She let her words trail off, as if she was unwilling to give voice to the terrible possibility.

Maggie nodded, remembering the sight of those ominous, bird-like shapes approaching in the night sky. "They must be new ones," she murmured. "The old doodlebugs, they announced themselves, but these... well, no noise at all."

"The boys are hungry," Birdie said, her voice low.

Maggie closed her eyes, trying to think. Then a memory surfaced, and she brightened. "Boys, you like my jam, don't you?"

"Yes, Ma," James said, his small face pinched with hunger. "But we don't have any bread."

"Well, just for once, we'll eat the jam right out of the pot!" Maggie declared, mustering up a smile. "It's over there, Birdie, I think, on the shelf in the corner."

Once Birdie had handed it to her, she pried off the lid, and soon, the boys were giggling as they dipped their fingers into the sweet, sticky jam, their spirits lifted by this small, unexpected treat.

"Did I ever tell you how I made this jam?" Maggie asked, settling herself beside them as they shook their heads. "No? Well, it was before the war, and you two were just tiny wee boys when we all went to visit your aunt in the country..."

As she spun the tale, Maggie felt some of the tension ease from her shoulders. They were alive, and they were together. That was what mattered most.

Eventually, the boys drifted off to sleep, their small bodies tangled together under an old tarp Birdie had found. Maggie was just beginning to doze off alongside them when a sudden, loud scrabbling noise jolted her awake.

It was too loud to be mice, she realised, her heart racing. Gently, she eased herself out from under the children's limbs, trying not to wake them.

"Ma?" Birdie murmured, her voice thick with sleep.

"Shh now, listen," Maggie whispered, straining her ears.

There it was again, and this time, she was certain she could hear voices, muffled and distant, but unmistakable.

The boys stirred, blinking owlishly in the candlelight. "Shout!" Maggie commanded, her voice ringing out in the confined space. "Help! Help! Down here!"

They took up the cry, their voices rising in a desperate chorus. The noises above grew louder, a series of thumps and bangs that sent their hearts racing with renewed hope.

And then, just as they dared to believe that rescue was at hand, the wall of the cellar collapsed around them.

The room shook with the force of falling concrete, showering them with dust and debris. Maggie threw herself over the children, shielding them with her body as chunks of brick and plaster rained down from the ceiling. She squeezed her eyes shut, certain that this was the end, that the entire house would collapse and bury them all alive.

But then the rubble stopped falling, and the dust settled. An eerie silence descended, broken only by the ragged sound of their breathing and the distant, muffled wail of sirens.

Maggie raised her head, hardly daring to believe that they had survived. And then she heard it—a voice, calling out through the dust and the rubble.

"Mrs Carroll?" A man wearing a tin hat popped his head through a gap that the door had once occupied. "Mrs Carroll, is that you? Are you alright?"

Chapter 8

GUY'S HOSPITAL, LONDON.

Delaney decided to visit the morgue and talk to Dr Holberg in person. He opted to walk the two miles from the Victoria Embankment to Guy's Hospital where the morgue and Dr Holberg's laboratory were located, fittingly enough in the basement.

It was late afternoon, and the light was fading, but he wanted to clear his mind, to think about what he would say to Maggie. When she'd come back into his life the previous year, he'd felt the same connection to her as he had all those years ago in Ireland. What he hadn't told Whaldon, what he hadn't told anyone, ever, was the passionate embrace he and Maggie shared as they parted company in the dead of night outside a British military safe house near Dublin.

"You'll be safe now," Maggie said, as she pulled back the sackcloth which had covered him in the back of the horse-drawn cart.

"What will happen to you?" Delaney had asked, as he slid to the ground, nearly shrieking in pain from the gunshot wound on his leg.

"You'll need proper medical help," Maggie replied, ignoring his question. "I must go."

Delaney had caught her arm. "Stay. They'll help you. You can't go back, Maggie. They'll kill you for sure."

Delaney had stayed at the safe house long enough for his wound to be tended to by a medic. He'd insisted that the British military look after Maggie. The officers who debriefed him had been impressed by Maggie's courage.

"Maybe she can be of use," the officer had commented. As Delaney got ready to leave for Belfast and then back to England, he'd said his farewells to Maggie.

"I don't know how I'll ever thank you."

"No need," Maggie had said quietly. "A bheith sábháilte." *Be safe.*

"Will you be safe?" he'd asked, "What will you do?"

"They have a job for me," Maggie said. "I'll stay in Ireland, for now."

Delaney didn't know to this day whether it was gratitude or love or both, but he had pulled Maggie into his arms and kissed her. She hadn't pulled away, but had whispered in his ear afterwards, "Go n-éirí an bóthar leat, a stór."

May the road rise to meet you, my darling.

He'd loved Elizabeth, his wife, and missed her every day, but he'd never forgotten Maggie. After working the murder case together, she had invited him to Christmas dinner. He had seen her devotion to her daughter and twin boys and had resolved never to talk of that impulsive moment. Yet, he'd studied her closely, the way she tilted her head before she laughed, the way her voice rose and fell, and her expansive hand gestures as she told a story, and had felt the echo of the passion of that moment, back in Ireland all those years ago.

Delaney wanted to work with her again. But was he being selfish? Did he agree with Whaldon because he believed her skills would be an asset, or did he just want an excuse to be near her?

This mission would put her in danger. She was a wife and mother. He must be professional and dispassionate, for her sake.

When he arrived at the morgue, he glanced up at the cloudy night sky, hoping that meant the Luftwaffe would take a night off.

When he went inside, Delaney found Dr Holberg bent over the half-covered corpse of Patrick Dowd, laid under the harsh electric lights of the morgue.

Dr Joseph Holberg was unassuming and serious, the kind of man you might think was a bank clerk or bureaucrat, Delaney thought. Nobody outside the criminal justice system would guess he was the pioneer of police forensic work and one of the most revered pathologists in England.

"Why do you do it?" he'd asked Holberg once, after a particularly gruesome case where the murder victim was set on fire. He'd watched Holberg working on the charred remains, seemingly unaffected by the stench of burnt flesh.

Dr Holberg had considered the question before answering. "Two reasons, Detective Chief Inspector. The first is merely professional curiosity and satisfaction. Every day is different. Every body is different. They each have a story to tell and I find it immensely satisfying to 'read' that story, if you will. The other reason is to remind myself of the sanctity of human life. Nobody has the right to take it away. That is what I believe. In death, we are all equal. I have the honour of treating each victim with respect, regardless of the life the person may have led."

Watching the meticulous way Dr Holberg worked, Delaney saw the reverence in the way Holberg moved the dead man's limbs, and replaced the white cloth over the body, to afford the man some dignity in death.

"Ah, Detective Chief Inspector, you have arrived at an opportune moment. I am concluding my examination of poor Mr Dowd. Would you be so kind as to wait a few minutes while I write the last of my notes?" Dr Holberg straightened up and removed his gloves.

"Please, take your time, Doctor."

Delaney stood back while Dr Holberg scribbled his notes, then he gestured for Delaney to join him at the autopsy table.

Holberg pointed to the victim's hands. "Multiple fractures to the phalanges and metacarpals, consistent with repeated blunt force trauma. Likely inflicted with a heavy object, perhaps a hammer or a pipe." He moved to the head of the table, his fingers tracing the edge of a small, round hole at the base of Patrick Dowd's skull. "And here, a single gunshot wound to the back of the head. Close range, judging by the powder burns. Death would have been instantaneous."

"He must have been held down," Delaney mused. "More than one assailant?"

"Indeed," Holberg agreed. "As I said when I initially examined the victim at the crime scene, it's my opinion there were at least two or three assailants. One to hold the victim, the others to carry out the torture. And look at the man's wrists."

Delaney leaned over to look. "Bruised. So he was bound."

"Yes. I've extracted some fibres from his wounds. Rope of some kind. I'll see if I can identify it further. The poor man was bound so tight, he was bleeding. Or he was struggling hard against his restraints."

Delaney frowned, his mind racing. "So they tortured him, then executed him. This was planned, deliberate." He paused, considering the implication that Whaldon was right. Dowd must have blown his cover without realising it and then walked into a trap.

Holberg nodded. "It seems that way. The extent of the injuries, the systematic nature of the torture... this was a message. A warning, perhaps, or a punishment? But there's more here, Detective Chief Inspector."

He moved to the foot of the table and lifted one of Dowd's legs.

"See there on his calf? Grazed. It's the same on the other leg and on his back. It's consistent with the body being dragged."

"Post-mortem? So he wasn't killed where he was found?"

Dr Holberg shook his head. "I didn't think he was moved last night. There just wasn't enough blood at the scene. But these markings confirm it. He was tortured, killed by a gunshot to the head, and then dragged and dumped outside the pub."

Delaney's thoughts turned to the pub owner, Bill Knowles. "The pub where we found the body... the owner, Knowles, he's a shifty sort. Seemed nervous when we questioned him. I think he knows more than he's letting on, but it's possible he was telling the truth. He might not have heard or seen anything if the murder took place elsewhere."

"He found the body?"

Delaney shook his head. "No, one of Knowles' unfortunate customers found him."

"Well, your Mr Knowles is not in the clear just yet." Holberg pointed to a glass jar filled with murky liquid which looked like he dredged it from the River Thames.

"That's the contents of Mr Dowd's stomach. No solid food to speak of, but definitely beer. He'd been drinking somewhere very recently. Given the estimated time of death, it most probably was the Leinster Arms."

"So he was drinking inside the pub, he leaves, gets tortured and killed somewhere else, and then the killers drag his body back to the pub? Why would they do that?"

Delaney was thinking out loud, but Holberg answered him. "Because they wanted him to be found."

Delaney looked at Dr Holberg. "Doctor, last night you didn't find any identification on the body. How did…"

Dr Holberg took his glasses off and polished them with a handkerchief he'd pulled from his pocket, before putting them back on and meeting Delaney's eyes.

"Detective Chief Inspector, I'm not sure how much I can tell you…"

"It's alright Doctor. I know some of it," and Delaney told him about his meeting with Chief Superintendent Whaldon.

Dr Holberg nodded. "Alright. Well, I didn't identify him. A short while after I got the deceased back here, I received a strange telephone call. The caller said, 'Your body is Patrick Dowd. Tell Special Branch this is what we do with rats'. And so I called Special Branch. They later instructed me to send the preliminary report to Chief Superintendent Whaldon."

"I see. Thank you, Doctor."

"What are you thinking, Detective Chief Inspector?" Holberg asked. "Do you have a theory yet?"

"Not really. But Whaldon thinks this might be connected to those murders before Christmas. We always suspected there was more to it, some larger conspiracy at play." Delaney began pacing the room, his mind whirring. "And with the Irish connection…"

Delaney let his sentence trail off. He stared down at the lifeless Patrick Dowd. "This is what we do with rats."

What was he thinking? He couldn't be responsible for persuading Maggie to put herself in danger. Not like this.

His thoughts were interrupted by a telephone ringing.

"I'll just be a moment." Dr Holberg excused himself and disappeared through a door at the back of the morgue.

Delaney could hear the murmur of his voice for a few moments, and then the doctor reappeared.

"A message for you, Detective Chief Inspector. That was your secretary, Mrs Berkley. She has sent a car for you. You are needed urgently at the office."

Delaney frowned. What could be so urgent Mrs Berkley would send a car for him?

"Thank you, Doctor. I'll look forward to your full report."

"Just one thing, Detective Chief Inspector, before you go," Holberg said, as Delaney turned towards the door.

"What's that, Doctor?"

"Are you familiar with Leinster Gardens? I think I know where Dowd may have been killed."

Delaney listened to Holberg, and then quickly made his way to the entrance of Guy's Hospital, where Constable Hunter was waiting for him in a police car.

Mrs Berkley eased herself out of her office chair as Delaney walked down the corridor. Constable Hunter was following him. As he got nearer, he could see her face was flushed red.

"Whatever is the matter, Mrs Berkley? What is so urgent?" he asked, concerned to see his usually unflappable secretary so agitated.

She was holding a file.

"Sir, Patterson Road, is this the current address for Mrs Carroll? She hasn't moved at all?"

Delaney nodded. "I believe she's still there. Why?"

"Oh, sir." Mrs Berkley stopped to catch her breath. "Oh, sir....." Her hand flew to her mouth.

"Mrs Berkley, calm yourself. What on earth is the matter?" Delaney said in concern.

"Sir, the bombing last night? Patterson Road took a direct hit."

Chapter 9

PATTERSON ROAD,
PLUMSTEAD.

Maggie blinked as she emerged into bright daylight, her eyes struggling to adjust after the darkness of the cellar. She clenched her fists in an attempt to stop herself from shivering, but her body was shaking so violently that her teeth chattered uncontrollably. The cold air stung her lungs and the acrid smell of burning filled her nostrils.

"Come here, love," a man's voice said, cutting through the chaos. Maggie squinted, trying to make out his features, but the daylight blinded her. For a fleeting second, she wondered if she had succumbed to her injuries and was now in the presence of an angel.

Then she felt a firm hand grasp her wrist, anchoring her to reality.

"Hold on to me, love," the man said again, his voice calm and reassuring. "Go slowly. The rubble is unstable."

"My children..." Maggie croaked, her voice hoarse from the dust and smoke.

"Don't worry. They're all safe. Keep moving, love, we need to get you out of here."

Maggie stumbled forward, her body aching with every step. She kept her head down, focusing on the ground beneath her feet, as the man guided her through the debris. His hands gripped her wrists firmly, providing support and comfort until, at last, she stood on solid ground. Only then did she look up into the eyes of the air raid warden.

"Mrs Carroll? It's me, Arthur Daniels, from the butchers, remember?" His voice was familiar, but all the sounds Maggie could hear seemed to come from a distance and she was having trouble getting her brain to process the words properly. Daniels squeezed her hands. "Don't worry, love. Your children are all safe. We have them wrapped up warm. We'll get them something hot to drink. You too."

Maggie turned to see Birdie with her arms wrapped tightly around the twins, huddled together in the back of a military ambulance. Her children's faces were ghostly white, their eyes wide with shock and fear. Maggie raised a trembling hand to them, trying to force a smile, but they didn't respond. Their gazes seemed distant, looking through her as if she were a ghost.

It was then that Maggie became fully aware of her surroundings. The sounds of sirens screaming, men shouting, and the crackling of fires filled her ears. The stench of burning assaulted her senses, making her eyes water and her throat hurt. As she turned slowly, taking in the scene of destruction, her knees buckled, threatening to give way beneath her.

The once-familiar street was now a wasteland of crumpled houses and twisted metal. Only fragments of walls remained standing, like broken teeth in a shattered jaw. Maggie's eyes were drawn to a bedroom, its contents exposed like a grotesque doll's house. The bed was made perfectly, the yellow curtains flapping in the breeze. With a gasp, she recognised them as Birdie's curtains. The rest of the houses were reduced to piles of debris, obscured by plumes of black smoke that rose like funeral pyres into the grey sky.

Arthur Daniels stood beside her, his face grim. "We took a direct hit," he said, his voice heavy with sorrow. "Bastards."

"What... I mean, I saw... something... before we ran," Maggie stammered, her mind struggling to process the devastation.

"Bombs. Damn Luftwaffe, bloody bastards. "'Cuse my language. Set off from France, they reckon." Arthur shook his head sadly. "We didn't have a chance. They must 'ave been aiming for the Arsenal. But you were lucky. If you'd gone to your shelter..." He trailed off, his gaze shifting to the back garden where George had laboured for three days to build their Anderson shelter. Now it lay buried beneath a mountain of fallen masonry.

Maggie closed her eyes, offering a silent prayer of thanks for their miraculous survival. But the gratitude was short-lived, as the reality of the situation sank in. Her home, her possessions, her entire world had been destroyed in an instant. She was immediately overwhelmed and couldn't stop tears from flowing.

"Are there any others?" she asked, her voice barely above a whisper.

"Not many, love. Not many," Arthur replied grimly, knowing exactly what she meant. "An older couple, they did the same as you. Went to the cellar instead of the shelter. We found them and got them out, but I'm not sure if they made it."

"The Bernsteins?" Maggie asked, thinking of the kind elderly couple who had always greeted her with a smile.

"I don't know, love. But they would have had to be looking out to see the bombs comin'. Because we had no warning. No time for the sirens, even. It's been a terrible night. The worst I've seen. And I was here in '41 when they bombed the Arsenal. But come on now. Let's get you to the hospital. That's a nasty cut on your head."

Maggie allowed herself to be led to the ambulance, her body numb with shock and exhaustion. Arthur helped her inside, where she collapsed onto the bench beside her children.

"Oh, Mum, have you seen? Mrs Grenfield... she must be..." Birdie burst into tears, her small body shaking with sobs.

Maggie gathered her daughter into her arms, stroking her hair and murmuring words of comfort. The twins huddled closer, their small faces streaked with tears. As the ambulance drove through the ruined streets, Maggie held her children close.

Chapter 10

MEMORIAL HOSPITAL, PLUMSTEAD.

"Here you are love,"

An elderly woman handed Birdie a pile of clothing. Maggie rubbed her daughter's shoulder, as Birdie gazed despondently at the jumble of faded material with frayed edges in her arms.

The woman sighed.

"It's all we have, I'm afraid. Try them on, love. And you'll need some shoes. What size?"

Maggie remembered her daughter rushing down the stairs with Mrs Bernstein, carrying a bundle of colourful silk dresses. She knew how Birdie felt. But they had nothing now, so beggars could not be choosers.

"It's just for now, Birdie. We need some clothes, and then we'll get set up properly again, I promise."

Birdie nodded and took the clothes with a tired smile.

Maggie was exhausted. Arthur Daniels had driven them all to the Memorial Hospital on Shooter's Hill. It had been converted to a military hospital, but the nursing staff had been mobilized to look after the wounded from the bombing.

Maggie's cut was not serious, so they sat for hours in the hallway waiting for someone to come. Maggie knew now how lucky they'd been. They watched as nurses, rustling in their starched uniforms, pushed stretchers carrying bloodstained people through the corridors. All the victims were from last night's attack. Maggie found out more from a hospital porter

"It were deadly," he said stoically, as the survivors were wheeled past, some crying out in pain, others mute in their suffering.

"Over a 'undred dead, they're sayin',". He looked at Maggie and then her children, who were exhausted and in shock.

"You are some of the lucky 'uns. Him upstairs must 'ave been looking over you."

Maggie nodded, trying hard not to imagine what might have happened if she hadn't been looking out her window and seen the approaching aircraft.

"It'll be a long wait," the porter said sympathetically, and he disappeared through a door in the corridor. He emerged with a blanket for the boys and Birdie and a cup of tea for Maggie.

"Drink this, love," he said, winking at her. "Extra sugar, but don't tell no-one." She smiled gratefully.

Maggie sipped the tea and shared it with Birdie. They sat silently, breathing in the antiseptic smell, and trying to ignore the dull echoes of screams from somewhere down the hallway.

Maggie must have dozed off in her chair, because she jumped when the click-clack of heels on the polished floors neared and stopped in front of her. She looked up into the exhausted face of a nurse.

"Your head?" the nurse said without preamble. "Let me look."

Maggie eased from under the sleeping twin's limbs and followed the nurse down the corridor and behind a screen.

Twenty minutes later, her head wound was cleaned up. The nurse looked at Birdie and the boys.

"You can change in there," she said and gestured to a closed door behind her.

It was only then that Maggie realised they were all still in their night-clothes and coats and the boys were sleeping on the bundle of clothing Birdie had been handed earlier.

"I'm sorry," the nurse said. "But you can't stay here. You should find a shelter for the night, before it gets dark."

"What time is it?" Maggie asked. She wasn't certain what day it was, either.

"Nearly three o'clock in the afternoon," and then the nurse was click-clacking down the hallway again.

When they were dressed, Maggie asked the hospital porter where they should go.

"Well, love, there's a shelter in Plumstead High Street, but if I were you, I'd go to one of the churches, away from the town. They say there's bound to be another attack, seeing as they missed the Arsenal last night. Try St Mark, near the common."

It was usually a short walk to St Marks church from Shooters Hill, but they were all tired. The light was fading as they left the hospital. Maggie hurried them along, feeling vulnerable as it got darker. She wanted to be settled before the blackout.

"Can we go home?" Patrick asked. "I left my bus." He was teary at the thought of his abandoned tin toy.

"Sorry, darlin'. It's not safe. But we'll go soon, I promise." Maggie hoped they could, but doubted they would ever salvage anything from their home.

"Come on, now, we'll find your bus, and if we can't, we'll get you a new one," Birdie said, taking Patrick's hand, and leaving Maggie with James.

Maggie smiled gratefully at her daughter.

When they arrived at St Mark's Church, the pews had been moved to make room for rows of makeshift beds. A woman sitting at a table took their names and wrote them on a list.

"In case someone is looking for you," she explained.

Maggie nodded. There was nobody looking for her, she was sure. George was far away on the front line and she had no other family than her children. But she gave their names, anyway. A group of women handed out bowls of hot soup and bread, which they took gratefully. Maggie and Birdie took blankets from a pile at the door. They found a space at the back of the church near the altar and arranged their bundles on the floor. Birdie found some red cushions between the pews.

"Can we use them?" she said doubtfully to Maggie.

"I think so," Maggie said. The cushions were for comfort when people kneeled to pray. She was sure God wouldn't mind them using them as pillows. After they'd eaten soup and bread, Maggie settled the boys down for the night. Birdie was asleep quickly, but Maggie lay on the thin blanket staring up into the rafters. She tried to process the events of the last twenty-four hours. The realisation that she and her children could have been buried alive hit her with a force that made tears well up in her eyes.

"Thank God," she whispered under her breath, the only prayer she could muster. "Thank God."

The stream of people coming into the church finally slowed, and the large wooden doors were closed. Even then, the church was draughty and cold as the winter air seeped through cracks under the stained glass windows and door.

"Lights out" someone called, and candles and lamps were extinguished. Plunged into darkness, conversations became muted, and finally, the church echoed with the sounds of people snoring and muffled crying. Maggie tried to get comfortable, her head resting on the hard red cushion, and said a prayer of thanks, and tried not to think of what might have happened. She gave herself a shake.

"You'll be no use if you fall apart now," she muttered to herself and shut her eyes, willing sleep to come.

She slept a little, and then she woke. It was pitch black in the church. If it was light outside, Maggie couldn't tell because of the thick blankets which served as make-shift blackouts over the Church windows. Maggie sat up, looking over the shadows of the sleeping forms of her children, and tried to think. What now? Where would they go? Housing was in short supply and expensive. She had some money saved. Birdie's wages helped, but she didn't want her daughter working at the Arsenal. This time the munitions factory had been spared, but what if those new rockets had better aim next time? What if the next attack came during the day when Birdie was on shift? She fought down panic, knowing that she couldn't look after the children if she were falling apart.

She wished she could speak to George. She lay back down again and closed her eyes. When she slid finally into a fitful sleep, she had a dream that George had arrived home from the War and had come looking for them. She could see him across the mountains of rubble and was trying to call out to him. But as was the case with dreams sometimes, she found she couldn't move to get closer, and when she opened her mouth to call his name, a strange wind tore her words away. Then her husband turned to look at her. He wasn't pleased to see her, she thought. His face was contorted with anger.

"You betrayed us," he shouted. "You betrayed us."

"George!" she'd called back. "Let me explain." He didn't answer, and when she looked at his face again, she saw it wasn't George at all. The dream had morphed her husband into a monster from her past.

Chapter 11

LEINSTER GARDENS, LONDON.

Delaney was lost in thought when Constable Hunter picked him up early the next morning. When Delaney had received the news about Patterson Road from Mrs Berkley, the extent of his sorrow had taken him by surprise.

Mrs Berkley must have seen the devastation on his face, because uncharacteristically, she'd patted him on the arm and said, "Don't worry, Detective Chief Inspector. There's still some hope. I'll try to find out if any casualties were taken to the hospitals or shelters."

Delaney hoped she was right.

"Here we are, sir," Hunter said as he parked the Wolsey.

"Right then, Constable," Delaney said grimly, shaking off his thoughts and turning his full attention to the murder investigation. "Let's see what Mr Knowles has to say."

The weak light of a grey London morning filtered through the grime-streaked windows of the Leinster Arms, casting a sickly pallor over the worn wooden tables and scarred bar top. Delaney paused in the doorway, his keen eyes taking in the scene before him. Beside him, Constable Billy Hunter shifted uneasily, his face screwed up in an expression of disgust.

"Not exactly the Ritz, is it, sir?" Hunter murmured, eyeing the sticky floor with distaste.

The last time they had both been inside the pub was the night of the murder. Delaney had been focused on the victim, not the shabby decor, and now he had to agree with Constable Hunter. This place was a dump.

Delaney cleared his throat, intending to catch the attention of the man behind the bar. Bill Knowles was a large, fleshy man with small, deep-set eyes and a sheen of sweat on his upper lip. He was methodically polishing a set of pint glasses with a stained rag, his movements mechanical and precise, and his eye on Delaney and Hunter.

"Mr. Knowles," Delaney said, stepping forward towards the bar. "Detective Chief Inspector Delaney, and this is Constable Hunter. We met the other night." Delaney held out his identification. "I believe you know why we're here."

Knowles looked up, his expression carefully blank. "Can't tell you any more than I did the other night," he said, his voice a raspy drawl. "I don't know nuthin' about that poor soul. I didn't see nuthin' and I didn't hear nuthin.'"

Delaney felt a flicker of irritation at the man's feigned ignorance, but kept his expression impassive.

"Patrick Dowd," he said, watching Knowles closely for any reaction. "He was the man found dead in the alley behind your pub two nights ago. Tortured and then shot in the head. You saw the body. Hard thing to forget, I would think."

Knowles' hand stilled on the glass he was polishing, but only for a moment. "Oh, I 'aint forgotten, officer. Terrible business, that," he said, shaking his head. "But I don't see what it has to do with me or my establishment. As I told you lot at the time and," he emphasized, "as I am telling you now."

"The body of a man was found outside your establishment, Mr Knowles. So I would say it very much has something to do with you. The man was bound and tortured. It must have taken some time. So if you don't mind, Constable Hunter and I will be here until we have the information we need."

Knowles sighed and set down the glass he'd been cleaning so hard that Delaney was surprised it didn't shatter. "Outside, Officer. The poor man was found outside. I don't have nuthin' to do with what happens outside. I don't go out much these days. Dangerous times, Detective, dangerous times. I mind my own business."

Delaney took a step closer, his shoes sticking slightly to the tacky floor. "Mr Knowles. I have reason to believe that the murder victim was in your pub the night he died. And that he might have been meeting someone here."

It wasn't the entire truth, but Delaney let the words hang in the air, watching as Knowles' jaw tightened almost imperceptibly. The man was hiding something, that much was clear. But getting him to talk would require a delicate touch.

"I run a respectable establishment, Inspector," Knowles said, his voice rising. "I don't know nuthin' about no meetings or no murders."

"Respectable?" Delaney raised an eyebrow, casting a pointed glance at the bottle of black market whisky sitting on a shelf behind the bar. "That's not the word I would use, Mr Knowles."

Knowles flushed, his eyes darting away from Delaney's gaze. "Times are hard, Inspector," he muttered. "A man's got to make a living somehow."

Delaney leaned forward, bracing his hands on the grimy bar top. "I'm not interested in your petty crimes, Mr Knowles, so let's start again. Was the victim, Patrick Dowd, in your pub the night of his murder?"

Knowles was silent for a moment, and then he said, "He might have been. It was busy. I don't take notice of everyone who comes in and out."

"It was a Monday night, Mr Knowles, not usually a busy drinking night, I wouldn't have thought. So, he may have been in the pub before his murder? Was Patrick Dowd a regular? Had you seen him before?" And as Knowles started to bluster again, Delaney held up his hand. "Mr Knowles, we can do this here or we can interview you somewhere not as convenient. So please just answer the question. Had you seen Patrick Dowd in this establishment before the night he was murdered?"

Knowles nodded. "Once or twice, mebbe," he muttered.

"Good. Did he come alone?"

"No. We get a lot of Irish navvies in here. He came in with his mates. They all live in the boarding houses around here."

"You knew he was Irish?"

"Course I did."

"Was he with anyone on the night of the murder?"

Knowles held up another glass to the light and then continued his polishing. "He was on 'is own as I remember."

"Came in on his own," Delaney repeated. "Did he speak to anyone here?"

This time, Knowles placed the glass carefully on the bar before he answered. "Not that I saw. 'E had a pint, and then left. Didn't see 'im leave. He was there, then 'e was gone. Then poor old Charlie Sutton went out for a piss and fell over the body. Then I called you lot. That's all I know, God's honest truth."

Delaney doubted God had much to do with anything in the Leinster Arms. He exhaled and closed his eyes briefly. He wasn't going to get much more out of Knowles. Yet.

"Thank you for your time, Mr Knowles. But if I find out you have been lying to me, first my officers will pay a visit and inspect your inventory, and second, I will arrest you for your part in the murder of Patrick Dowd. I am sure you know what sentence a murder conviction carries, Mr Knowles. So I invite you to contact me, should you remember something that helps my investigation. Good day to you."

Delaney and Hunter left the pub. Delaney breathed in some fresh morning air, glad to be out of the fug of the Leinster Arms.

"What now, sir?" Hunter asked.

"I wish I had more manpower Constable," Delaney replied. "I would have Knowles and the pub under constant surveillance."

He stood in the street, looking around. "Dr Holberg believes Dowd was not killed outside the pub, but somewhere else. Then the killers dragged him back to be found."

"More than one killer, sir?"

"Yes. Dowd was tortured before he was killed, so at least one other man must have held him down. Holberg had a theory about where he might have met his death."

"So Knowles might be telling the truth?"

"Oh no, Constable. Dowd was definitely in the pub earlier that evening. The contents of his stomach confirms that. But, at some point, he left—either by himself, or he was forced—and then he was tortured and killed nearby, and his body dragged back to the Leinster Arms. The question is, why?"

"Why he was dragged back?"

"The killer or killers wanted him found. They even made an anonymous telephone call to Dr Holberg, confirming Dowd's identity. They called him a 'rat'. The question I have is why did they drag him back here? Why not leave him in the street?"

Constable Hunter thought for a minute. "The killer wanted to implicate Knowles?"

Delaney nodded. "That's what I think. I think they want Knowles to sweat a bit. Come on, Hunter, I want to have a look around."

Delaney and Hunter walked along the street, leaving the car parked in the same place. Delaney kept stopping to look at the tall Victorian terraced houses that lined Leinster Gardens.

"What are we looking for, sir?"

"Something Dr Holberg told me this morning. Do you know this area at all, Constable?"

"No, sir."

"Me neither. But see all these houses? Some of them are not what they seem."

"What do you mean?"

Delaney didn't reply. He kept walking for a minute, stopped, and then looked up at the houses again, on his left-hand side.

"Here we are. Number 23 and 24. They're not houses at all. Just facades."

Constable Hunter looked at him in surprise. "Really?"

Delaney explained, "When the Metropolitan Tube line was being built back in the last 1800s, these two houses were demolished. But rather than re-build them, the railway company built these facades."

"So, there is nothing behind them?"

"No. But it wasn't just for looks. The railway needs air vents. So behind these facades are open spaces with vents to let off steam from the underground railway."

"I see, sir. And you think Patrick Dowd was killed behind these facades?"

"I do, Constable. What better place to torture and kill someone where you wouldn't be seen or heard from the street? Let's take a look."

Delaney and Hunter found a narrow alleyway that led behind the fake houses and a large concrete area with an iron grate across the centre. Looking up, they saw iron girders fastened to the actual houses on either side of the facades.

"Take a close look, Constable. We might find enough to get Holberg's team out here."

Both men walked slowly around the space, keeping their heads down and eyes examining the ground and the walls for any sign that a violent encounter had occurred there.

After a few minutes of finding nothing, Hunter exclaimed, "Over here, sir."

When Delaney joined him, he pointed to two large rust-brown stains on the concrete. "I think that's blood, sir."

Delaney squatted down to inspect the stains. "I think you're right, Constable. Good work. We'll get Holberg out here. He might find other evidence that proves Dowd was killed here."

Constable Hunter tapped him on the shoulder. "Look up there, sir. It's possible we might have witnesses."

When Delaney looked up, he saw a small window, high on the next house along.

"Well spotted. Let's knock on the door, shall we? That window is on the third floor of number 25."

They walked back to the street and went up the steps to the front door of number 25. Delaney rapped on the door. There was no answer. He banged again, with a little more force. Still no answer, and Delaney couldn't hear any movement inside.

"We'll come back, Hunter. You never know, someone might have seen something useful."

As they turned to leave, Delaney spotted a handwritten card in a small window by the front door.

Help Needed. Ask for Mrs Doyle.

"Right. We'll be back to interview Mrs Doyle soon," he said to Constable Hunter.

He shivered as a chilly February wind scattered litter around them. "Let's go back to the office. I think I know how to rattle our Mr Knowles. And we have made good progress today."

"And there might be some good news about Mrs Carroll and her family, sir," Hunter added.

"I hope so, Billy. I hope so."

Chapter 12

LEINSTER GARDENS, LONDON.

Bill Knowles waited for twenty minutes before he left the bar and walked over to a grimy window which gave him a wide view of the street. There was no sign of the two coppers, although the car was still parked out there.

Then he went into his small windowless office at the back of the pub. He lit a cigarette and inhaled deeply to steady his nerves, and sat down at his desk, which was piled with bills and receipts, some of them yellow with age. He stared at the telephone on his desk and contemplated his options again, before picking up the receiver and dialling a number he knew by heart.

"I told 'em nuthin'," he said without preamble when the call was picked up at the other end. "Just like you told me. Now, I want out. I'll see to the delivery and then that's it. I'm finished, do you hear? I'm not swinging for this murder."

Chapter 13

ST MARK'S CHURCH, PLUMSTEAD.

That morning, Maggie had woken with a start, the images of her dream still so vivid that she reached out to check that George hadn't turned into a monster, but was still her good-natured husband, sleeping peacefully beside her. Her hand touched cold concrete, and she flinched, the foggy images from her dream receding out of reach, to be replaced by the reality of their predicament.

Maggie was stiff from sleeping on a thin blanket. She sat up and stretched and looked around.

There wasn't an inch of space on the church floor or in pews which weren't occupied by people, either hunched under blankets or just sitting, huddled together for warmth and comfort. There are so many of us, Maggie thought, and we're all homeless.

"Oh, George," she whispered to herself, "what do I do now?"

"What's that, Ma?" Birdie asked, her head poking out from under her covers.

Maggie realised she must have spoken aloud. "Nothing darlin'," she said, attempting a smile. "I just had a bad dream. How did you sleep?"

"Alright," Birdie replied as she stretched. "Oh, Ma, what do we do now?" she asked, echoing Maggie's thoughts.

"Don't worry darlin'. We'll get by." But even as Maggie attempted cheerfulness, her words sounded hollow, and she felt a heavy knot of anxiety form in her stomach.

Just the shock setting in, she told herself. After everything they had suffered in the last twenty-four hours, it was normal that she should worry. Maggie pushed her dark feelings away and stood. She stretched her arms and back again, easing away the aches and stiffness from the chilly night. She touched her forehead. The bandage was still in place, and her fingers didn't feel any moisture, so the cut must have stopped bleeding. Her head still throbbed though.

The twins were stirring under the thin blankets.

"Come along, boys," Maggie said brightly. "Let's rouse ourselves. We need to fill out some forms so I can get my ration book and we can find somewhere to live. We'll need to leave soon. There'll be plenty of people needing the same thing, so I want to be first in line."

Grumbling a little, the two boys rubbed sleep from their eyes and then helped Birdie fold the blankets.

The door of the church creaked open to allow damp winter air to billow in, but Maggie was glad to see the same cheery women from the night before carrying urns of tea.

"I'll get us a cuppa, Ma," Birdie announced, and Maggie nodded gratefully. She'd need a strong brew to get her through the day.

As Maggie smoothed down her sons' hair and tried to decide on a plan of action for the day ahead, her attention was caught by men's voices, raised above the general hubbub.

"Police. Wonder what they want." Birdie materialised at Maggie's side, holding a steaming mug of tea.

"I don't know, love," Maggie answered, taking the tea, but her knot of fear tightened as two uniformed officers bent over the table where Maggie had registered the previous evening. As Maggie and Birdie watched, they shuffled through paperwork and spoke to the same volunteer who'd welcomed them when they arrived.

After a few minutes, one officer held up a sheet of paper and pointed to it. Maggie couldn't hear what they were saying to the lady, but her apprehension grew as the officers looked in Maggie's direction.

"They're coming over here, Ma. Do you think it's about Dad?" Birdie's face had drained of colour and she gripped Maggie's arm.

Maggie could see the two men approaching, both with serious expressions on their faces.

"No, I'm sure not," Maggie replied, trying to keep her face calm, but feeling her heart hammer in her chest.

As the officers got nearer, Maggie felt a rising sense of panic. She tried to keep her expression neutral, but her mind was racing. What could the police possibly want with her? And why now, when her world had already been turned upside down?

"Mrs Carroll?" the taller of the two officers asked, consulting a notebook. "Margaret Carroll?"

Maggie nodded, her throat too dry to speak.

"I'm Officer Barnes, this is Officer Hollis. We've been sent by Detective Chief Inspector Delaney. He has been looking for you."

Maggie gazed at the officer in confusion. "Delaney?" she said at last. "You mean Robert Delaney? I don't understand. Why is he looking for me? How did he know..."

"Sorry Mrs Carroll, that's all we know. DCI Delaney's orders were to find you and take you to Scotland Yard."

Maggie glanced at Birdie and saw the fear and confusion in her daughter's eyes. She couldn't leave her children, not now.

"All right," she said at last, "But my children…"

"We'll take them with us," Officer Hollis said. "They'll be safe at Scotland Yard. You all look like you need something to eat."

Maggie looked down at herself and then at Birdie and the boys. They were wearing the rumpled clothes the nurse had given them. There were smears of dirt on their faces and dust in their hair. They were in no fit state to visit Scotland Yard. And yet, Robert Delaney might be able to help them.

"Alright," Maggie said, realising she didn't have the energy to argue. All four of them followed the officers out of the church to a car waiting outside.

The boys settled in the back seat, excited to be in a car, and Birdie slid in beside them.

"Where are we going, Ma?" Patrick asked.

"You remember Mr Delaney? He visited us at Christmas? Well, we're going to see him," Maggie said. "Isn't that nice?"

"Will he find us a new house?" James asked.

"Well, now, I don't know about that," Maggie replied, trying to smile. She was grateful when one of the officers offered to show the twins how to turn the siren on.

As she climbed in, she turned to thank the officer who closed the door behind her, and she glanced back at the Church. A man stood outside, and although he had his back to Maggie, his figure looked familiar.

It was his hair, Maggie realised as the police car drove away. The man had red hair. Why was that familiar?

She was just tired and confused, she told herself. The drive to Scotland Yard passed in a blur of grey streets and bombed-out buildings. Maggie stared out the window the whole time, her mind whirling with questions and fears.

Chapter 14

SCOTLAND YARD, LONDON.

Mrs Berkley was speaking on the telephone when Delaney and Hunter arrived back at the office.

He waited until she finished her call and replaced the receiver.

"Good news, sir," she said immediately, and with a rare smile. "There were survivors from the bombing on Patterson Road, including a mother and three children who were taken to hospital with minor injuries. We are certain it's Mrs Carroll and her family. They were at the hospital last night, but this morning, two officers checked the churches and shelters and located them at St Mark's Church. They are on their way now."

"Thank God," Delaney said, feeling relief wash over him.

"Quite," Mrs Berkley said briskly. "The good Lord was certainly watching over them."

"So far, he's been watching over all of us today, Mrs Berkley."

Chapter 15

SCOTLAND YARD, LONDON.

"Maggie!"

Delaney was sitting behind his desk, his shirtsleeves rolled up and his hair dishevelled, engrossed in his case files. He looked up as Maggie, Birdie, and her twin brothers were ushered in by two constables. His eyes widened slightly at the sight of their dusty clothes and pale faces.

Seeing the weariness on Maggie's face and the bandage on her head, he had an immediate urge to rush over and wrap his arms around her. Instead, he said, "Thank God you are alright. You are alright, aren't you? Any injuries? What happened to your head?" He got up from behind his desk and took Maggie's arm.

"Sit down here," he said, helping her to the chair which faced his desk.

Maggie nodded her thanks and said, "We are all fine. Just a cut on the head. It was truly a miracle, Robert. And then, your officers found us. How did you know where we were?"

Delaney explained, "Mrs Berkley did all the work. We'll get you all looked after."

"Robert," Maggie said, her voice tired, "I'm glad to see you, but what are we doing here? Why were you looking for us?"

"First things first, Mrs Carroll," a voice said behind them. "These children need a bath, a good meal, and then rest. They've been through a terrible ordeal."

"Mrs Berkley." Maggie turned and smiled at the older woman. "We were blessed. There were many of our neighbours who didn't... well..." Her voice cracked as she couldn't finish her sentence.

"Oh, my dear." Mrs Berkley patted her arm. "Don't think about any of that now. Let's get you fed and clothed."

"Yes, yes, of course," Delaney said, feeling like an idiot. "All of you need some rest and clean clothes."

A thought struck him. Where would they go?

"Er, I do have room at my house," he started, but Mrs Berkley cut him off with a glare.

"Detective Chief Inspector, Mrs Carroll is a married woman. That won't do at all. No, if you will permit me to leave work now, I will take Mrs Carroll and her children to my house. They will be comfortable there until other arrangements can be made."

"Thank you Mrs Berkley," Delaney said, relieved.

Maggie glanced back at her children, huddled together in the office. "Are you sure?" she asked. "It's such an imposition..."

"Not at all," Mrs Berkley insisted. "Detective Chief Inspector Delaney needs to talk with you, but that will wait until tomorrow. Isn't that right, sir?"

It didn't sound like a question to Delaney, so he nodded. "Of course." Mrs Berkley beckoned for Maggie and her tired family to follow her.

"Do you have a tin bus we can play with?" Delaney heard one of the boys ask as they walked down the corridor.

Delaney shook his head and smiled. Mrs Berkley never ceased to surprise him. It was entirely possible, he supposed, that she did have a tin bus for the twins to play with.

Chapter 16

MULGRAVE ROAD, SHREWSBURY COMMON.

"I can't thank you enough," Maggie said for the third time to Mrs Berkley.

"Now, I won't hear any more of that," the older woman said firmly. "We all need to pull together in these dark days and do our bit for the country. It's our duty."

She and Maggie were arranging bedding for the boys. The twins were to sleep downstairs in Mrs Berkley's living room on a bed of cushions while Maggie and Birdie shared the bed in the spare room upstairs.

Mrs Berkley's home was a Victorian terrace on a quiet residential street in Shrewbury Common, not far from the Carroll's demolished house in Plumstead.

Usually, Mrs Berkley took a train to Woolwich and then it was a brisk twenty-minute walk to her house on Mulgrave Road, but today, Constable Hunter had volunteered to drive them all there.

Maggie had smiled to herself when he made the offer. She had seen the way the young constable looked at Birdie, and the blush on her daughter's cheeks as he gallantly held his arm out to assist Birdie out of the car when they arrived at Mrs Berkley's house.

Even wearing ill-fitting hand-me-downs from the hospital lost and found, and after being practically buried alive, Birdie still held her chin high and rewarded Constable Hunter with a beaming smile.

Mrs Berkley's house was warm and comfortable. There was a spacious kitchen with a round table, which they all sat around while Mrs Berkley made tea and toasted some crumpets, to the delight of the twins, who had never tasted them before.

"Use all the hot water you need," Mrs Berkley insisted afterwards, and Maggie felt her shoulders relax a little as she scrubbed her body free of all the grime and dust which had settled in her pores and matted her hair.

Birdie was delighted that Mrs Berkley had an inside toilet, and Maggie was the most grateful she had ever been when the older lady produced a tin car for the boys to play with.

"My neighbour has a grandson the same age," she explained to Maggie as they both watched the boys lying on the rug in front of the living room fire, pushing the car backwards and forwards and laughing.

For a short while, Maggie could persuade herself that life was getting back to normal.

Chapter 17

SCOTLAND YARD, LONDON.

"You want me to go undercover? I don't understand, Robert."
Maggie stared at Delaney in obvious astonishment.

"I know it's a lot to take in," Delaney replied. "I'll explain what I can."

Delaney had been glad to see that Maggie looked rested when she arrived with Mrs Berkley at the office the next morning. Her face was still etched with worry lines, though.

"The children? How are they?" he'd asked.

"They are grand, thank you. They are staying with Birdie at Mrs Berkley's. I don't know what we'd have done without her. She's been so kind."

Mrs Berkley had made tutting noises and waved her hand dismissively.

Delaney had got straight to the point. Chief Superintendent Whaldon had made it clear that this mission was of the utmost importance.

"Mrs Berkley, I need to chat with Mrs Carroll in private. Please hold any telephone calls."

"Yes, sir. I'll bring you both a cup of tea, then you'll not be disturbed."

Maggie had taken a seat in Delaney's office, and he'd sat behind the desk.

She looked expectantly at Delaney. "This is all very mysterious, Robert. I hope nothing is wrong?"

Mrs Berkley delivered a tray with a teapot and cups and then left the office, closing the door behind her. Delaney waited until she was gone and Maggie had poured the tea before he answered.

"If you are worried about Connor Byrne, then I can put your mind to rest. He's still firmly behind bars and facing the gallows," Delaney said, seeing, by the relief on Maggie's face, that he had guessed correctly and she had been worried about the man who had tried to kill Birdie.

"Oh, thank goodness, Robert. I was sure that you were going to tell me he had escaped or been released somehow."

"No, nothing like that," Delaney had said slowly, "but what I have to tell you is connected to Byrne, I'm afraid."

Maggie sat with her cup of tea in her hand, looking worried again.

"We need your help," he'd said at last. "We need you to go undercover."

Maggie had nearly dropped her tea in surprise.

When she had gained her composure and put the teacup down, she asked, "We? Who is 'we' Robert? The police?"

"The British Government."

"I don't understand, Robert. How can I help the government? I'm just a mother and a housewife. Although I don't have a house at present," Maggie gave a small laugh.

Delaney waited a moment, then leaned forward, his elbows on the desk. "Maggie," he said quietly. "What I'm about to tell you is top secret. It cannot leave this room, do you understand?"

She held her hand up to stop him from speaking. "Robert, please don't tell me government secrets, I can't..."

"Maggie, you can. You know you can," Delaney said firmly. He opened a desk drawer and pulled out a manila file.

He reached across the desk and gestured for Maggie to take the file.

"The contents of that file tell me you are not 'just' a mother and house-wife. It tells me you have run successful undercover operations many times for the British Government. And they are asking you to help them one more time."

Maggie's whole body stiffened as she opened the file, scanning the pages.

"The government has been keeping tabs on me all this time?" she asked, frowning.

"No. When you arrived in England and married George, there was nothing to monitor. But when you helped with the Connor Byrne busi-ness, you attracted some interest. Good interest," he added.

"Robert, this is very flattering, to be sure, but I helped you because I was worried about Birdie. I am just a mother and housewife now," she said as she closed the file and placed it on Delaney's desk. "This girl, here," she tapped the file with a finger, "she does not exist anymore. There must be many fine officers the British Government can ask for help now."

Delaney sighed. "That's the problem, Maggie. There are none. None available for this operation. And I wouldn't involve you if I had any other choice. But this is a request from higher up. Please, would you at least listen to what I can tell you? And if you agree to help, there is a full briefing with MI5 tomorrow."

Maggie sat in silence for a moment.

Delaney knew what he was about to say was manipulative.

"If you help, you would help make the country a safe place for your children. For everyone's children."

"Alright," she said at last. "I'll listen."

"We've had intelligence that suggests a splinter group of the IRA is plan-ning an attack on London," Delaney said. "But this time, they're targeting something specific. Something that could turn the tide of the war."

"And Connor Byrne is part of that group?" Maggie guessed.

"Yes. At the time of his arrest, we believed he was working for German secret services, to gather intelligence in exchange for weapons or other support of the IRA. But they are doing more than just gathering information, and they have help."

"Who is helping them?"

Delaney shook his head. "I don't know at the moment. I haven't been fully briefed either.

"Connor Byrne won't talk at all?"

"No. MI5 has never got him to talk, even when there was an offer to reduce his sentence from hanging to life imprisonment. But, they did trace contacts of his back to a boarding house in Leinster Gardens, and for weeks now, an informant has been feeding back information. Until the other night. The night of the bombing."

"What happened?" Maggie was sitting forward in her seat now.

"The informant, Patrick Dowd, was murdered. His body was found outside a pub in Leinster Gardens, off the Bayswater Road."

"Oh." Maggie sighed. Delaney could see she had guessed what was coming. He carried on.

"MI5 needs a new informant," Delaney said, his tone direct. What was the point of beating around the bush?

"Robert, you can't be serious? I have a family now. And we are homeless. My job is to keep them safe, and I'd be putting them in danger all over again..."

Delaney held up his hands as Maggie became more agitated.

"Maggie, I understand, I really do. But MI5 will put your children somewhere safe. And they will rehouse you, where ever you want. Look, I don't know the whole story, but this group has resources. They are planning something big and it's imminent. We just don't have the manpower or the time to infiltrate the group. We need someone who they don't suspect, just to get a piece of information MI5 can work with."

"I suppose by someone they don't suspect, you mean someone Irish. Is that it?"

Delaney nodded. "Yes, I do."

Maggie sighed again.

"Maggie, at least take the briefing. You'll be bound by the Official Secrets Act. I'm sure Mrs Berkley won't mind the boys and Birdie staying with her another night. And if you decide not to do this, then I'll help the best I can to find you somewhere to stay."

Maggie closed her eyes as if she were trying to gather her thoughts. Delaney sat in silence, allowing her time.

"You are sure that I am the right person for this job?" she asked hesitantly. "And MI5 will make sure my children are safe?"

"Of course."

"Then I'll come to the briefing."

Later that evening, when the twins were sleeping soundly, and Birdie was getting ready for bed, Maggie and Mrs Berkley sat in the kitchen sharing a pot of tea.

"Robert has asked me for my help," Maggie said tentatively. "He wants me to…"

Mrs Berkley held up her hand. "No, you mustn't say another word, my dear. As I understand it, the matter is highly confidential."

"Oh, I know. I would not break any confidences," Maggie said hastily. "I was going to say that he wants me to do something that is quite… well, dangerous. And I am in two minds. On one hand, my first concern is the children, although Birdie is nearly a grown woman. They have been through so much, what with George away at war and the bombing. But, I think I can help with this matter of national importance. It's so hard to decide, and I don't have much time."

"Are you asking for my advice?" Mrs Berkley topped up both teacups.

"I suppose I am," Maggie said, smiling. "It's been a long time since I could confide in anyone. Not since George left."

"You've no family?"

Maggie shook her head. "George was an only child, and his parents are both gone now. He had an aunt, but she died last year. And… well, I lost touch with my family in Ireland years ago. So I've no one to go to, to help me sort through problems. I'd be grateful for any advice you have."

Mrs Berkley smiled. "My dear, I have known Detective Chief Inspector Delaney for many years. He is a thoughtful, intelligent man of great integrity. And I believe he is a great judge of character. So if he has asked you to help him, he knows that you have the skills he needs, and he wouldn't send you into danger unless he had no other choice."

Maggie nodded.

Mrs Berkley continued, "I am sure that he will do everything in his power to make sure the children are safe."

"So you think I should do this?"

"Only you can make that decision. But these are extraordinary times. And I believe we must all rise to the challenge, and as hard as it is, we must do our duty, even if that means suffering some hardships."

Maggie sighed. "You are right. I just hope that Robert can find somewhere for the children to live away from London. Maybe somewhere in the countryside. I have to go to a briefing tomorrow. I'll know more then, I suppose."

There was a rustling sound behind Maggie, and she turned her head.

"I'm not going to the countryside," Birdie was standing in the doorway, her hands on her hips. "I don't know what it is you have to do, Ma, but I intend to go back to work."

"Birdie, how can you go back to work? You have nowhere to live, and what about the boys? Who will look after them?"

"I have to do my duty too," Birdie argued, and Maggie could see tears shining in her eyes, "Just like Mrs Berkley said. I'll find a flat, or..."

"Bernadette can stay here," Mrs Berkley interrupted, "As long as your mother agrees, that is," she said firmly to Birdie. "She gets the last word."

Maggie laughed. "It's been a long time since I got the last word with my daughter. Alright, Birdie. If I can arrange for the twins to stay somewhere safe, I will allow it. It's very kind of Mrs Berkley and you are to help her and not be a bother. And no going out with Billy Hunter. You'll behave yourself like a lady."

"Ma!" Birdie cried, her face flushing red, but then she smiled. "Thank you so much, Mrs Berkley."

After Birdie had left, and they heard her footsteps going up the stairs, Mrs Berkley patted Maggie's hand. "Don't worry. It's all going to be alright, you'll see."

Maggie smiled back, but inside, she didn't feel as confident as Mrs Berkley.

Chapter 18

MULGRAVE ROAD, SHREWSBURY COMMON.

Mrs Berkley knocked gently on the bedroom door early the next morning. Maggie was already awake. She hadn't slept much and had been laying in bed beside her sleeping daughter, just watching her breathe, not wanting to face the day ahead.

When she opened the bedroom door, Mrs Berkley was already dressed and ready for work. She held out an armful of clothes.

"Here," Mrs Berkley said. "One for you and the other for Bernadette. You're both going to work today, so you'll need suitable clothes."

"Oh, thank..." Maggie started to say, but Mrs Berkley was already walking away, talking over her shoulder. "None of that, please. I have arranged for my neighbour to watch the boys today, so Birdie can resume her shift. There's a pot of tea downstairs when you are ready."

"Good morning," Delaney said when Maggie met him in the cobbled courtyard of Scotland Yard. "I was worried you might change your mind."

"If it wasn't for Mrs Berkley, I might have," Maggie answered.

"Mrs Berkley is a wise woman," Delaney said. "Shall we? Before you change your mind?"

There was a black Wolsey waiting for them, with its engine idling. Maggie noticed that Constable Hunter was not driving today.

"Where are we going?" Maggie asked as Delaney opened the car door for her. She slid into the back seat and he went around the other side of the car and let himself in.

"Blenheim House," Delaney answered, once he'd slammed the car door.

"Actually, sir, we're not going to Blenheim today," the driver said over his shoulder. "I've orders to take you to another location."

Delaney smiled at Maggie and shrugged his shoulders. "Sorry about all the hush hush, Maggie."

The Wolsey's engine hummed smoothly as it carried Detective Chief Inspector Delaney and Maggie out of London, leaving behind the bomb-scarred streets and the constant threat of enemy aircraft overhead. Delaney sat in the back seat, his mind drifting as he watched the city give way to the green countryside of Surrey.

Beside him, Maggie sat still, her hands clasped together in her lap and her face drawn with worry. Delaney knew she was thinking about her children. He reached over and touched her shoulder.

"They'll be alright, Maggie," he said, his voice gentle. "I promise you."

Maggie nodded, but the concern didn't leave her eyes.

As the car wound its way through the narrow country lanes, Delaney found his thoughts turning to happier times. He and Elizabeth had often taken drives like this on lazy Sunday afternoons, stopping to walk in the countryside, the sun warm on their faces as they laughed and talked about everything and nothing.

They had been particularly fond of the Epsom races, Elizabeth's eyes sparkling with excitement as she watched the horses thunder past. Delaney had never been much for gambling, but he loved to see the joy on his wife's face as she cheered for her favourite.

Now, as the car passed by the rolling hills and quaint villages of Surrey, Delaney felt a pang of longing for those simpler days. The war had changed everything, and sometimes it was hard to remember what life had been like before the bombs, blackouts, and the constant fear.

Beside him, Maggie was still silent, her gaze fixed on the passing scenery. Delaney wondered what she was thinking; if she too was remembering happier times.

As the car passed through small villages, Delaney noticed they had left Surrey and entered West Sussex. Delaney saw a change in the driver's demeanor when they passed a signpost to Midhurst. The man, who had been silent for most of the journey, suddenly cleared his throat and spoke up.

"We're nearly there, sir," he said, his voice crisp and efficient. "The hospital is just ahead."

Delaney frowned, confused. "Hospital? I thought we were going to an MI5 office."

The driver nodded. "Yes, sir. The office is located within the Edward VII military hospital."

Maggie sat up straighter, her eyes widening. "A military hospital? Why on earth would they put an MI5 office there?"

Delaney shrugged. "Security, I suppose. No one would think to look for it in a place like that."

He'd heard rumours of MI5 offices hidden away, deep in the English countryside. He'd never paid much attention, but here they were. It spoke of secrets and subterfuge, of a war being fought, not just on the battlefields of Europe, but in the shadows and back rooms of Britain itself.

The car turned into a narrow lane and continued for a mile before Delaney could see a large red brick building, partially obscured by trees.

As the car pulled up to wrought-iron gates, Delaney felt a sense of trepidation settle over him. Whatever they were about to walk into, he had a feeling it would be unlike anything he had ever encountered before.

The driver showed his identification to a guard at the gate, who waved them through with a curt nod. As they drove up the long, winding gravel driveway to the hospital entrance, Delaney took in the sprawling building, surrounded by manicured lawns and gardens.

As the car came to a stop outside the main entrance, Delaney took a deep breath and straightened his tie. Beside him, Maggie smoothed down her skirt, her face set in a determined expression.

"Ready?" Delaney asked, his hand on the door handle.

Maggie nodded, her jaw tight. "As I'll ever be."

A stern faced woman in a starched matron's uniform greeted them at the hospital entrance.

"Good morning," she said, nodding curtly at Delaney and then looking Maggie up and down. She checked their identification before saying, "This way, please."

Delaney and Maggie followed the nurse along dimly lit corridors, with high ceilings, smelling of a mixture of floor wax and disinfectant. Delaney caught glimpses of wards through partially open doors, lined with beds filled with patients, tended to by nurses who moved purposefully about, dispensing pills and checking charts.

There was an air of calm efficiency.

At the end of one corridor, the matron stopped. "Follow the signs for the operating theatre," she said. "They are waiting for you, and she pointed to double steel doors to the right."

Delaney and Maggie followed her instructions and pushed through the heavy double doors. They were then standing in a corridor that looked exactly the same as the one before, but instantly Delaney thought he was in a different world.

Around him, the muffled sounds of urgent conversations and the clacking of typewriters seeped through the walls. The air was heavy with the scent of cigarette smoke and the musty odour of people working in cramped conditions.

They followed the sign to the operating theatre and this time, when Delaney looked through open the doors, he could see rows of men and women, bent over desks and working at machines which looked similar to typewriters or examining large maps fastened to the walls.

Delaney and Maggie exchanged glances.

"Quite the set up, isn't it?" Delaney mumbled. "Here's the operating theatre."

A small man wearing a tweed jacket and carrying a briefcase stood outside another set of double doors. He reminded Delaney of a schoolteacher.

"Detective Chief Inspector Delaney and Mrs Carroll?" he asked.

"That's right," Delaney replied, and Maggie nodded.

"We're ready for you in the briefing room," he said, gesturing for them both to follow him through the doors.

Chapter 19

KING EDWARD VII HOSPITAL, MIDHURST, WEST SUSSEX.

The MI5 briefing room was a cold, windowless room, and when the door closed behind them, the chatter from outside was muted.

There was the faint scent of antiseptic still present in the air, a reminder of the room's past use. Maggie shivered slightly as she stepped into the converted operating theatre, her eyes taking a moment to adjust to the harsh fluorescent lighting that cast shadows in the corners.

In the centre of the room was a long table surrounded by chairs where five men were already seated, browsing through files piled up in front of them, while at the end of the table was a film projector facing a blank wall.

"Take a seat, please."

The man who had greeted them pointed to empty chairs and hurried to the end of the table, where he fiddled with the projector.

"Lights, please," he called out after a minute, and another man got up and dimmed the fluorescent lights.

Maggie sat in the darkness, and they all waited for one of them to finish shuffling the paper as they remained in awkward silence until the man finally said, "Welcome everyone. I'm Director Hawkins. Thank you for coming on such short notice." He didn't wait for any response, and Maggie noticed he didn't introduce anyone. She glanced around the room, thinking that all the men at the table could merge into any crowd in London and she would have difficulty recognising them again. They all wore grey, unremarkable suits and could be bankers or bureaucrats.

Director Hawkins cleared his throat, drawing her attention back to him, where he stood at the foot of the table. "We've called you here today because we believe a new Irish Republican terrorist cell is planning a major attack on British soil," he said gravely. "Some of you may recall the Sabotage Campaign of 1939."

He leaned forward and pressed a button on the side of the projector, causing a spool of film to whir into life, and grainy footage of people running about appeared on the blank wall.

Maggie recognised Hammersmith Bridge. As they watched, Maggie could see shots of twisted metal and debris, and blurry figures of people pointing and gesturing. Hawkins continued to speak, raising his voice above the clatter of the projector.

"The S-Plan, launched in 1939, was a campaign of bombings and sabotage against civilian, economic, and military targets across Britain. The IRA's goal was to force the British government to withdraw from Northern Ireland and to establish an independent Irish republic encompassing the entire island of Ireland. I must acknowledge that the S-Plan had its successes. The IRA carried out a series of devastating attacks, causing significant damage to infrastructure, as well as a great deal of fear and panic, forcing us to divert valuable resources to counter their efforts."

Hawkins gestured at the footage. "This is the aftermath of the Hammersmith Bridge attack. You may recall the coordinated attacks in June

1939, and then the bombing of Coventry in August 1939, which killed five people and injured over fifty. That was a particularly shocking example of their ruthlessness."

Hawkins turned off the projector, and the spool of film shuddered to a stop.

"Lights please," Hawkins said. One of the men pushed his chair back and got up. In a moment, the harsh fluorescent lights flickered on.

The room fell into an uncomfortable silence while Hawkins re-arranged some papers in front of him. Then he cleared his throat and started speaking.

"In 1939, a Scotland Yard task force was able to apprehend most of the perpetrators, most of whom were sentenced to hanging. The S-Plan brought the IRA a great deal of publicity and support, both within Ireland and among Irish communities in this country. They portrayed themselves as freedom fighters, struggling against the oppressive British regime, and hence gained some domestic support from disaffected men who harboured resentment against our government."

Hawkins paused again, as if to gather his thoughts.

"However, the S-Plan also had significant drawbacks for the IRA. First, the campaign was immensely costly in terms of resources and manpower. The IRA had to stretch their limited funds and personnel to carry out attacks across Britain, which ultimately led to a dilution of their effectiveness, and also the killing of innocent civilians alienated many potential supporters."

He paused again and looked around the room. "Thanks to increased intelligence gathering by ourselves, and the introduction of enhanced security methods by our government, we believed that by 1940, the S-Plan was largely defeated, and the IRA had been forced to scale back their operations dramatically. Many of their key personnel had been arrested or killed and even their leaders, according to our intelligence, admitted that the S-Plan was a failure. However, gentlemen, and lady," Hawkins acknowledged Maggie with a nod in her direction, "we have received credible intelligence that there is a power struggle within the leadership of the IRA and a splinter group is planning another campaign of attacks on British soil."

Hawkins pointed to the files in front of Maggie and Delaney.

"Please turn to the first page of your files," he instructed.

Maggie opened the file and had to swallow back a gasp of recognition when she saw the first picture.

"Connor Byrne," Hawkins said, "Identified as an IRA operative responsible for three murders and one attempted murder, in the course of his mission to steal our nation's secrets. We believe he was working for the Nazis. Although he refuses to cooperate, we have identified several of his co-conspirators. Please turn to the next page."

Maggie did so and found another photograph. It showed a man in his mid-forties, with a heavy brow and deep-set eyes that seemed to glitter with malevolence even in the black-and-white image. Maggie recognised the pub in the background of the photograph—The Crown and Cushion—on Woolwich High Street.

As if reading her mind, Director Hawkins said, "This is Sheamus McClary. Former IRA loyalist. We believe he's been recruiting and training a new cell, intending to launch a series of coordinated attacks across England. We think he is being funded by the Germans, and helped by some of the criminal underground, whose primary motivation is profiteering. He was located in Woolwich, but now he and his operatives work out of Leinster Gardens. It's an area well-known for its boarding houses for Irish workers."

Hawkins tapped the desk to emphasise his point. "Sheamus McClary is a ruthless killer and a cunning operative. But, he is also a drunk and we do not believe he is the brains behind this operation. According to our informant, he reports to an individual who has only recently arrived in the UK, and who is the liaison with their German counterparts."

"Dowd?" Delaney spoke for the first time. "Patrick Dowd was this informant, correct?"

"Correct, Detective Chief Inspector. Patrick Dowd, found deceased on the 3rd of February, was presumed murdered by McClary and associates. So now we have no direct information coming from the inside."

"And now McClary knows we're on to them?"

Hawkins inclined his head in agreement. "Correct again. He made this very clear by leaving Dowd's body where it could be found and by making a telephone call to the morgue, with a message for us. For those of you around the table who don't know, the message said, 'This is what we do to rats'. Their arrogance makes them all the more dangerous. And time, gentlemen and lady, is running out."

Hawkins paused and took a breath. "The increased bombings over the last month are a consequence of Hitler's frustration. Operation Steinbock, as he calls it, is a re-invigorated campaign by the Luftwaffe with the simple goal: to break British morale, and repeat the impact of the Blitz. But that's not all. Our intelligence tells us that this is only the beginning."

The Director's face grew grim and his tone grave. "Operation Steinbock is just the start. Hitler has been working on a new weapon, one that will enhance his airborne capabilities and could be the turning point in this war for our enemy."

Maggie noticed all eyes were on Hawkins. Everyone, including Delaney, was sitting up straight, focusing on the Director's words.

"The V-1, they call it," Hawkins explained, "is a pilotless aircraft, powered by a pulse jet engine and guided by a primitive autopilot system. It can fly for hundreds of miles, carrying a warhead of over a ton of high explosives, and deliver it with devastating accuracy to its target. And our sources inform us that the McClary's gang is planning to launch a new campaign of terror against London just as the city is reeling from the V-1 attacks."

The hairs on Maggie's neck stood up. Delaney shifted in his seat, and spoke again, "How much intelligence did Dowd share before…"

"Not much, I'm afraid. We know the first attacks are imminent, maybe weeks or even days. They are apparently waiting for supplies. We believe that a large amount of explosives is being shipped to Birmingham and then down to London, and then it will be a short time before the attacks start, possibly to coordinate with bombing raids from across the channel."

"If we know explosives are coming, why don't we just intercept them?" Delaney asked.

One of the other men in the room answered him, sounding faintly amused at Delaney's suggestion. "We could do that, ol' chap, but then they'd re-group, get some more, and start up again."

"That's correct," Hawkins jumped in. "The goal is to stop this campaign for good."

He leaned forward and placed his hands on the table. "If we don't nip this in the bud right now, and the attacks are a success, then their confidence will grow. Who knows where it might lead. Maybe a full-blown conflict that could last for decades. And this is why you are all here today."

Hawkins allowed his words to sink in before he looked at Delaney and Maggie.

"We have lost the element of surprise. McClary will expect us to replace Dowd. He will be suspicious of any newcomer professing sympathy for his cause. But we have to get eyes and ears near McClary, and divert their attention, if possible until we have gathered information we can work with. That is why Detective Chief Inspector Delaney and Mrs Margaret Carroll are with us today."

The men around the table finally acknowledged Delaney and Maggie.

Hawkins continued, "The Detective Chief Inspector here will continue to investigate Patrick Dowd's murder following normal procedure. He will, however, use the investigation to pull in and lean on known associates of McClary. The threat of being charged with murder may loosen some tongues. Mrs Carroll will work undercover to obtain two pieces of critical information for us. First, the identity of McClary's boss. The second is the location of a warehouse where we think they'll take delivery of the explosives."

Maggie felt all the eyes in the room rest on her.

"Mrs Carroll will be undercover in the Leinster Boarding house where Dowd was living. Please turn to page four."

Maggie turned the page and found a photograph of a row of Victorian terraced houses. On the page, one of them was marked, '25'. She heard Delaney clear his throat and say, "Maggie, I mean, Mrs Carroll will apply to be a housekeeper there? That's how she's going in?"

"Quite so, Detective Chief Inspector. We understand from Dowd that the landlady, a Mrs Doyle, has a high turnover of staff, because of the rough nature of the men living there. We believe Mrs Carroll, with her... erm, background, will be a suitable candidate and will not raise any suspicions. She'll be our eyes and ears there."

One man stared at Maggie but directed his question to Hawkins. "Does she have enough experience for this role?"

Maggie's face grew hot, but before she could answer, Hawkins flipped open another file and read, "Margaret Carroll, nee McVeigh, born in Belfast 1901. Lived with her aunt and uncle, Margaret and Ryan McVeigh in Dublin after her mother and sister died. Uncle Ryan and cousin Sean were both active members of the IRA. McVeigh worked as a maid, gathering information on the Cairo gang, a group of British intelligence officers working in Dublin collecting information on the IRA. She ceased working for them when cousin Sean murdered an elderly neighbour he suspected to be an informant. McVeigh then helped Robert Delaney," Hawkins broke off to nod at Delaney, "escape the killings of 20th November, 1920, known afterwards as Bloody Sunday. Delaney and one other were the only surviving members of the Cairo Gang. McVeigh could have escaped to England with Delaney. Instead, she spent a year working for the Igoe Gang, proving herself to be an invaluable and courageous operative until finally leaving Ireland in 1922. McVeigh married George Carroll in 1923 and has lived in London ever since."

He looked up at Maggie. "Did I leave anything out, Mrs Carroll?"

Delaney spoke before Maggie could respond.

"You did, Director Hawkins. Mrs Carroll was instrumental in the successful arrest of Connor Byrne. Her analysis of the case files allowed us to make connections between his victims and ultimately uncover his motivation. Without Byrne, we wouldn't have any of your intelligence. So yes, sir," he nodded at the man who'd asked the question, "Mrs Carroll has enough experience, and if there is any doubt, she has great loyalty to this country."

The man inclined his head in acknowledgement. Director Hawkins looked around the room. "Any more questions?"

"No, sir."

For the next hour, Director Hawkins laid out all the intelligence Patrick Dowd had gathered about the McClary's gang: where they lived and worked, their daily schedules, and where they drank.

Maggie could see Delaney's expression darken once or twice and realised he must be connecting this new information to his murder case.

At the end of the briefing, Hawkins dismissed everyone except Maggie and Delaney. The other men stood and filed out of the room, and one by one, offered their hands to shake both Delaney's and Maggie's as they passed.

Delaney and Maggie were left in the room with Director Hawkins.

"You understand what we are asking of you, Mrs Carroll?"

"I do, sir."

"And you are willing to answer the call of duty for your country?"

Maggie hesitated for a moment. Her country? For a second, the image of her now deceased neighbour, Mrs Grenfield, flashed into Maggie's mind, and she saw the disdain on the woman's face as she shut the door on Maggie and her children.

But her children would forever live in England now, and even if she was considered a second-rate citizen, she knew she would do anything she could for the future of her family. She would do her duty.

"Yes, sir."

"Excellent."

"But, sir," Maggie spoke urgently. "I have children. We were bombed out and..."

"Yes, yes, we are aware, Mrs Carroll. Arrangements have been made for your children to be evacuated to a safe house, close to here, actually. A special agent, Mrs Hazelton, has been assigned to take care of them. This evening you will return to London and tomorrow, a driver will take you and the children to the safe house where you can meet Mrs Hazelton. After that, you will come back here to prepare for your undercover work. We will only have a short time. You must be ready to start in two days."

He smiled at her. "The British government is grateful for your service, Mrs Carroll. And rest assured, we take care of our own."

Chapter 20

SCOTLAND YARD, LONDON.

The soft glow of the desk lamp illuminated the scattered papers and photographs that littered Detective Chief Inspector Delaney's desk. The air in his cramped office was stale, and Delaney's head was thumping. Delaney leaned back in his chair, his brow furrowed as he studied the murder file of Patrick Dowd for what felt like the hundredth time.

Maggie was taking her boys to a safe house in the country before she prepared for her undercover assignment. Delaney wished Birdie was going with them, but she'd begged to stay in London. He'd been there the previous evening when Maggie tried one more time to persuade Birdie to go with her brothers.

"What about my job, Ma? We need the money more than ever," she'd argued. "And Mrs Berkley will look after me, and I promise I'll go right home after my shifts."

Mrs Berkley had confirmed this.

"She'll be fine with me, Mrs Carroll. It will be nice to have some young company."

Reluctantly, Maggie had agreed. Delaney had noticed the glances exchanged between Birdie and Constable Hunter and guessed the reason for Birdie's pleading was more than just her job at the Woolwich Arsenal. He decided to keep that observation to himself.

Constable Billy Hunter was sitting opposite him now, his eyes fixed on the papers in front of him.

Hunter didn't have security clearance to know the details of Maggie's undercover mission, but Delaney had explained that this case was bigger than the murder of Patrick Dowd, and they couldn't leave any stone unturned.

"It's important that we investigate the murder for all the public to see," Whaldon had told Delaney when he reported back to him that morning. "They know Dowd was an informant, but we have to hope he didn't tell them what we know."

Delaney had sighed. "He was tortured, sir. Who knows how much he could stand before he cracked? And won't they smell a rat when Maggie turns up, looking for a job?"

Despite Director Hawkins' confidence, Delaney had his doubts. Whaldon had agreed with Hawkins.

"No, I don't think so, ol' chap. It's wartime, and help is hard to find. Maggie has a good cover story. She got bombed, needs a job. The best cover stories are the true ones."

Delaney still wasn't sure. But if he cracked this case, then MI5 might get all the information they needed, and Maggie could go home to her children. He resolved to double his efforts and focused on the file, reading it again and making notes, hoping that something would jump out at him.

And then something did. Delaney had been turning an idea over in his mind, and now he knew what to do next.

"What do you make of this, Billy?" Delaney asked, tapping a finger on one of the crime scene photographs. It showed the exterior of the pub where Dowd's body had been found, but while most of the photographs were taken facing away from the back of the pub, this one had caught the back entrance of the pub and a stack of crates full of empty bottles.

Hunter leaned forward, squinting at the image. "What am I looking for, sir?"

Delaney pointed at the crates, his expression thoughtful. "Remember what Knowles said about black market booze? He practically admitted to it, didn't he?"

Hunter nodded. "We could bring him in, put some pressure on him. But he's probably poured it all away by now. And I don't see how that would help, sir?" He looked questioningly at Delaney.

Delaney grinned back at him. "Remember I said that I have an idea to loosen up Knowles, Constable? I think it will work. I'll work on that, and I have a task for you. Have another look at the fellow who found the body. What was his name?

He reached for another file, flipping it open until he found the notes. "Here it is. Charlie Sutton. Bring him in. Let's see if he has any previous. If so, let's lean on him a bit, too."

Hunter nodded, "Right you are, sir."

Delaney knocked on Whaldon's office door for the second time that day. "Come!"

Whaldon was sitting behind his desk. Only the top of his head and a plume of smoke from Whaldon's customary pipe were visible behind a pile of files.

Whaldon stood and stretched his arms above his head, before walking around the desk and pumping Delaney's hand in welcome, as if he hadn't seen him for ages.

"Come in, come in. You're a welcome sight, Bob. I needed a break from all this damn paperwork. Never thought I'd end up a bureaucrat when I joined the force. What can I do for you?"

"Well, sir," Delaney began, taking a seat as Whaldon gestured for him to sit down. "It's your time in the force I've come to ask you about."

Whaldon perched on the edge of his desk and raised his eyebrows in surprise. "I see. Anything in particular you wanted to know?"

Delaney hesitated. Whaldon had been a legend in the Met for as long as Delaney could remember. He had a reputation of fairness as a senior officer, but rumours had always swirled about his enviable crime clean-up rate. The whispers were that Whaldon had a long list of confidential informants buried deep in London's gangster underworld.

Delaney was just about to test that theory. He hoped it wouldn't backfire. Whaldon's hot temper was also famous.

"Sir, I need some information," he said at last "Information which I believe you might have access to. Or know someone who could help me. Someone unofficial, if you see what I mean."

"Righto," Whaldon said, his eyes narrowed as he re-lit his pipe and puffed a couple more times. "And what information are you after?"

"I need something on Bill Knowles, the publican at the Leinster Arms. He knows more than he's saying, maybe something that will lead us to the IRA, but I can't lean on him, not without some leverage. If I pull him in for a few bottles of black market booze, he'll just go quiet and I'll tip off the gang. I need something... something off the books, as it were, sir."

"Hmm."

Whaldon was quiet for so long, Delaney thought he had definitely overstepped.

Then Whaldon took his pipe out of his mouth and pointed it at Delaney. "Did I ever tell you about that night in Piccadilly? With the bomb?"

Delaney shook his head. "No, sir."

"It was quite the night, Bob, quite the night. We'd been on full alert for a while. You heard about it all in the briefing, of course, but Piccadilly was one of the first attacks, in June of '39. I was on night duty at Vine Street when the bomb went off, around ten o'clock, I think. I don't know what I thought, at the time. Maybe it was an attack from the Germans, was my first thought, but I ran all the way to Piccadilly Circus."

Whaldon paused and seemed lost in the memory for a moment before he asked, "Have you ever been on the scene immediately after an explosion, Bob?"

Delaney shook his head. He'd heard explosions, of course. It had become part of life in London since the war began, but he'd been lucky enough to avoid a direct hit.

"Oh, it's chaos. It was chaos that night. Dark too, because all the lights had been blown out. People wandering in confusion, covered in muck and blood. Some of 'em couldn't hear a thing because their ears were ringing. It took a while before I saw the other bomb. I don't mind telling you, Bob, I was as frightened as I have ever been."

"How did you know it was a bomb, sir?"

Whaldon laughed. "Because I picked it up, Bob! Goodness me, I could have blown myself and the rest of Piccadilly to kingdom come."

He shook his head. "It was a brown paper parcel, tied with string, but when I held it, it was hot. And as I held it in my hand, it seemed to get hotter, so I knew I had to do something."

"But how did you know—" Delaney started to ask, but Whaldon laughed again.

"I didn't know a thing, ol' boy. But I did think that there should be fuses and something to detonate the bomb, so I opened the parcel and found seven sticks of gelignite. Every one had fuses stuck in them, so I reckoned that if I removed all the fuses, the gelignite couldn't blow."

He frowned. "What I didn't know then was a knife blade rasping against the gelignite could have set it off. But I got lucky."

Delaney waited, and Whaldon continued, "While I was standing there, surrounded by more explosives than Guy Fawkes, I heard a familiar voice asking me if he could help. It was Charlie Burgess, one of London's most notorious thieves. I had nicked him a few times. I told him to get the hell out of there, and he said, 'take care, Guv,' as he left."

Whaldon took another puff at his pipe. "You know the story after that, Delaney. There were six other explosions that night, and the next day, we began the manhunt. I worked with Special Branch, and we rounded up most of those bastards, and we had help from a policewoman who went undercover too. It took a while, but we got 'em."

"Great result, sir," Delaney said. He was confused. Everyone in the force knew this story. Why was Whaldon telling it now?

As if reading Delaney's mind, Whaldon continued, "I suppose you are wondering why I'm bringing up that old story. It's not to blow my own trumpet."

Whaldon stood up abruptly and walked around to the back of his desk. Delaney heard him open a drawer behind the mound of paperwork and rummage for a moment.

Then he came back and sat on the edge of the desk again, holding two small boxes in his hand.

"A few days after we arrested those Irish boys, I received a telephone call. I didn't recognize the voice, but I was invited to the Billiard Saloon, just off 'Dilly Circus. I was told to ask for Bill and the voice said 'who knows but yer might find out somefink, guv'."

Whaldon mimicked a cockney accent and grinned. "Of course, I had to go. What detective ignores a lead like that? Anyway, I went to the Billiard Saloon and Charlie Burgess was waiting for me. He showed me into a dingy back room, and there must have been fifty people in there, Bob. All of them known to police. Every single gangster known to be in the London underworld was standing there with drinks in their hand."

Delaney blinked in surprise.

"Then one gang leader—I won't say his name, but you'd know of him—he shoved a large whisky in my hand and thanked me for saving lives that night. He said he hoped I would accept a small token of their appreciation."

Whaldon held out one of the boxes. "Here, open it."

Delaney took the box and opened the lid. Inside was a bronze medal on a blue silk ribbon. One side was inscribed with a rose, the other with the message 'To Detective Inspector Charles Whaldon, for saving lives, 24th June 1939, from his Friends in London.'

Delaney looked up at his senior officer. "This was well deserved, sir," he said, and he meant it.

"Thank you. That's not why I showed you, or why I shared that story." Whaldon pursed his lips. "I know the rumours about me, Delaney. I know officers think I have some vast informant circle which I tap for information, and that's how I got all my promotions, but I can tell you, I have never approached any of these men for information or help. For one night, we were all on the same side. After that, they received no favours from me, and they knew better than to ask."

Then he looked down. "But today, Delaney, we are facing the same threat as we were back in June 1939. The same enemy who doesn't care about taking innocent lives to make a political point. And I believe that the men who gave me this medal five years ago would help us in any way they can today. So, leave it with me, and I'll arrange a meeting. But, Delaney?"

"Yes, sir?"

"This is between you and me, you hear?"

"Yes, sir. Thank you." Delaney turned to leave the office.

"Hold on, Bob."

"Sir?"

"Connor Byrne. I think you should have a crack at him," Whaldon said.

"Byrne? But MI5 has been all over him. I don't think I can squeeze any information out of him if they can't."

"He's a cool customer, Bob. But I just got word that he's due to hang in three weeks. Sometimes, facing death in the eye can change a man's heart and mind. And you were the one who put him there. I think it's worth a try."

Delaney doubted Byrne would talk now. He was a fanatic, an extremist who believed in a cause. He believed he would die a martyr.

But anything was worth a try.

"I'll see him, sir. You never know, he might say something. Or maybe he's been talking to other inmates? I'll talk to the guards."

"Excellent."

Delaney walked to the door and then stopped and turned back to Whaldon.

"Just one question, sir."

"What's that, Bob?"

"The other box. What's in it?"

Whaldon laughed. "This?" He held up the other small box. "His Majesty presented this to me at Buckingham Palace on the 6th February 1940. It's the King's Medal for Gallantry."

"I see. Well, you deserved that one too, sir."

Delaney found Constable Hunter impatiently pacing his office.

"Sir, I think I've found a lead," he declared. Before Delaney could say a word, he held up a file. "The man who found the body? Charlie Sutton? You asked me to check his statement."

"Yes, you found something?"

"I did. In his written statement, he says he arrived at the pub late, he'd been drinking elsewhere—and I checked it out. He was in another pub before the Leinster Arms and there are witnesses to back up his story. He says they were drinking late, but it wasn't a rowdy night, and then he leaves by the back entrance to relieve himself and finds the body. He was genuinely in shock too, sir. I believed him."

"So what's the lead, Constable?"

"His written statement doesn't match what he said to me that night."

He tapped the file again, his expression growing serious. "There was something he said that's stuck in my mind. Something about a woman, a drunk woman who was outside the pub that night."

"I don't remember that."

"No, sir. You were outside with Dr Holberg. And he just made a passing comment when I asked him if he'd seen the victim before he found the body, whether he recognised him from earlier in the evening. And he said, No, there were just the regulars, except some woman who was leaving."

"Did Knowles say anything about a woman?"

"He brushed over it, saying sometimes they get the odd 'woman of the night' touting for business, and he always throws them out."

Constable Hunter blushed. "Sorry, sir, I should have thought about it before. But it wasn't until I saw he'd left it out of his written statement that I thought it might be significant."

Delaney nodded, his eyes distant as he turned the information over in his mind. "Don't worry, Constable. You've remembered it now, and it could be important. She could have seen or heard something. Get on to it, Hunter. See if you can find her and bring her in."

Hunter nodded. "I'll do that, sir. It's a long shot. I mean, how do we even know she was there at the same time as Dowd? For all we know, she could have been in and out of the pub hours before he ever showed up."

Delaney nodded. "That's right, but we need to chase down every lead. Bring Sutton in too. Ask him why he left the woman out of his statement. See if he is frightened of Knowles, and was pressured to leave it out. And any other information he might be withholding. Good work, Billy."

"Another thing, sir, Dr Holberg telephoned. He wants you to drop in and see him. He has some new information."

"Thank you, Constable. The doctor will have to wait. I'm off to Wormwood Scrubs."

Chapter 21

WORMWOOD SCRUBS, LONDON

I t had been a long time since Delaney had walked through the grim corridors of Wormwood Scrubs.

During the Blitz in 1940, Delaney remembered, the prison had suffered damage from one of the most intense bombing attacks. One of the cell blocks had been obliterated, along with the infirmary and the chapel.

The prison had continued to function, although no significant repairs had been made. The prisoners were just crammed into smaller cells.

The overcrowding was evident to Delaney. The air was acrid with the stench of sweat and other bodily fluids Delaney didn't want to think about, and the noise was deafening.

The prison guard escorting Delaney seemed unperturbed by the constant shouts and screams from the prisoners and the clanging of metal on metal as men bashed their tin plates on the iron bars of the cell doors.

Occasionally, he'd gesture and point out a corridor leading to another wing, as if he were giving Delaney a guided tour.

"Deserters, conscientious objectors down there," he muttered at one point, with a sneer on his face. "Should be in with the murderers, if you ask me."

Finally, they reached a heavy metal gate. The guard unlocked it and went through, gesturing for Delaney to go into a small windowless cell. A table and two chairs stood in the middle of the concrete floor.

"Wait there," the guard said, before he disappeared, the metal door clanging shut behind him.

Delaney steeled himself for the confrontation ahead. He hadn't seen Byrne since the sentencing at the Old Bailey. The man was defiant then, refusing to show remorse for the murders he'd committed, spitting on the courtroom floor before being led away to serve his remaining days behind bars. Byrne's death sentence was scheduled for three weeks' time. Then, he'd be taken to the 'hanging shed' where a priest would read his last rites before he was hung from the neck until he died.

It was a barbaric, undignified death, in Delaney's opinion. Until now, Byrne had refused to talk to MI5, even with the promise of a commuted sentence on the table. But Delaney wondered, as he sat in the stinking cell waiting for Byrne, if death by hanging might be preferable to a bare existence in a hellhole like this. But even this negotiation tool was off the table now. MI5 had made it clear that Connor Byrne had been given his chance and had turned it down. Delaney had no authority to make any offers; Byrne was on his way to the gallows. Delaney's only hope was to appeal to Byrne's conscience and human decency—if he had any left at all.

The door opened, and the guard led Connor Byrne into the room. Byrne was shuffling, his legs shackled with chains, and his hands cuffed in front of him. He wore the prison garb of drab grey trousers and shirt, made of coarse material, which hung off him. Byrne was considerably thinner than when Delaney had seen him last, and his shoulders stooped.

His face looked hollowed out, and there were rough patches on his skin. Prison life always took a toll on men, but Delaney was shocked at the drastic change in Byrne's appearance. Gone was the attractive, vital man who charmed his victims. Birdie wouldn't recognise Byrne now, Delaney thought.

The guard pushed his prisoner into the chair opposite Delaney's, and Byrne rested his cuffed hands on the table. Delaney could smell the man's odour and see the grime around his neck and face, masking the prison pallor. Byrne's eyes were still hard and defiant, Delaney noted. He held Byrne's stare for a long moment and then studied the man's face for any sign of weakness or vulnerability. He didn't see any.

Delaney waited until the guard left the room and they were alone.

"Conner Byrne," Delaney began, his voice calm and measured. "I'm here to offer you a chance. Give me the information I need about the IRA's plans, and you can face God with a clear conscience."

Byrne let out a harsh, mirthless laugh. "What makes you think I don't have a clear conscience, Detective Chief Inspector?"

"Thou Shalt not Kill," Delaney quoted. "Doesn't your God tell you it's a sin to take another life?"

Byrne snorted but didn't answer.

"You've killed three innocent women, Byrne. Doesn't that weigh on you?"

"I'm a soldier, Detective Chief Inspector. I'm fighting a war, fighting for a righteous cause. Blood is always spilled in a war. Think of all the lives lost in the name of your king and country," Byrne spat the last words out.

"You're no soldier, Byrne. You are a common criminal, working with a bunch of thugs. Remember, in 1939? What did you call it? The S-Plan? What an embarrassment that was. Even your own leader went underground until we hunted him down like a dog. And we know the real IRA does not sanction your pathetic little outfit, Byrne."

Delaney hoped his words were rattling Byrne, but the man sitting across from him remained impassive.

Delaney continued, "You think they'll sing songs about you, Byrne? You think you're going to die a martyr for your cause? When you hang and get dumped into an unmarked grave, nobody will know or care. They've already forgotten you exist, Byrne."

Conner Byrne flinched and then he snarled, "You know nuthin', you fool. You have no idea what's comin' for you."

Delaney smiled to himself. At least he'd confirmed there was a plan, and Byrne knew about it. Maybe someone was keeping him up to date in here.

"Whatever you and your thug friends have planned, it won't work, Byrne. It failed before and it will fail again. And you know something? I don't think you care about any cause. I think you like killing. That's all, plain and simple. There's no secret war, no cause, no plan. Just a gang of killers, running around London, making mistakes."

Byrne said nothing, but Delaney could see his chest rising and falling.

"Patrick Dowd? You remember him? He told us a lot before he turned up dead."

Byrne shrugged. "Who? Never heard of him." And then he sneered at Delaney. "You sit and talk all you want, officer. All the time I'm sittin' here, I'll not be cleaning the latrines."

Delaney knew he was wasting his time. "No, I'll leave you to your last few days on earth, Byrne. I won't be at your hanging. I have better things to do."

Delaney got up and walked to the door. He banged on it and heard the guard on the other side unlock it, and then the door swung open.

He was about to walk through when Byrne said, "Go n-éirí an bóthar leat, Detective Chief Inspector."

Delaney didn't turn around and was glad Byrne couldn't see his expression. It had been over twenty years since someone had said that phrase in Irish to him.

Was it a coincidence? He hoped it was.

Chapter 22

MIDHURST, WEST SUSSEX

Maggie's heart felt heavy as the car wound its way through the narrow lanes, the countryside a stark contrast to the bustling chaos of London. The boys had been uncharacteristically quiet, their faces pressed against the windows as they watched the unfamiliar landscape roll by. Maggie could feel their nervousness, their uncertainty about what lay ahead, and it broke her heart to know that she was the cause of it.

They hadn't wanted to leave Birdie and Mrs Berkley. In just two days, they had become attached to the older lady who had welcomed them into her home. Now they were leaving that safe haven and heading into the unknown.

They didn't understand why they had to leave.

Not for the first time, Maggie was regretting her decision to take on this job.

The driver, a taciturn man with a thick moustache and a flat cap pulled low over his eyes, had barely spoken a word since they left the city. Maggie was grateful for the silence, for the chance to gather her thoughts and steel herself for what was to come. She knew that leaving her children, even in the care of a trusted MI5 agent, would be the hardest thing she had ever done.

Maggie recognised the countryside when the car got near to Midhurst. They drove past the turnoff to the hospital, where Maggie was to meet with Director Hawkins' staff to prepare for her undercover mission.

It was a ten-minute drive from the turning to King Edward VII hospital to the small market town of Midhurst, through narrow leafy lanes, and then past rows of stone cottages with doors and window panes painted bright yellow.

"Those are all owned by Lord Cowdray," the driver told Maggie, finally speaking when she'd asked about the yellow paint.

"Most of 'em are rented to his workers."

"What's a Lord?" Jimmy asked.

"Someone who was born lucky," the driver said with a chuckle. And then he added, "We're nearly there. If you look out the window in a minute, you'll see Cowdray Ruins."

"What's that?" Patrick asked.

"You'll see in a minute," the driver said.

"Look," Maggie announced, as the car turned right, passing a sign that announced they'd arrived at Midhurst.

The imposing structure of the remnants of a once-grand Tudor manor house came into view, rising hauntingly from the tranquil Sussex countryside.

In between the road and the ruins were farmer's ploughed fields, but Maggie could see some sections of the walls still standing tall, while others had crumbled to the ground, leaving behind piles of ancient masonry. The empty window frames, like soulless eyes, stared out onto the surrounding landscape. Maggie thought it looked eerie. The boys were fascinated.

Beyond the ruins were rows of green canvas tents.

"What are the tents for?" she asked the driver.

"Military," the driver replied, "Training camp, I think."

"It's a castle," Jimmy cried. "A tumbled-down castle." He turned to Maggie. "Can we go see the castle, Ma?"

"Maybe Mrs Hazelton will take you," Maggie said. "It'll be a grand adventure."

Just past the fields and the view of the ruins was a market square with a clock tower. Opposite was a sign for Midhurst Grammar School and a driveway that led to a large stone building with an oak door. Outside, Maggie could see boys dressed in smart uniform kicking a ball. The car passed rows of small shops on either side of the cobbled street.

Apart from the military tents around the ruins, Maggie thought that this country town seemed untouched by the war, reassuring her that this was the right thing to do. Her twins would be safe here, she told herself.

The car turned into a narrow, tree-lined street that wound up a hill. There was a cluster of stone cottages at the foot of the hill and then fields again until the car reached the top.

Maggie could see a row of terrace houses with fields stretching out on either side.

The driver stopped the Wolsey in the narrow lane. He turned in his seat and said, "This is it, Mrs Carroll. Number 12 is the one with the blue door."

He got out and walked around to open the passenger door. Maggie got out and helped the boys slide across the seat.

"I'll wait for you here," the driver said.

"Come on boys, let's find out what's next on this big adventure," Maggie said cheerfully, but already she could see tears forming in the boys' eyes, as they knew she was about to leave them.

Before they were halfway down the path, the front door opened, and a tall woman stepped out. She had silver grey hair to her shoulders, brown eyes that sparkled, and a wide smile on her face. At her feet, a small, shaggy dog yapped excitedly, its tail wagging furiously.

"Hello there," Mrs Hazelton said, her voice warm and welcoming. "I'm so happy to have you boys to stay with me. And this is Baxter."

The boys' faces lit up at the sight of the dog, and they rushed forward to pet him, their sadness at leaving their mother momentarily forgotten.

"Can we take Baxter for walks?" Jimmy asked, as the little dog jumped up and licked his face. "Can we take him to the castle?"

"The castle?" Mrs Hazelton said questioningly, looking at Maggie.

"He means the ruins," Maggie explained. "We saw them a few minutes ago, just before we arrived."

"Well, the ruins and Cowdray grounds have been turned into a military compound for the war, but we can have a walk by the river and we can still get near enough to see them. And we can take Baxter. How does that sound?"

The boys nodded in agreement, still playing with the dog.

Mrs Hazelton leaned towards Maggie. "I know it's hard," she murmured. "But it won't be for long. Don't worry, I will look after them."

She nodded at the car, still idling in the lane. "You should go," she said. "While they're distracted with Baxter. They'll be fine."

Maggie nodded. "Well now," she said brightly, "you boys be good for Mrs Hazelton, and I'll be back in a few days."

"When is Birdie coming?" Jimmy asked as they both rushed to hug her.

"She's staying in London with Mrs Berkley. She has to go to work."

Maggie leaned forward to kiss the boys. "I'll tell you what," she whispered. "I'll ask Birdie to write you a letter, and then you can write back to her and tell her all about the castle and Baxter. How about that?"

Finally, she extracted herself from the boy's hugs and thanked Mrs Hazelton. She willed herself not to look back as she took the longest walk of her life to the waiting car.

Chapter 23

MILE END ROAD, LONDON

Delaney stared at himself in the mirror. He wasn't as pale and gaunt as Connor Byrne, but there were dark shadows under his eyes. He needed a good night's sleep, but not tonight. He had another appointment, courtesy of Chief Superintendent Whaldon.

It had been late afternoon when he got back to Scotland Yard after meeting Byrne. The inmate's last words were still echoing in his ears. Was he being paranoid? Or did Byrne know something?

"May the road rise up to meet you," he repeated to himself in the mirror. It had been the last thing that Maggie McVeigh had said before they parted ways after leaving Dublin.

"It's just a saying," Delaney said to himself. There was no possible way Byrne could know about Maggie. Before he'd left Wormwood Scrubs, he'd checked with the prison guard about Byrne's visitors.

'Just his priest', the guard told him. And Byrne didn't speak to other prisoners, didn't boast about his crimes. He just kept his head down.

That's it then, Delaney told himself sternly, straightening his tie. Just a coincidence.

Delaney stepped into the street, the chill of the London night air biting at his face. A taxi cab was waiting for him. Whaldon had told him to go alone, so this time Constable Hunter was having the night off.

"Mile End Road, please," Delaney told the driver.

The taxi cab dropped him at the end of the Mile End Road in Whitechapel. Delaney was now within walking distance from the Regal Rooms nightclub, where he was to meet the leader of one of the most notorious criminal gangs operating in London: the Hoxton Mob.

The Mob had wielded the most power during the 1920s. Their primary activity was extortion and protection rackets, but they turned their hand to bank robberies and illegal gambling. Since 1939, they operated a black market network, cracking down on any other criminal who dared to wander onto their 'patch'.

Harry Coster was in charge. He had a fearsome reputation, not only with the police, but throughout the criminal underworld. Nobody in the Hoxton Mob had ever been successfully prosecuted for any crime.

Delaney had heard many rumours about the mob and Chief Superintendent Whaldon, including that Whaldon was taking back-handers to turn a blind eye. Delaney didn't believe it. He hated the idea of approaching the mob for help, but the ends justified the means, he told himself.

Harry Coster had taken over the leadership of the Hoxton Mob when his brother-in-law, Alfie Solomon, had been murdered. Solomon, Whaldon told him earlier, had presented him with his medal.

"Alfie was ruthless," Whaldon explained. "And the rumours are that Coster was the one who murdered Alfie. But he was with Alfie and all the others the night Alfie gave me the medal, and so he's agreed to meet you."

Whaldon had put his hand on Delaney's shoulder. "Be careful, Bob. The reason I've never asked these boys for anything is that nothing in their world is ever free. There will be a price to pay."

Delaney knew he was crossing a line. He hoped it was worth it.

Delaney pulled his coat tighter around himself and walked briskly, glad of the moonlight. He'd been to the Regal Rooms before, but it hadn't been a social visit.

Back in 1936, when he'd been in uniform, he was part of a large-scale operation targeting the Regal Rooms and other nightclubs in the area. The force had got multiple tip-offs about illegal gambling and the sale of alcohol outside permitted hours.

During the raid, the police arrested several individuals, including patrons and employees of the nightclub. Some of those arrested were carrying knives and razors. In the end, only a few charges had stuck. And nothing had stuck to the mob.

In a few minutes, Delaney was looking at the sign marking the entrance of the Regal Rooms. He checked his watch in the moonlight. Right on time. He walked towards the entrance, his footsteps echoing on the damp pavement. As he approached the door, a figure emerged from the shadows; a tall, broad-shouldered man with a face that looked like it had seen its fair share of fights.

"You Delaney?" the man asked, his voice rough and gravelly.

Delaney nodded. "That's right. And you are?"

The man grinned, flashing nicotine-stained teeth. "They call me Tommy. Mr Coster is waiting for you."

The nightclub was busy. Delaney hadn't taken much notice of the decor the last time he'd been inside. He'd been too busy chasing the patrons as they scattered when the police entered.

There was a spacious main room with a large dance floor at the center. The floor was made of polished hardwood, perfect for dancing to the live music. A band played jazz on a stage that was flanked by large palms and ferns, adding a touch of greenery to the otherwise dimly lit interior. Behind it, there was a backdrop featuring the club's name in large, stylised letters. Surrounding the dance floor were numerous tables and chairs where guests could sit, drink, and socialise.

Delaney noticed American GIs leaning on the bar, chatting to glamorous-looking women.

Nobody paid Delaney or Tommy any attention.

Delaney contrasted these opulent surroundings with the average Londoner's austere existence and felt a flash of bitterness towards the wartime profiteers like Harry Coster.

This was no time to stand on his principles, he told himself.

Tommy led him past the bar and dance floor to a door marked 'Private' at the back of the club.

"Wait here," Tommy grunted as he opened the door. "I'll see if Mr Coster is ready for you."

Delaney stood outside the closed door, waiting for Tommy to return, struggling with the impulse to walk away. Before he could change his mind about the meeting, the door swung open, and Tommy reappeared.

"Come in, Mr Delaney," Tommy said, and Delaney followed him into a dimly lit corridor. Tommy knocked softly on the door at the other end, and not waiting for a reply, opened it and stood back for Delaney to go inside.

It was a small room, partially filled by an oversized oak desk.

"Mr Delaney," said a small balding man from behind it, sitting in an oversized leather chair. "Or may I call you Bob?"

The man, who looked more like a banker, stood up. He was clean shaven, wore horn-rimmed glasses, and was dressed in an expensive, but tasteful pin-stripped suit. He was the kind of man who would blend into the financial organisation and corporate offices in the City of London.

It was only when he smiled, and Delaney glimpsed a gold filling, and then came round the desk and held out a hand which was heavy with diamond rings for Delaney to shake, that the man gave a hint of his real occupation.

"Mr Coster?" Delaney shook the man's hand. "I'm Detective Chief Inspector Delaney."

"Of course." Harry Coster's smile widened as if he found this amusing. "Well, sit down, Detective Chief Inspector. May I get you a drink?"

Delaney declined while he sat in a smaller leather chair, facing the man across the desk. "Mr Coster..." He started to speak, but Coster waved his hand and sat behind the desk again.

"Harry, please. We're all friends here."

"Mr Coster," Delaney continued, "I'm here because I need some information."

"Of course you are," Coster said, his smile not retreating, but his tone a little less welcoming than before. "So tell me, Detective Chief Inspector Delaney, what information do you think I have? And why should I help you?"

Coster leaned forward, his elbows on the desk and his hands clasped.

"Mr Coster, I believe you have information which I can use to help me solve a murder and a wider conspiracy which is not only a threat to the general public, but also to your business," Delaney said.

"Go on," Coster said casually, but Delaney caught the twitch of his hands at the mention of Coster's business.

"Black market deliveries on your patch," Delaney said. "Deliveries which include gelignite. Maybe firearms."

"Gelignite? Same bog-trotters who blew up the 'Dilly I assume? That's why Charlie Whaldon called."

Delaney nodded. "They got to one of our informants. We have someone else undercover, but we don't have much time. I believe that the Irishmen have a number of people working for them and one of them is likely a customer of yours. Bill Knowles of the Leinster Arms? I need to know when the delivery of explosives is due and where it's going."

"And you want me to find out?" Coster leaned back in his chair.

"I do."

"And what do I get in return, Delaney?" Coster's tone was all business now.

"Chief Superintendent Whaldon saved lives back in 1939. Consider your help a payment of that debt."

Harry Coster laughed. "Delaney, that was Alfie Solomon's debt. It died with him. No, I'll need more than that."

Delaney sighed. "What do you want, Coster?"

Harry shrugged. "I'll get my boys to do a little digging. We'll lean on Knowles. And then you'll owe me, Delaney. That'll do for now."

Delaney knew he couldn't argue. "Alright, Coster. But make sure you don't tip Knowles off that we're on to the Irish conspiracy. Make it look like it's all about business."

Coster tapped his nose. "Don't worry, Delaney. I've dealt with the Paddies before. I'll get what you need."

Delaney stood. "Thank you for your time, Mr Coster."

Coster shouted, "Tommy!"

The door opened instantly, and Delaney guessed Tommy had been listening the whole time.

"Show Mr Delaney out and get him a drink. Mr Delaney, you should relax a little before you go. Listen to the music and Tommy here will find you a companion for the evening. My treat."

Delaney left The Regal Rooms without taking up Coster's offer. He already felt compromised, but what could he do? Maybe the only course of action they had was to fight dirty.

Chapter 24

FULHAM, LONDON

Delaney was still tired the next morning when he woke up. When he arrived home after his visit to the Regal Room, he'd gone to bed and fallen into a deep sleep.

He splashed cold water on his face to wake himself up and shivered in the February morning chill as he dressed. At least the Luftwaffe had taken a few nights off, he thought. Although he doubted if even the air raid sirens would have woken him.

His leg was aching where he'd been shot over twenty years ago. He sat on the side of his bed and rubbed the scar until the pain dulled.

Delaney was meeting Maggie later that day. She had been fully briefed now, and all that was left to do was to agree on how she would communicate with Delaney while she was undercover.

Director Hawkins had reluctantly agreed for Delaney to be Maggie's handler after Delaney had insisted. "I need to keep her appraised of the murder inquiry," he'd told Hawkins. "The more information she has, the better."

It wasn't the only reason, if he were honest with himself. He wanted to make sure she was safe. His stomach churned every time he thought of putting Maggie in harm's way.

As he sat there in the dull morning light, his mind went back to Dublin. That fateful Sunday morning when he and Maggie had fled for their lives.

"We need to move fast" he'd said, after listening to a wild-eyed, drenched Maggie. He'd stuffed a few clothes in a bag and made sure he had his official documents in a pocket. "You have to come with me."

Maggie had protested, but Delaney had shoved her out the door. "You can't stay here, Maggie. They'll know it was you. You have no choice unless you want to end up like Mrs Doherty."

At that moment, Delaney had heard a commotion in the street.

"They're coming," Maggie said, her eyes wide with fear. "I bolted the front door, but they'll kick it down."

"Down the back stairs," Delaney said urgently.

As they had run through the back entrance, they could hear a crash and then men's boots thumping on the stairs up to Delaney's room.

Delaney and Maggie pressed up against the back wall of the boarding house in the pouring rain. They heard men shouting.

"Over there," Maggie whispered. "Down that alley. It leads to the river. The only way out of Dublin is over the bridge."

"I have to warn the others," Delaney had said desperately. "They'll all be killed."

Maggie shook her head. "Too late. They're already dead. I only got to you because the others were first."

The sounds of shouting got louder.

"Quick," she cried. "They'll look for you."

Delaney and Maggie made a dash for the alley. Delaney pushed Maggie in front of him as he heard the shouting get louder. Maggie was running ahead while Delaney glanced over his shoulder and, in doing so, slowed down. It was an error of judgement.

A shot rang out, echoing down the alleyway and at the same time, Delaney felt a stinging pain in his calf.

He cried out.

Maggie swung round.

"Keep going, keep going," Delaney shouted. "I'm alright. I'm right behind you."

Delaney had been painfully aware he was leaving a trail of blood as they raced down alleyways, through the maze of tenement buildings on the outskirts of the city until they reached the River Liffey.

"I can't hear anything," Maggie whispered, as they crouched in the undergrowth.

"We'll keep going," Delaney told her. "I have friends who can hide us. We have to keep going. Just a mile over the river and we'll be safe."

They had made it.

Delaney was alive because of Maggie McVeigh. Did he have the right to ask her to risk her life all over again?

Chapter 25

GUY'S HOSPITAL LONDON.

Before seeing Maggie, Delaney had an appointment with Dr Holberg. An hour after leaving his house, he stepped into the morgue, the familiar sterile scent of disinfectant greeting him.

Dr Holberg stood over the body of Patrick Dowd, which was partially covered by a white sheet.

"Detective Chief Inspector Delaney, thank you for coming. I think I've found something that may be of significance to your case."

Delaney approached the table. "What is it, Dr Holberg?" he asked. "The name and address of our killer?" Dr Holberg smiled politely at Delaney's attempt at humour.

"I'm afraid not. I have, however, found some fibres on our victim's body."

Delaney frowned. "Isn't this already in your report?"

"I found fibres from the rope that bound Dowd's hands and feet. The rope is commonplace and sadly gives us little useful information. No, these are additional fibres and I have been able to do a thorough analysis. The results are most interesting."

"Fibre analysis? Is this a new technique, Doctor?" Delaney knew the science of forensics was advancing at a rapid pace, but this was the first time Dr Holberg had used fibre analysis on one of his cases.

"It is relatively new, yes. Have you heard of the Greenwood murder case? Back in 1936?"

Delaney shook his head.

"A forensic scientist in Huddersfield—Conrad Lattes, I believe—used the analysis of fibres found on the murder victim's body, Mabel Greenwood, to match them to fibres found in a particular cloth used to make the lining in men's suits. Lattes was able to match the exact fibres to the suspect's clothing. The evidence was instrumental in the conviction."

"I see. And you think we can do the same thing here?" Delaney was intrigued.

"It's possible." Dr Holberg gestured for Delaney to inspect Patrick Dowd's head. "Do you see where Dowd was gagged?"

Delaney saw the bruising around Dowd's mouth immediately. It was clear, even to his untrained eye, that the man had been gagged, likely to silence his screams as he endured the torture before the gunshot which ultimately claimed his life.

"I do."

"The bruising pattern suggests he was gagged tightly for a period," Holberg explained, tracing the outline of the marks with his finger. "Tight enough for fibers to become embedded in the skin around his mouth. Now look over here."

He pointed to a nearby microscope, a state-of-the-art piece of equipment that had only recently become available to police laboratories. Delaney walked over and leaned in to take a look.

"It's blurry," Delaney declared, straightening up.

"Adjust this knob here." Dr Holberg showed him as Delaney looked through the microscope again, and suddenly the blurry image came into sharp focus, making the fibres look like thick worms.

"Silk," Holberg explained, answering Delaney's unspoken question. "High-quality, too. Not the kind of material you'd find in your average department store."

Delaney straightened again, his mind already racing with the implications. In a time of rationing and scarcity, silk was a luxury few could afford. The fact that the killer used it as a gag suggested a level of wealth and sophistication that could narrow down the list of suspects considerably.

Delaney thought of Bill Knowles. He couldn't imagine him wearing or owning expensive garments.

"So the next step is for you to find a suspect, and then I can match these fibres to any silk clothing or garments."

"Ah," Delaney said, his initial excitement dampened. "That's the hard part."

Then Delaney remembered something from yesterday's meeting with Constable Hunter. "The silk fibres could have come from women's clothing, couldn't they?"

"Of course," Dr Holberg replied. "But I highly doubt our killer is a woman. Not alone, anyway. Dowd wasn't a big man, but looked like he was quite strong. A woman could have been one of several people involved in his killing though."

"And they could have used a silk scarf, maybe? Or a large handkerchief?"

"Very likely."

Constable Hunter mentioned that Charlie Sutton, the man who'd discovered the victim, had seen a woman at the Leinster Arms. It was now even more important that they find that woman.

"Thank you, Doctor," Delaney said as he left the morgue. "This has been very useful."

Delaney hurried back to Scotland Yard to share this new information with Constable Hunter. Maybe Sutton could remember what the woman at the pub had been wearing that night. And then, Delaney thought, he could pass that information to Maggie at their meeting. If she could identify a woman who was glamorous enough to wear silk and also fraternised with the men at the boarding house, it might be the lead they needed.

Chapter 26

LYON'S CORNER HOUSE, THE STRAND, LONDON.

The windows of the Lyon's Corner House on the Strand were misted up. The frost of the early morning had given way to a persistent grey drizzle. Inside the teahouse, there was the low hum of conversation and the clatter of crockery from the kitchen. Delaney was early for his meeting with Maggie. He chose a seat at a table facing the door and ordered for himself and Maggie while he waited for her.

When he'd got back to the office after leaving the morgue, Mrs Berkley had told him that Hunter was still tracking down Charlie Sutton.

"Any other calls or messages, Mrs Berkley?"

It was unlikely that Coster would contact him so soon, but Delaney still hoped they could nail Bill Knowles and get all the information they needed from him, so Maggie would not have to go through this mission.

The sight of Patrick Dowd's body in the morgue and the evidence of the vicious battering he'd taken had troubled Delaney deeply. What on earth was he thinking, sending Maggie into danger like this?

Exactly on time, the doorbell jangled, and he looked up to see Maggie standing in the entrance. She placed her umbrella in the stand and looked around the cafe until her eyes met Delaney's.

He raised a hand in acknowledgement, and she smiled in reply as she slipped off her coat and hung it up. As she stood with the grey light from the windows behind her, Delaney glimpsed the girl he'd first met over twenty years ago, in her silhouette and the grace of her movements as she walked through the teahouse to join him. An unfamiliar emotion stirred in his soul, but he pushed the feelings away. Maggie was a married woman, he reminded himself.

"I ordered tea and scones. I hope that's alright," he said as he stood and pulled out the chair for her.

"That's grand, thank you."

She sat, and Delaney caught the eye of the waitress and indicated they were ready.

Maggie smiled up at the waitress as she delivered a tray of tea, with teacups, milk, and sugar, as well a plate of scones to their table.

Maggie waited until the waitress walked away before she turned to Delaney, her face serious now.

"Is everything alright, Robert? You look worried. Has there been a change in plans?"

Delaney sighed and shook his head. "No, nothing like that." He stopped and struggled to find his next words. "Maggie, I know you have agreed to… to help with this mission, but I have to tell you something. And after I do, if you want to change your mind, I will understand and I'll make Whaldon understand too."

Maggie was silent and Delaney watched her face for anxiety, but all he saw was a slight weariness or resignation, as if she sensed what he was about to say.

He told her about Patrick Dowd and the way he died. He left nothing out.

Maggie reached for the teapot.

"It should be brewed now," she said. "Shall I?"

Delaney nodded and watched as Maggie poured tea for both of them. She added milk to hers. She didn't seem to show any reaction to what he had told her, but her hand shook a little as she stirred her tea.

"Real milk," she remarked, "Makes a nice change from the powder."

"Maggie—" Delaney started, but she held up a hand.

"It's alright Robert. I am aware of how vicious these people can be. Even my own family..." She left the sentence hanging in the air between them.

"It's different now though," Delaney pressed. "You have the children."

"Robert, do you think I haven't thought about that? The possibility of leaving my children without a mother? And who knows if their father will ever come back from this damn war?"

Her voice was low but fierce.

"Of course, I just—"

Maggie interrupted him again. "Robert, I don't have any choice. We are homeless. At least this way, the children are safe. And if Special Branch is to be trusted, then we'll have somewhere to live when this is all over."

"I'll make sure of it," Delaney reassured her as he reached out his hand to hold hers, but he stopped when the waitress appeared at the table. He shooed her away with a wave of his hand.

Maggie took a sip of her tea before she carried on speaking. "You know, we would be last on the list for a home," she said. "We are tolerated, but not liked."

"You mean..."

"Because we're Irish, yes. And if this bombing campaign is not stopped, then I fear we won't be tolerated either."

"I hadn't realised it was that bad for you," he whispered. "I'm sorry."

She looked earnestly at Delaney. "I had to leave Ireland, Robert. Especially after all that I did back then. I was a traitor. I still am in many people's eyes. But it isn't fair."

Her voice was matter-of-fact now, but Delaney saw her jaw tighten.

"Everything I did for this country, and I am still despised. I don't believe in The Cause, at least not the twisted campaign of the IRA and I hate the violence and killing, but I wish the future was a little brighter for my children in this country."

"I'm sorry," Delaney said again. He didn't know what else to say. "You're right. It isn't fair. But you know, if it wasn't for you, I wouldn't be here now. I owe you my life, and I don't want to send you back into danger without knowing everything about these bast... I mean..."

Maggie smiled. "I will do this, Robert. I know how dangerous it is."

"Does your husband know what you—"

"What I did? What I was? Or what I still am, I suppose," Maggie finished his sentence. She fell silent, and Delaney wondered if she would answer, then she said,

"George knows my life was... not good, in Ireland. But he never asked questions." She looked directly at Delaney and said softly, "He is a good man, Robert. I am blessed with him and the children."

It was as if she were making sure he knew exactly where he stood, and Delaney wondered if she ever thought of the embrace they shared, but he decided that it wasn't fair to ask. It was a long time ago and nothing could happen between them now. That was what she was telling him.

"What happened when you left Ireland?" Delaney asked instead, his curiosity overwhelming him. He didn't want to upset Maggie by talking about her past, but there were gaps in the file Whaldon had given him. He knew Maggie was a survivor, but he was amazed at how she had managed to escape Ireland and end up in London, happily married with a family.

Maggie gave a short laugh. "It was an adventure, indeed," she said. "There were other people I worked for, after you..." She left that hanging, and Delaney remembered from the file that she'd worked for other intelligence agents. "They helped me get to Belfast, and I took the ferry to Liverpool. I didn't know what to do, and I didn't have much money, so I took a position as housekeeper for a family in the city."

Her face broke into a genuine smile. "The thing is, Robert, the family was Jewish. And me, being an ignorant Catholic girl, I didn't know what that meant." She laughed. "The first morning, I was up early and trying to impress, so I planned to have a full breakfast ready for them. I went to the butchers and bought the best bacon I could find, and I fried it up, and thought they would surely be pleased."

"Oh dear." Delaney laughed too. "I suppose they weren't as pleased as you thought?"

"No! The lady of the house walked into the dining room, picked up all four corners of the tablecloth from the table I'd laid for breakfast, and threw everything out, including the crockery and then me. I had no idea what I had done. It was only when I got to London and told someone about it I realised what a terrible sin I'd committed."

"But you weren't to know," Delaney said.

"No, it's true. After that, I decided to try my luck in London, and I found a job as a maid at the Hill's Hotel in Mayfair. I met George there."

Maggie looked into the distance as she recalled the memory. "He was a pastry chef back then. He stole my heart with a slice of Victoria sponge."

Then her face darkened. "He has been such a good husband and father. I must not fail him, Robert. I must keep the children safe."

Robert reached over and touched her hand. "I'll make sure they are," he said, "and you are not to take risks, Maggie. Just gather as much information as you can, and then we'll get you out of there, I promise."

Maggie nodded. "I'll do that."

"And then, a new life, away from London," Delaney said, and to his surprise, those words tugged at his heart.

An hour later, Delaney and Maggie stood outside the tearoom. They had discussed details of Maggie's cover story, and how they were to pass messages and information while Maggie was undercover.

"We have intelligence that the IRA gets explosive materials, such as gelignite, from a supplier in Birmingham. They must have a storage unit somewhere. We believe they will coordinate attacks with the ongoing bombing campaign, so they must have communications with the Germans," Delaney explained. "We need information which will help us sabotage their efforts, and specifically, the identity of the leader."

Maggie was to apply for the job of housekeeper at the boarding house in Leinster Gardens. According to the information Dowd had gathered, there were three boarding houses, all owned by a Mr and Mrs Doyle. Mrs Doyle hired the help, and there was a vacancy right now. Delaney remembered the notice in the window of Number 25, Leinster Gardens. McClary boarded there, so it was where Maggie would be most likely to pick up useful information.

Delaney had wanted to know the details of Maggie's cover story.

"Maggie Carlon, recently widowed. Myself and my children were bombed out, my children are with relatives in the country, and I need work," Maggie relayed easily. "The best cover stories are the ones which are nearest the truth."

Maggie was to receive and leave messages in a tiny cafe on Portobello Road.

"It's about a mile from Leinster Gardens," Delaney had told her, "and it's busy with the marketgoers. Also, there's a Catholic Church nearby, so they would believe that you could attend Mass there. The owners of the cafe are friends of the Intelligence Service. They will keep the closed sign up on Sunday mornings, but keep the door open. I will leave messages for you, and they will call me when you have been in."

Then Delaney remembered. "There were silk fibres on Dowd's body. They might have come from a woman. If you see a woman visiting the boarding house, try to get a name."

When they shook hands awkwardly and said their goodbyes, Delaney was feeling better about the whole thing.

"Please take care, Maggie," he said and reached out to touch her arm.

"I will, Robert," she promised him before she turned to walk away. Then she stopped and looked back. "May the road rise up to meet you, Robert Delaney."

Delaney met her eye and nodded his thanks, but an icy shiver of fear ran through his body and he didn't know why.

Chapter 27

LEINSTER GARDENS, LONDON.

Maggie stood looking up at the boarding house in Leinster Gardens, holding a small bag which held a change of clothes. She must get hired today, Hawkins had told her. There would only be one shot at this.

A faded sign in the window said, 'Help wanted'. It looked like it had been there for some time.

Maggie made her way up the front steps, her sensible shoes clicking against the weathered stone. The door was a dull green, the paint peeling in places to reveal the wood beneath. Maggie took a deep breath, steeling herself, before she knocked firmly.

Moments later, the door swung open to reveal a woman in her fifties, her hair piled on her head and a cigarette in the corner of her mouth. "Yes?" she said, her voice sharp, and her eyes narrowed with suspicion. "Can I help you?"

Maggie forced a smile. "Mrs Doyle? I'm Maggie Carlon. I'm looking for work, and the butcher on the corner said you were looking for a housekeeper."

Mrs Doyle looked her up and down, her gaze lingering on Maggie's left hand and her wedding band. "You married?" she asked. "This is a live-in job."

"I am, but my husband is away fighting the war, and me-self and my children, we were recently bombed out. I need the work, Mrs Doyle, and I am very reliable."

Maggie emphasised her soft Irish accent as she spoke.

"We can't have no children here," Mrs Doyle replied. "This is no place for children. These boarding houses are for men. And some of 'em are rough."

"My children are away in the countryside with my husband's sister," Maggie said hastily, as Mrs Doyle moved to close the door, "and I really need the work. And don't you worry, I grew up with brothers in Dublin, so I know how to deal with working men."

"Well, I suppose it would be a nice change to have a respectable married woman working here." Mrs Doyle sucked on her cigarette and coughed as the smoke filled her lungs. She narrowed her eyes again and Maggie thought for a moment that Mrs Doyle didn't believe her story.

"Alright then," Mrs Doyle said when she'd caught her breath. "When can you start?"

Maggie was relieved. "As soon as you like, Mrs Doyle," she replied as she held up her bag. "I can move in today."

The interior of the boarding house was much like the exterior—shabby, with a lingering air of faded gentility. The hallway was narrow, the wallpaper a dingy floral pattern that had likely been fashionable before the last war. A threadbare runner stretched down the centre of the floor, muffling Maggie's footsteps as she followed Mrs Doyle to the kitchen.

"You'll start with the washing up," Mrs Doyle instructed, gesturing to a large sink piled high with dirty dishes. "Then you can start on the rooms. The lodgers expect their beds made and their rooms tidied every day."

Maggie nodded, setting her bag down in a corner. "Of course. I'll get started right away."

Mrs Doyle handed her an apron and watched as Maggie tied it on and began to fill the sink with hot, soapy water.

"Your room is up in the attic," she said. "I'll cook dinner tonight, and show you where everything is, and your day will finish when the kitchen is cleared. You'll be up early to make breakfast. They rise at 5 am, so don't be late."

"Don't you worry, Mrs Doyle," Maggie said cheerfully, "I'm an early riser."

Chapter 28

SCOTLAND YARD, LONDON.

Three days later, Delaney sat at the desk in his office, staring out the window.

He had heard nothing from Maggie. He had even phoned the teashop in Portobello Road to check, and a frosty voice informed him he would be notified the moment they received a message. The line went dead before Delaney could thank them.

He tried not to worry, but it was impossible.

There was a sharp rap on the door and Mrs Berkley entered with a tray of tea and biscuits.

Delaney raised his eyebrows when he saw the biscuits.

"Are we celebrating?" he asked.

"No, sir. But you haven't eaten breakfast this morning, have you?"

"No, Mrs Berkley, I haven't," Delaney admitted.

She set the tray on his desk. "You know, all the worrying in the world will not help Mrs Carroll. You need to trust her to do her job, and you concentrate on yours. If you don't mind me saying so, sir," she added, her face serious.

"Yes, Mrs Berkley, you are quite right. How is Birdie, I mean, Bernadette?"

Delaney noticed Mrs Berkley's face soften as she said, "She's a very sensible young lady. She misses her mother and brothers, but she is very focused on her work."

As I should be, Delaney thought.

"Chief Superintendent Whaldon would like to see you in his office. When you have a minute," she announced before she left his office.

Delaney sighed. Whaldon would want an update. The thing was, there wasn't anything to report.

He drank a cup of tea and ate all the biscuits and then went to Whaldon's office.

Whaldon was as impatient with the lack of progress as Delaney.

"Nothing at all? No word from Coster's lot?"

"Nothing, sir." Delaney had reported back about his meetings with Harry Coster and Connor Byrne already.

Delaney still couldn't shake the feeling of unease about Connor Byrne's last words to him. But really, a line from a poem? It wasn't exactly evidence, was it? Whaldon would think he had bats in the belfry, he decided.

"I don't like the thought of London's safety in the hands of Harry Coster," he said instead. "I don't trust the man. I get the feeling he'll use the situation to his advantage somehow."

Whaldon rubbed his chin, then reached for his pipe and lit it.

"You might be right ol' boy. Coster is not like Alfie Solomon. There's no honour among thieves these days. We'll have to hope that McVeigh gets some useful intelligence. When will you get a message from her, do you think?"

Delaney shrugged. "Soon, I hope. Hopefully, she'll have something and we can pull her out of there. Anything from MI5?"

"Nothing that helps us. They expect Hitler to ramp up his air strikes soon, and they believe that will be the signal for the terrorist attacks to start. Kicking us when we're down, the damn bastards."

It was rare to hear Whaldon use strong language, but Delaney shared his frustration.

"Any other leads in the Dowd murder?" Whaldon asked.

Delaney told him about Dr Holberg's discovery of silk fibres on Dowd's body and how they could be used as evidence.

Whaldon shook his head in amazement. "One day, there'll be no need for policemen," he said. "Scientists will replace us all."

"Not yet, sir. We have to connect the fibres with a person. Dr Holberg still needs us to do that. We think... well, I think... it might be a woman."

"You think a woman was involved in the murder?"

"Possibly, sir. A woman was spotted leaving the pub around the time we think Dowd was killed. But unfortunately, we haven't been able to track her down, or the witness who saw her."

Constable Hunter had visited the address Charlie Sutton gave him. He wasn't there.

"A neighbour told me Sutton got a visit from two rough-looking men and then left shortly afterwards. Someone got to him, I reckon," Hunter had reported to Delaney.

"So no leads at all?" Whaldon puffed on his pipe for a moment, seemingly lost in thought.

"We'll just have to hope that McVeigh comes through with the goods, as our American friends would say," Whaldon said at last, "We are relying on her now."

Maggie stood at the kitchen sink and washed the last of the dinner dishes. There was a window over the sink, and she looked out at the moonlight and stars as she thought of her children before pulling the blackout curtain into place.

It was a strange thing, Maggie thought, the large space where two houses should be. Mrs Doyle had pointed this out.

"The railway runs underground here. Number 22 and 23 were pulled down so they could vent the steam from the underground railway. So the front of the 'ouses are fake."

Every so often, Maggie felt the boarding house tremor and there would be a billow of steam from a vent in the space where number 23 and 24 used to stand.

Maggie had been working hard for three days now. There were twelve bedrooms on three floors to be cleaned each day. Then there was a large kitchen and a living room with chairs, a sofa, and a card table where the men would go after their evening meal. There were two other rooms on the ground floor of the house, but Mrs Doyle hadn't mentioned them, and when Maggie tried the doors, they were both locked.

Every day she got up at 4.00 am before the men and went downstairs from her tiny room in the attic to tidy up the living room, clean out the grate of the coal fire, and make porridge for the men's breakfast. After they left for their work, which was mainly clearing bomb sites and demolishing condemned houses, Maggie methodically cleaned every room.

The second day, Mrs Doyle inspected her work and nodded approvingly. "Very nice, Mrs Carlon. Very nice indeed."

On the first evening, Mrs Doyle had stayed to cook dinner and to show Maggie around the kitchen. The men barely noticed Maggie when they arrived back. One or two of them had grunted their thanks when she set a plate of food in front of them, but apart from that, there had been little in the way of talking at the dinner table.

Sheamus McClary was clearly in charge. Mrs Doyle introduced him, but Maggie had already recognised him from the picture in the MI5 file.

"Any trouble with the men, you come to me," he said, giving Maggie a cursory look up and down. Maggie hadn't expected him to be a short man, but he had muscular arms and a thick neck, which made him look like a bulldog. He also had large, calloused hands, and he walked with an arrogant swagger. He wasn't above cuffing the younger men around their heads if they spoke out of turn. From the expressions the other men displayed, McClary was not well liked, but was feared enough for them all to do as he said.

Maggie was getting anxious. She hadn't seen or heard anything useful to report back to Delaney. And so far, she hadn't had an excuse to leave the boarding house without arousing Mrs Doyle's suspicion.

After their dinner this evening, the men had sat around the table, drinking. Maggie had tried to hover around the table as long as possible, clearing plates. In her experience, a few drinks often loosened tongues.

But abruptly, McClary stood up and gestured for all the men to go into the living room, where he'd closed the door, and the voices of the men became muffled.

As Maggie placed the last dish on the drying rack, she heard footsteps behind her. She turned to see a young man standing in the doorway. His name was Liam, Maggie remembered. He was younger than the rest of them, a thin, gangly boy who didn't look like he had the strength for manual labour.

McClary and the other men teased him constantly, and his pale face was often flushed with embarrassment. Maggie felt sorry for the lad.

"Can I help you with something, Liam?" Maggie asked, wiping her hands on her apron.

"Sheamus, I mean, Mr McClary says to tell you there will be two more for dinner tomorrow. He says to tell Mrs Doyle, and he says that she is to do the cooking," Liam mumbled, not able to look Maggie in the eye.

"I see. Well, I'm be sure to pass the message on when I see Mrs Doyle tomorrow," Maggie said, smiling.

"There's something else," Liam added. "He says that you are to stay in your room tomorrow night. Take the night off."

"Well now, that's very kind of him, I'm sure," Maggie replied. "Please say thank you to Mr McClary for me. I'll be glad of the rest."

Liam bobbed his head in acknowledgement and disappeared back into the living room.

Maggie hung the tea towel to dry and took off her apron. One thing was certain, she thought as she made her way up the flights of stairs to the attic. She wouldn't be staying in her room the next evening.

Chapter 29

LEINSTER GARDENS, LONDON

Maggie woke early. She lay on her thin mattress for a few minutes. Her shoulders and arms ached from the scrubbing and cleaning that had filled the days she'd been at the boarding house. She focused on relaxing her limbs before getting up and dressing quickly, ready for the day's work.

She splashed cold water on her face from the bowl on her shabby dresser and smoothed her hair back into a bun.

Before Maggie left her room, she caught sight of her face in the cracked mirror attached to the wall above her dresser. She barely recognised the pale, tired face that looked back at her.

I'm too old for this. I need to finish this assignment, she thought. She felt an ache in her heart. Lord, she missed her children.

But tonight, two more people were joining McClary and the other men. She must find out who they were and try her hardest to identify them, or get some tidbit of information for Delaney. Then she'd have to make an excuse to leave the boarding house and get a message to him.

Today was Friday. Maybe Mrs Doyle would let her go to Mass on Sunday. That would be the perfect excuse to leave the boarding house for a few hours.

The fug of lingering cigarette smoke and stale beer greeted Maggie in the kitchen. The floor was sticky, and empty glasses and bottles littered the countertops and table. Maggie put on her apron and quickly lit the stove where set a large pot of water to boil for cleaning. Once she'd tidied up, she went into the living room and did the same, straightening cushions and brushing crumbs onto the floor for sweeping later.

The men had stayed up late last night. Maggie had finally heard the creak of footsteps on the stairs and the banging of bedroom doors hours after she had climbed into her narrow bed.

There would be sore heads this morning, judging by the number of empty beer bottles strewn around the living room. As she cleared up the last of the mess, Maggie noticed something unusual.

The door to one of the other rooms was open a crack. Someone must have forgotten to lock it. Maggie stared at it for a moment and then pushed the door wide open. She didn't have much time before the men appeared, so she would have to be quick and listen out for footsteps. Maybe she'd find something useful in here. Why would the doors be locked, unless there was something Mrs Doyle or McClary didn't want anyone to find?

The room was dim, the only window covered by a blackout curtain. She dared not light a lamp, so she waited until her eyes had adjusted.

The room was sparsely furnished. There was a desk in one corner and two worn leather chairs. Bookcases lined the two walls but were empty of any books.The room wasn't used as a study, Maggie thought. Maybe just a meeting room?

Maggie stood and listened, but the house was still silent. She moved behind the desk quickly and pulled on the drawer handles. They were all locked. She ran her hand over the leather which covered the top of the desk, and underneath, trying to find a nook or cranny where a key could be hidden, but nothing. McClary or Mrs Doyle must keep the keys on their person, Maggie thought. If there was any information worth having in here, then that was the most likely scenario.

If she had longer, she might try picking the locks of the drawers, but soon the men would come downstairs wanting their breakfast. As if her thoughts could be read, Maggie heard the squeak of floorboards above her. She backed out of the room, making sure there was no trace of her being there. Just before she pulled the door, so it was in the same position as she had found it, Maggie saw something glinting under one of the chairs. As quick as she could, she stepped back in the room, picked it up, and dropped it in her apron pocket.

Then she left the room, positioned the door once more, and busied herself cleaning out the fireplace and starting a fire to warm the room and the rest of the house.

An hour later, and all the men had left for work and Maggie had time to dig into her pocket and examine the shiny item she'd found. It was a tiny silver cross on a pin. A lapel pin? Maggie couldn't imagine McClary or any of his men wearing a lapel pin. She slipped it in her skirt pocket. It might be nothing, but she'd hold on to it for now.

Just as Maggie was finished cleaning the downstairs, Mrs Doyle arrived.

Maggie passed on Liam's message from McClary. Mrs Doyle pursed her lips and seemed annoyed.

"You'll have to do the shopping," she snapped. She pulled open a drawer in the kitchen and found a scrap of paper and a pencil before she sat at the kitchen table and scribbled a list.

"Take this and the ration book," she said, handing them both to Maggie. "Go to Portobello Road market. There are two places where we get a little extra to help us out. I've written them down. Tell 'em that I sent you."

"Ah, I see," Maggie said, understanding at once that Mrs Doyle was referring to black market traders.

"There's a bus if you want, but it's not far to walk, not for a young woman like you."

Maggie couldn't believe her luck. She didn't have to sneak out to leave a message for Delaney. She had the perfect cover.

The bustling market of Portobello Road was a welcome distraction for Maggie as she navigated through the crowds, her wicker basket in hand. The vibrant colours of the fresh produce as well as the lively chatter and cries from the stall holders helped to lift her spirits, momentarily pushing aside the fear and uncertainty that had become her constant companions since she began this undercover mission.

Maggie decided to do her shopping before heading to the tea shop to leave a message for Delaney. She didn't have anything definite to report, but she wanted to leave word about the mysterious guests expected that evening, and that she'd try to report back on Sunday morning.

Maggie walked from stall to stall, using the coupons in the ration book and tucking the 'extras' out of sight. She wished she was shopping for her family and wondered how the boys were coping in the countryside. Mrs Hazelton had been reassuring, but the boys had endured a lot and Maggie missed giving them a hug and tucking them into bed.

She worried less about Birdie. Mrs Berkley was so sensible, and Maggie had a feeling that young Constable Hunter would pay special attention to her daughter.

Lost in thought, she almost didn't hear the familiar voice calling her name. But when she turned, she found herself face to face with someone she thought she would never see again.

"Mrs Carroll? Maggie Carroll, is that really you?"

Standing before her, with a look of shock and disbelief etched across her face, was Mrs Bernstein, her neighbour from Patterson Road.

Maggie's heart leaped into her throat as she stared at the woman, her mind reeling with a hundred questions. She thought the Bernsteins were dead, killed in the same blast that destroyed her home. But here she was, alive and well, and looking at her with a mixture of joy and confusion.

"Mrs Bernstein," Maggie managed to choke out, her voice barely above a whisper. "I... I thought..."

But before she could finish her sentence, Mrs Bernstein had pulled her into a tight embrace, her arms wrapped around Maggie's shoulders as she sobbed with relief.

"Oh, Mrs Carroll, my dear girl. I can't believe it's really you. I thought you were dead."

Maggie hugged her back, tears stinging her own eyes as she tried to process the shock of seeing her neighbour again. But as glad as she was for Mrs Bernstein's embrace, she became immediately uneasy. If Mrs Bernstein recognised her, if she started asking questions about where she had been and what she was doing here, it could blow her cover entirely. And with so much at stake, Maggie knew she couldn't let that happen. Maggie glanced around, but to her relief, nobody was paying them any attention.

Gently, she disentangled herself from Mrs Bernstein's arms, taking a step back and forcing a smile onto her face. "It's so good to see you. I can't believe it either. I thought you and Mr Bernstein..."

She trailed off, unable to finish the sentence, but Mrs Bernstein understood, her eyes clouding with grief as she shook her head.

"Mr Bernstein didn't make it," she said softly, her voice thick with emotion. "The bomb... it took him. But I survived, by some miracle. I've been staying with my sister ever since, trying to put the pieces back together."

"I'm so sorry, Mrs Bernstein," Maggie said, her heart aching for the elderly lady, and she reached out to squeeze the woman's hand. "I can't imagine how hard it must have been for you."

Mrs Bernstein nodded, wiping away a stray tear with the back of her hand. "It's been a struggle. I won't lie. But I'm getting by, one day at a time. And what about you, Maggie? Where have you been all this time? And Bernadette and the boys, are they..."

"They're safe," Maggie told her. "We were so lucky. We were trapped in the cellar for a while, but we all made it out with just a few scrapes and bruises. The children are in the country now, with George's sister. I thought it best to move them. But I must carry on working and look for another home."

It wasn't all a lie, Maggie thought.

Mrs Bernstein smiled, relief washing over her face. "Thank God for that," she said, squeezing Maggie's hand. "I've been so worried about you all, ever since that awful night. I thought for sure that nobody could have survived..." Her voice tailed off. "But then, I heard that a family had been rescued, and I so hoped it was you. Poor Mr Larkham and Mrs Grenfield. I'm afraid they didn't make it. I tried to look for you, Mrs Carroll. I even went to the Catholic church to ask if you had gone there for help. I met a Father Thomas who couldn't tell me anything, and I didn't know where else to look."

Maggie froze, her heart pounding in her chest. Father Thomas? But that couldn't be right.

"Father Thomas? Are you sure it wasn't Father Brennan? A young man with red hair?"

Mrs Bernstein stared at her.

"Oh no, it was an elderly man. But he wasn't very helpful."

"Well, never mind, you found me now. And Birdie and the boys will be so happy to know you are alright," Maggie replied, forcing a smile.

Mrs Bernstein squeezed Maggie's hand again. "It made my day to see you," she said, her voice choked with emotion. "You take care now." With a final hug and a promise to keep in touch, Mrs Bernstein disappeared back into the crowd, leaving Maggie standing alone with her thoughts and her fears.

If Father Brennan hadn't found out about her from Father Thomas, then the only way he could have known that Maggie existed at all was from the newspaper article about Birdie. Why was he so interested in that? And why lie about it?

A thought struck her. Maggie put her shopping on the ground and pushed her hand in her pocket. She pulled out the tiny silver pin and turned it over in her hand, staring at the cross. A silver cross and a priest were surely connected, weren't they? But then she shook her head. No, this was just a coincidence, she told herself. Father Brennan was just a young upstart priest, trying to make a name for himself. Maybe he was working for Father Thomas, but was trying to make himself sound more important than he was.

Time was getting on, so Maggie didn't have time to think about this now. She had to visit the tea shop and get back to the boarding house in time to finish her chores before the men came home from work.

The tea shop was down a narrow alley, just off the Portobello Road. Maggie pushed open the door to find a stout woman with curly black hair sitting behind a counter, reading a newspaper.

"Cuppa tea, love?" she asked, as Maggie set her basket down on a small table by the window.

"Yes, that'll be grand," Maggie replied and remembered what Delaney had told her to say. "I'd love a scone with that if you don't mind." Then she added, "I love a toasted scone with strawberry jam."

"Strawberry jam is hard to find in the war, love," the lady said, "but I'll see what I can do."

Maggie sat and waited and a few minutes later, the lady brought over a cup of tea, and a plate with a buttered scone and a large dollop of jam. Sure enough, when Maggie picked up the scone, there was a folded piece of paper underneath for Maggie to leave a note. Tucked under the side of the plate was a pencil.

Maggie drank her tea and ate the scone. When she was finished, she scribbled a quick note to Delaney.

Safe. Two guests expected tonight. Will report Sunday.

Then Maggie stood up and took the empty cup and plate back to the counter. She tucked the note under the plate and slid it over to the lady.

The lady nodded her thanks.

"How much for the tea and scone?" Maggie asked.

"On the 'ouse, love," she said. "Come again soon."

"I will," Maggie told her as she pulled open the door. Next time, she hoped she'd have something significant to report.

Chapter 30

MULGRAVE ROAD, SHREWSBURY COMMON.

The night was chilly and damp when Birdie finished her Friday shift at the Woolwich Arsenal. The heavy factory gate clanged shut behind her. She pulled her coat tightly around her and said her goodbyes to the other girls who were going to the pub. They'd invited her and she'd hesitated before refusing. A night out would be so much fun and would take her mind off the bombing and the aftermath. It was just what she needed. But she'd promised Ma she would go straight home every night. At least she had two days before her next shift. Tomorrow she might go to Woolwich covered-in market. Mrs Berkley would want to her to go to church on Sunday. Birdie felt a bit funny going to Mrs Berkley's church with a vicar instead of a priest, but Mrs Berkley said God wouldn't mind. Birdie wondered if God would mind if she missed it altogether and met Constable Hunter for a walk over Plumstead Common instead.

Birdie quickened her pace. Mrs Berkley might be worried if she was late home. Birdie shivered as the wind whipped through the street. If she hurried, she thought, she could catch the last tram. But, she reasoned, she could save two pence if she didn't, and anyway, there were so many tram stops on the route to Mrs Berkley's home that it would be quicker on foot. It was only a twenty-five-minute walk.

Satisfied she'd made the right choice, she turned left and headed towards Plumstead Road. Birdie knew she'd walk past the turnoff to the road they used to live on, where the entire street lay in rubble. There were barricades at the end, preventing anyone from going back to the bomb site. Not that Birdie wanted to, anyway. Even in the safety of Mrs Berkley's house, she couldn't sleep without having nightmares about being buried alive. She knew her mother had bad dreams too, after that night. They'd shared a bed that first night at Mrs Berkley's house and Maggie had tossed and turned and cried out in her sleep.

And now they were apart. The boys were somewhere in the countryside and her mother? Where was she? Birdie knew her mother's absence had something to do with the murderer who tried to hurt her. All she wanted was for the whole family, including her father, to be together in a new home. She sighed to herself. That wish seemed a long way off.

Rain started to fall and Birdie quickened her pace, her footsteps echoing off the cobblestones. The streets were empty now, and the houses were dark and silent during the blackout. Birdie hummed to keep her spirits up and to quell her growing sense of unease as she hurried along. She slid her hand into her pocket and felt around for the metal hairpin she kept there.

It wasn't much, but she remembered the paralysing sense of helplessness when Connor Byrne's charming smile transformed into a snarl and he'd grabbed her. She'd been so shocked, she hadn't been able to think about what to do. Her voice had refused to scream and her arms and legs turned to jelly.

She'd tried to think about what she could have done to escape and what she would do if it ever happened again since that night. Jabbing a metal hairpin into an attacker's eye seemed like a good plan, and just having the pin in her pocket made her feel better.

Birdie was walking down Shrewsbury Lane now, and about five minutes away from Mulgrave Road where Mrs Berkley lived. Birdie hoped Mrs Berkley was home and there was a pot of tea waiting for her.

Birdie turned into Mulgrave Road, and as she did so, she caught a movement out of the corner of her eye. She stopped and peered into the gloom. Mrs Berkley's house was at the far end of the Road, so Birdie hurried forward. Then she heard footsteps. They were heavy, but fast. Birdie turned and saw a shadow approaching her. Immediately, she felt her heart beating against her chest. The ominous shadow got nearer, and Birdie's fear grew, as her hand clutched the hairpin in her pocket. What should she do? Confront whoever it was?

But Birdie didn't wait to call out. First, she broke into a fast walk, and then, as the footsteps kept coming nearer and nearer, Birdie ran.

Her coat billowed behind her as she ran as fast as she could until she finally saw the wrought-iron gate at the end of the short path to Mrs Berkley's front door. Birdie flung herself through the gate and up the two steps, frantically banging on the door, willing Mrs Berkley to be home, so she didn't have to find the key in the dark and navigate the lock as her pursuer was nearly upon her.

"Bernadette! Whatever is wrong?"

Birdie could have hugged Mrs Berkley in relief. The older lady had opened the door and light flooded out, illuminating the path and the street beyond the gate. Birdie turned, expecting to see a man wielding a weapon, but there was no one there. Whoever it was had faded into the shadows. Mrs Berkley stared at Birdie. "You're soaked through, young lady. Come in quick, it's blackout and we're lighting up the street."

"There was someone following me," Birdie said, her voice trembling. "I'm sure of it. I heard footsteps."

Mrs Berkley's expression changed immediately. "Come inside quickly, but leave the door open a crack so I can see. And give me that walking stick."

"What are you going to do?" Birdie questioned as she passed Mrs Berkley the stick. "Shouldn't we go inside and lock the door?"

"I'm going to see who's there," Mrs Berkley said firmly before she marched down the path to the gate that Birdie had left swinging.

As she fastened the latch on the gate, she looked both ways down the street.

"Is there anyone there?" Mrs Berkley called, "Show yourself, please."

Nothing. Birdie was starting to feel embarrassed. Had she imagined it?

"There's nobody about," Mrs Berkley reassured her as she came through the front door, although as she closed it behind her, she bolted it top and bottom.

"Whoever it was has gone now. But I will report it to the Detective Chief Inspector first thing on Monday morning."

"Oh, but what if it was nothing?" Birdie said as she hung her wet coat on a hook. "I'm sure there was someone, but what if..." Her voice trailed off. She thought of Constable Hunter and didn't want him to think she was just a silly girl who imagined monsters everywhere.

"What if you imagined it?" Mrs Berkley finished her sentence. "If you did Bernadette, it would be quite understandable, after everything you have been through. But if you didn't and there was someone following you, then I must report it. But don't worry. Nobody will think badly of you. Not even young Constable Hunter," she added with a smile, which made Birdie blush.

"Come on into the kitchen and warm up. I've got a pot of tea ready."

Chapter 31

LEINSTER GARDENS, LONDON.

Mrs Doyle shooed Maggie out of the kitchen as soon as McClary and the men arrived back from work that evening. As Maggie took off her apron, she said, "Mrs Doyle, if you don't mind, may I attend early Mass on Sunday? It's been a while since I've been to confession, and I should go, if you won't miss me for two hours. I'll do my chores before, and I'll leave porridge for the men."

Mrs Doyle swung round and, from her expression, seemed about to say no, but then the door opened and McClary barged in.

"What's she doing here?" he grunted. "I thought I told ya..."

"She's just leaving," Mrs Doyle interrupted him and then said to Maggie, "Yes, yes, go to Mass but be back quickly, you hear? Now, off to your room."

"Yes, thank you, Mrs Doyle."

Maggie hurried up the stairs to her room but left the door open. She heard the sounds of chairs scraping on the kitchen floor and doors banging.

It would take a while for the men to eat their dinner. She planned to creep downstairs to see if she could get a look at the two guests McClary had invited, and overhear any of the conversations. It was a dangerous move, but it might be Maggie's only chance to gather information before the gang put their plans into action.

After a while, Maggie heard the clatter of dishes. Mrs Doyle had already told her she was leaving the washing up for Maggie to do on Saturday morning, so Maggie was sure that Mrs Doyle would leave quickly once dinner was over.

Maggie crept slowly down one flight of stairs, across the landing, and then down the second flight.

She was now crouched down behind the bannisters and had a clear view of the kitchen and the door into the living room. If she was lucky, she would see all the men as they left the table and went to the other room.

They were all still sitting at the table. Maggie could see the back of McClary's head, but the guests were out of sight, although their voices were loud.

Maggie listened for a moment and quickly realised that an argument was taking place.

"Now listen, you promised us the delivery would be at—"

"Damn it, man, I've got coppers all over... after Dowd... you gotta give me—"

Someone, not McClary, thumped the table hard, and the voices quietened down.

Maggie could then hear a man's voice. It was too low to make out the words, but there was something about the way the timbre of his voice that caused an icy shiver to run down her spine.

Her legs were aching from being crouched in the same position behind the wooden bannisters, but Maggie willed herself not to move and strained harder to hear what was being said.

A loud thud followed by a shout of pain made Maggie start. Then a man's voice bellowed, "That delivery must be at Palmer's by Monday. Do ya hear me? Or you'll get the same as…"

Maggie didn't hear the end of the sentence, because a man had strode into view and was standing in the kitchen doorway.

Her hand flew to her mouth. It couldn't be. It just couldn't be.

As if the man sensed he was being watched, he turned his head, and for a moment, Maggie thought he was looking directly at her. She tensed every muscle and closed her eyes, praying that he hadn't seen her. When nothing happened, Maggie opened her eyes to find that the man had gone, but standing in his place was Liam. This time, Liam lifted his head, and Maggie was certain he knew she was there.

She waited for him to shout, but he stepped back and slammed the door.

Maggie waited until she heard movement in the kitchen, and then she raced silently back up the stairs to her attic room. She closed the door behind her and sank to her knees in shock. Surely her eyes must have been deceiving her. After all these years, was it really possible she'd just seen her cousin, Sean McVeigh?

Chapter 32

MULGRAVE ROAD, SHREWSBURY COMMON.

"Bernadette? It's six o'clock. Breakfast will be ready shortly." Mrs Berkley's voice followed a sharp tap on the bedroom door.

Birdie wasn't asleep. She had been wide awake for half the night, it seemed. When Birdie had closed her eyes and drifted off to sleep, her dreams were filled with monsters in the shadows who grabbed at her arms and throat and she'd woken, gasping for breath and trembling with fear.

Even in the daylight, she imagined bogey-men around every corner. Saturday morning at the market hadn't cheered her up at all.

"It's understandable," Mrs Berkley had said. "You've endured a lot over the last few months. What with that terrible business before Christmas and then the bombing. It could just be the shock of everything. You could be imagining it, and nobody would blame you. But we must be sensible. First thing on Monday morning, I'll tell Detective Chief Inspector Delaney and he'll know what's best to do."

Everything Mrs Berkley had said in that calm voice of hers made sense. Birdie had forgotten about her fears on Saturday evening as she and Mrs Berkley listened to the radio, and Birdie had written a letter to her brothers. She hoped they were having fun in the countryside. She'd felt much better as she addressed an envelope, and left the letter ready for posting on the hall stand before she climbed the stairs to her bed. She was even looking forward to going to church on Sunday morning. But when her eyes closed, the nightmares had come again.

Mrs Berkley smiled at Birdie as she sat down at the kitchen table. "Bad night, dear? You look a little pale."

The table was laid, and a pot of tea and two teacups were ready in the middle while Mrs Berkley stirred a pot of porridge on the stove.

"I suppose," Birdie muttered, pouring herself a cup. "I had silly dreams," she said, giving Mrs Berkley a half smile.

Now she was sitting in the warm kitchen, with the darkness outside giving way to silver grey as the sun rose, Birdie felt silly.

"Now, don't you worry," Mrs Berkley said, bringing two bowls of porridge to the table. "The Detective Chief Inspector will look into it. And if necessary, I am sure he'll spare Constable Hunter to make sure you get home safely after work on Monday."

Birdie smiled. She liked Billy Hunter. He was handsome, and a war hero.

They ate their porridge in silence.

"Just time for another cup of tea," Mrs Berkley said, "and then we'll leave for church." Before she could reach for the teapot, there was a loud banging on the front door.

Mrs Berkley's hand froze for a second. "Now, who can that be, at this hour on a Sunday morning?" she said, her voice steady, but Birdie's heart was thumping.

"I'm sure it's just a neighbour," Mrs Berkley continued, "but Bernadette, just to be sure, why don't you slip out the back and wait in the scullery?"

Birdie nodded and tried not to show her fear as she opened the back door and stepped into the chilly scullery. She closed the door behind her and shrank back into the dark corner, behind the shelves which were lined with tins and jars.

Birdie could hear Mrs Berkley's muffled footsteps fading as she went to the front door.

'Who's there please?' Mrs Berkley's voice held not a hint of fear. It was clear and commanding. "I'm afraid you have the wrong house. I live alone," was her response to a muffled voice.

Maybe they would go away, Birdie hoped. It was just the wrong house. Somebody had got the wrong address and Mrs Berkley would pop her head around the door, and they would both have a good laugh at how silly they had been.

But Birdie was wrong.

From her hiding place, she heard a loud thump and a crash. Then she heard Mrs Berkley cry out in pain and fear. There were more thumps and running footsteps.

They were sure to find her. What should she do? In the corner of the scullery, there was a broom, but that was no weapon. Birdie felt along the shelves for something she could throw. Her hand reached into her pocket, but she'd left the hairpin in her other dress.

This was no use, she thought. She couldn't help Mrs Berkley. Maybe she should run? But where to? There was a gate at the back of the house, but it was kept bolted. What if there was a padlock too? Did she have time to get out there and check? She heard footsteps heading upstairs. There must be more than one person, she thought, and they were searching for her. Oh God, there's no time, she panicked. She'd have to find somewhere to hide.

What would her mother tell her to do?

Then her leg banged against something sharp and metal. It was the hatch to the coal cellar. The hatch was small, but Birdie eased it up, trying not to make a sound.

The opening was just big enough for her to get through. She didn't want to go head first, so she turned around and backed through the opening. Her feet touched the pile of coal and as she lowered her weight down, it made a crunching sound, which seemed as loud as a siren. She froze, her heart pounding, but all she heard was the creak of floorboards above her, as the men moved from room to room.

Birdie let her body drop and her feet sunk further into the coal. She let the hatch down quietly, leaving her in darkness. She crouched down and burrowed as far as she could into the coal, rubbing the dust all over her face and neck. If they opened the hatch, she hoped they wouldn't see her.

And then she lay still and prayed silently.

Chapter 33

LEINSTER GARDENS, LONDON

Maggie was up early on Sunday morning. She finished washing the breakfast dishes and swept the kitchen floor. She tried not to keep looking at the clock on the mantel. Another two hours and she would be in the teashop and she'd not be coming back here. It was far too dangerous. She thought about leaving early this morning before the men came down for breakfast, but she hadn't wanted to arouse suspicion. She'd do her morning chores, keep the same schedule, and leave as if she were going to Mass, as she'd told Mrs Doyle.

She hadn't slept at all for the last two nights. She'd half expected to be dragged out of bed at any moment, playing the scene over and over in her mind. Liam had seen her, she was certain. But on Saturday morning, she had made porridge and gone about her work as usual. The men were quiet, sullen even, and Liam didn't meet her eyes when she put his breakfast on the table.

Maggie had thought about leaving the boarding house right away. But before she could go, Mrs Doyle arrived and instructed her to clean out the pantry and change the bed linen on all the beds to prepare for Monday morning laundry.

Throughout the day, Maggie's mind had returned to the man she'd seen.

Was she sure it was Sean? She hadn't seen him for twenty years, but she'd recognised his voice; that lazy drawl.

At the end of the day, the men returned from work and ate their dinner, mostly in silence. There was tension in the air, Maggie thought. It wasn't just her own unease.

What she'd heard on Friday night about the delivery they were waiting for must be connected to their plans. 'Palmers' must either be the name of a person or a place. Maggie had to get the information to Delaney, and hopefully, that would be enough for MI5 to intercept the explosives and round up the gang.

And she had to get out of there and back to her children.

Finally, it was time to leave. Maggie took her apron off and hung it on the hook on the back of the kitchen door. She slipped on her coat and picked up her bag. She wasn't taking anything else with her. She had no intention of coming back to Leinster Gardens.

Detective Chief Inspector Delaney sat in the tiny tea shop near Portobello Market, his fingers tapping impatiently on the worn wooden table. The aroma of freshly brewed tea and warm scones filled the air, but Delaney barely noticed, his mind preoccupied with thoughts of Maggie.

He glanced at his watch for the umpteenth time, the minutes ticking by with agonising slowness. He had to get Maggie away from the boarding house. It was getting far too dangerous for her to stay.

Late on Friday evening, Mrs Berkley had come into his office.

"There's a man on the telephone. He wants to speak to you. He would not leave a message," she said, her tone disapproving.

When Delaney picked up the receiver, he recognised the voice at the other end immediately. It was Tommy, Harry Coster's henchman, who'd met Delaney at the Regal Room nightclub.

"We got wind of a special delivery comin' Monday. It's 'eaded to a ware'ouse at the Docks. We dunno where yet. That's all." And then the telephone went dead.

Constable Hunter and two other officers were spending their Sunday making discreet inquiries around the London Docks, trying to connect Knowles or McClary to a warehouse. It was like looking for a needle in a haystack, Delaney knew. He only hoped that Maggie had some information that would help. Her last message had said that McClary was expecting guests. Whatever the gang was planning, it was imminent. Delaney was sure. He hoped fervently that Maggie had managed to get away that morning. Maybe she had gone to Mass first.

The Sunday market was busy. Stall holders hollered at the crowd, hawking their wares. Spivs moved among shoppers, winking at women and opening their jackets to reveal stockings, lipstick, anything they'd got their hands on, and were selling for a tidy profit.

The war had been a golden time for criminals, Delaney thought. As well as the brave citizens who risked their lives digging for survivors in bombed-out buildings, were the looters. Sometimes, the looters were the emergency services. Delaney remembered a case during the bombings back in 1940, where six members of the auxiliary fire service had successfully extinguished a blaze in a pub near St Paul's Cathedral, but had also helped themselves to bottles of whisky and gin, and other items which they hid inside their fire tender. It was only the sharp eyes of a special constable that had been their downfall.

The six of them were sentenced to five years at the Old Bailey.

There had been an outcry in the newspapers after the sentencing. What was the harm, people had wondered. The stuff was only going to waste.

The void between right and wrong had grown since the first flush of patriotic fervour at the beginning of the war. At first, there seemed to be a genuine sense of all being in this together against Hitler, to make sure everyone kept the flag flying for the brave boys fighting the evil enemy. But years later, cynicism and weariness had set in, and now it seemed to Delaney it was survival of the fittest on the streets of London.

The war had brought the best and worst out in people, Delaney thought, and not only that, the same war shirkers who wandered around the market with their shiny suits and jaunty hats were the same people who thought themselves better than Maggie and the Irishmen who had come to England to work, and those who'd volunteered to join the British Army.

Delaney was jerked out of his reverie by a lady standing over him.

"Anything else, love? Another cuppa?"

Delaney shook his head. Maggie wasn't coming. Mass was over now. She must be stuck at the boarding house. There was nothing to do here. He just had to hope that Maggie got to the teashop on Monday and could leave a message.

Delaney nodded at the lady as she took his empty cup and plate. She raised her eyebrows questioningly, and he muttered, "no message," before leaving the teashop.

Delaney made his way through the market, his tall frame and demeanour marking him as a policeman, even in plain clothes. A couple of the men working the stalls turned their backs or averted their eyes.

But Delaney didn't care about their black market trading. Not today.

Chapter 34

PORTOBELLO ROAD, LONDON.

Maggie walked briskly to Portobello Road. She kept her head held high, and she was careful not to glance over her shoulder. She hummed a little to calm her nerves.

She was relieved when she reached the market and the usual crowd of people. She stopped to listen with other shoppers to a stallholder who was entertaining the crowd with his patter.

"Go on, darlin', these pots are cast iron. Best you'll get in London. You'll make beeooooutiful mash in these, and when you're done, you can bash the ol' man round his 'ead when he rolls in drunk... darlin' you won't get a better price..."

She joined in the laughter and took the risk of glancing around. She couldn't see anyone suspicious, and the tea shop was near. Maggie took a breath and moved purposefully towards the tea shop and Delaney. Nearly there, she thought. Mission over.

Then, as she stepped around a stall to get to the pavement, a hand gripped her arm.

"Mrs Carroll, it's God's miracle," a voice breathed in her ear. "Here you are, alive and well. And how are those beautiful children of yours?"

Father Brennan looked down at her, his baby-blue eyes full of amusement.

"Father Brennan," Maggie said, swallowing her gasp of shock and keeping her voice even. "What a surprise it is, seeing you here."

She thought back to his visit, the sense of unease she'd felt at his interest in Birdie. And then the information from Mrs Bernstein. Maggie remembered in horror the silver cross she'd found at the boarding house. Brennan was mixed up in all of this, and he'd known all along about Maggie.

Brennan confirmed her thoughts. "I'm sure it is a surprise to see me, Mrs Carroll." Father Brennan did not release his grip. "Or should I say Maggie McVeigh?"

Maggie's shock must have shown on her face because Father Brennan laughed. "Poor Maggie. You weren't expecting that, were you? Well, I shouldn't stand here chatting. Here's someone else who wants to say hello after all these years."

Maggie followed Father Brennan's gaze and there he was, Sean McVeigh. She hadn't been mistaken. It was him. Older, stockier, and his face fleshier under his flat cap. His skin showed the reddish veins of a hard drinker, just like his father. His lips were curved into the same vicious sneer she remembered, as he strode forward and grabbed her other arm. Maggie could hardly breathe as the same fear as she'd felt all those years ago, threatened to overwhelm her.

"If it isn't my lovely cousin Maggie," Sean whispered as he tightened his grip. "I've been looking forward to catching up with you."

He nodded at Father Brennan. "The good father here has to leave us now. He has a very important appointment in the countryside. He's going to pay a visit to those bonny boys of yours."

Maggie began struggling, and Sean laughed. "If you make a scene, then you'll never see 'em again. Walk with me and I promise that Father Brennan won't hurt a hair on their heads. After all, those boys are family, aren't they, darlin'?"

"You... Bastard," Maggie hissed, her fear dissipating into anger, as she saw the glint of metal in the light and then felt the tip of a blade pressed into her side. She was helpless.

"Come now, Maggie," Sean laughed. "That's no language for a lady."

Then he stopped laughing as a voice said, "Mrs Carroll. How nice to see you again."

Mrs Bernstein was smiling at her. Sean stepped back and touched his cap, but mouthed, "Don't try anything. Remember the boys."

"Mrs Bernstein, lovely to see you, too. I'm afraid I can't stop. This gentleman is a handyman, and I've been sent to find him to fix a leak." Maggie said brightly, desperately trying to think of something to say that would alert Mrs Bernstein to the danger she was in, but not tip off Sean.

"Well, I'll not hold you up, my dear," Mrs Bernstein replied.

Maggie reached out and touched Mrs Bernstein's shoulder. She saw Sean flinch and blurted, "Remember me to Mr Bernstein. Tell him that until we meet again, may the Lord hold him in the palm of his hand. Will you do that?"

A look of confusion spread over Mrs Bernstein's face, but she quickly recovered, and to Maggie's relief, she said, "I will do that, my dear. Of course I will do that."

Chapter 35

A WAREHOUSE, UNKNOWN LOCATION, LONDON.

Maggie had been led away from the Portobello market and down an alleyway.

Sean had bound her hands behind her back and gagged her with a filthy rag that tasted of stale tobacco. Maggie fought her rising panic as he covered her head with a sack. She knew if she gave way to her fear, she might not be able to breathe, so she closed her eyes and concentrated on calming her thumping heart.

She was shoved onto a hard surface and heard a door slam shut. It wasn't long before she realised it was a vehicle as she heard the roar of an engine.

Maggie didn't know how long they had been travelling when the vehicle finally came to a stop. Then she heard the door open and felt a blast of cold air.

A hand grabbed her shoulder, and she was hauled to her feet, where she staggered slightly.

Maggie heard Sean's voice near to her, barking orders. "Open the door. Quick now."

Maggie tried to focus on the sounds around her. She could hear men shouting, she thought, although she couldn't make out what they were saying. And then, just as a hand gripped her upper arm and pushed her forward, she heard the unmistakable cry of a seagull. She was near the water.

Was she at Palmer's Warehouse? With all her might, Maggie willed Mrs Bernstein to have understood her last message. She'd seen the confusion in Mrs Bernstein's eyes as Maggie had gripped her hands and talked about poor dead Mr Bernstein as if he hadn't perished in the bombing. Maybe it was enough for Mrs Bernstein to realise that something was wrong. Maybe she would go to the police station. Maybe Mrs Bernstein would remember Robert from the newspaper report of Birdie's escape from Connor Byrne and ask to speak to him. And then, maybe, there might be a slight chance that Robert would understand the significance of her cryptic message.

It was a long shot, Maggie knew. So she prayed.

Somebody had shoved her down onto cold concrete and she lay there shivering. Footsteps echoed around her and then faded away. It had been quiet for a long time. Maybe she'd had slept, she didn't know.

"Sit," a voice instructed. Not Sean's voice. A younger man. Liam?

She was dragged to a chair and her ankles were bound tight to the legs before the sack was pulled off her head. Her hands were bound to the arms of the chair.

It took a moment for her eyes to adjust, and then she could see that she'd been right; Sean had brought her to a warehouse. As Maggie blinked and looked around, she saw wooden crates stacked up high around her, but she couldn't see anyone in the gloom. Had they left her again?

The warehouse was dark and musty and there was a peculiar smell in the air. It reminded Maggie of Christmas somehow. Was it marzipan? Before she could identify it, from the shadows, a figure emerged, and Maggie felt her blood run cold.

"Ah, Maggie, this is lovely. A family reunion at last. You do not know how much I've looked forward to seeing you again. My cousin, traitor to her country and The Cause."

Sean stood in front of her, his arms folded and a smirk on his face, which matched his sarcastic tone.

"But where are my manners?" he said. "This isn't the way to catch up, is it now?"

Maggie flinched as Sean's hands came near her face, and she braced for a punch. Instead, he chuckled and removed her gag.

"Oh, I'm a changed man, cousin Maggie," he said as she coughed. "Punching a woman gives me no pleasure."

"You are indeed a different man, Sean," Maggie rasped. "You and your rotten father used my poor aunt as your punching bag, as I remember."

Sean's face darkened, and Maggie could see his hands clench. He hadn't changed that much, she thought.

"You'll not speak of my poor dead mother and father," he spat. "They took you in and you betrayed us all."

He seemed to struggle to compose himself. "And now, dear cousin, you are all the family I have left. Except for the beautiful Bernadette and those precious boys."

Maggie felt a wave of nausea overwhelm her at the mention of her children.

"Sean," she said, her voice trembling slightly, "what is this about? Why have you brought me here?"

Sean's smirk widened. "Why, Maggie, I thought that would be obvious. I brought you here to settle the score. To make you pay for your betrayal all those years ago."

Maggie shook her head, her mind racing. Her only hope was Delaney. And she needed time for him to find her.

"Betrayal? Betrayal of what? The Cause? You never cared about any cause. You just liked killing people."

Sean's face twisted in anger for a second and his fists clenched again. "I am a soldier fighting a war, Maggie. Fighting for the rights of our people. Delaney was an enemy of The Cause. He was an oppressor, and he deserved to die, and you... you helped him escape. You betrayed your own people, your own family..."

"What about Mrs Docherty? Was an old woman an enemy of The Cause? What about the women and children you slaughtered? Were they oppressors? You're no soldier, Sean. You might have believed in The Cause at the beginning, but you... you're just a thug. And now you think you are some kind of leader, is that it? You're going to kill more innocent people, are you?"

Sean shook his head and laughed, but Maggie could tell she had got under his skin. "It doesn't matter what you think of me. What matters is I have found you and now you are going to pay for what you did." Maggie felt some satisfaction that she'd rattled Sean, but his threat hit home and she struggled not to show her panic.

Sean stepped forward and brought his head close to her face. She could smell his stale breath as he whispered, "I know where your children are, Maggie. I know everything about you."

"You leave them alone," she replied, her voice trembling with a mixture of fear and rage. "They're just children, Sean. They have nothing to do with this."

"Guv?"

Sean straightened, and Maggie saw Liam standing behind him.

"What?"

"Delivery. It's here."

Liam looked at Maggie tied to the chair, and immediately dropped his eyes.

"I'm coming," Sean said. Before he turned away from Maggie, he reached out his hand and stroked her cheek. "Don't worry," he muttered. "I'll be back." A hot tear ran down Maggie's cheek as he turned away from her.

As Sean's footsteps echoed away, Maggie twisted her hands to see if she could loosen the rope. But it just bit into her skin. It was the same around her ankles. There was no way she could escape from this.

Maggie hung her head and allowed tears to flow. How had Sean found her children? How had he found her, after all these years?

"Hello, Maggie. Nice to see you again, my dear. Are you enjoying your family reunion?"

Father Brennan was standing in front of her, grinning. And then it all made sense. The newspaper article. Maggie remembered the first visit she'd had from Father Brennan—if he was a priest at all—and how he'd held the newspaper clipping in his hand.

"It was the newspaper, wasn't it?" she said. "That's how Sean found me."

Father Brennan chuckled. "Ah, Sean couldn't believe his luck. He's always talked about his little cousin, Maggie, and how she betrayed him. And what he'd do to her if he ever found her. And here you are, in the same city! Does the Lord not work in mysterious ways? Connor Byrne told us about a woman who rescued her daughter and who told him she was working for the British Government. And then there was the picture of your beautiful daughter, who is the image of her mother. It was easy to piece together after our little visit. Sean thought you had died in the bombing, but then, there was a miracle. You came knocking at our door. An undercover agent to replace Dowd. The poor deluded Detective Chief

Inspector Robert Delaney actually gave you back to Sean on a silver platter. A genuine miracle."

"Sean is the leader of this… gang, then?" Maggie sneered back at the priest. "You trust him to run your little campaign? You think you'll get away with it, with him in charge?"

"Look around you, my dear. You're sitting in the middle of the biggest stash of explosives in all of Europe. Hitler himself hasn't got as much as we do."

The almond smell. It was gelignite, Maggie realised.

Father Brennan followed her eyes. "Yes, don't move around too much," he grinned again. "That stuff could blow at any time."

"Not all of it," Maggie said. She'd spotted another stack of crates that didn't have fragile signs on the sides like the others. She nodded her head towards them. "Whisky. Black market, I suppose. Sean's a drunk like his father. Did you know that? He's bound to have made mistakes. He'll take you down with him."

Father Brennan threw back his head and laughed. "Oh, Maggie, Sean didn't give you enough credit. You are indeed an intelligent woman. But, I fear," he wagged his finger at her, "not intelligent enough."

He pointed at the whisky crates. "Sure, that's just a little business on the side. Just one more delivery of explosives tonight, then they get shipped out tomorrow, and while the British are trying to defend themselves from Hitler's new toys, we'll be hammering them from their own turf. They'll not know what hit them."

"What are you going to do with my children?" Maggie hissed.

Father Brennan shrugged. "I'll bring them to you, of course. A mother and her children should not be parted. And then… bang!"

He clapped his hands as he said the last word. "Sean will have the pleasure of detonating the last bomb. He's waited a long time for his revenge. I think he deserves it, don't you?"

Maggie could hear Father Brennan's laughter echo around the warehouse and fade as he walked away, leaving her alone and helpless.

Chapter 36

SCOTLAND YARD, LONDON.

When Delaney arrived at Scotland Yard on Monday morning, he sat at his desk and pulled out his notebook and file on Conner Byrne. His visit to see the condemned man had been a waste of time, but he needed to do something, to find something, which would move this investigation forward.

He flipped through the pages of his notebook. Byrne had given nothing away. Delaney remembered the contemptuous sneer on the man's face when Delaney offered him the chance to clear his conscience and reveal the name of the man who ran his IRA unit, or any information which might prove useful.

Byrne preferred to be a martyr to his cause.

Delaney had checked with the prison guards one more time for the records for any information on Byrne's visitors, but there was nothing. Just his priest, the guards had told him, arranging for his last rites before Byrne's date with the hangman.

But Delaney could not shake off the feeling that Byrne was mocking him with those last words as he left the cell.

May the road rise to meet you.

It wasn't a coincidence, Delaney knew. He'd heard those words from Maggie many times. It was almost as if it were a secret code between them. And Maggie hadn't shown up for the meeting at the tea shop. There was something wrong.

Delaney picked up the telephone receiver to call the tea shop. Maybe Maggie had been in later and left a message, but before he could dial the number, there was a knock at the door, and Constable Hunter came into the office without waiting for Delaney to invite him.

"Constable? What is it?"

Constable Hunter looked worried. "It's Mrs Berkley, sir. She hasn't turned up for work today. I came up to the office this morning to see you, and I thought she might be delivering a message or something, but I've been back twice and she still isn't at her desk. The duty sergeant on the front desk says he hasn't seen her, and nobody else has either."

"I see."

Hunter was still agitated. "The thing is, sir..." He hesitated.

"Go on, Constable, what else?"

"Birdie, I mean Miss Carroll, she didn't turn up for her shift today."

"What? Are you sure?" Delaney sat upright. Now his feeling of unease turned into worry.

"Yes, I know I shouldn't have, sir, because I was on duty and I shouldn't have taken the car, but with Mrs Berkley not at work, I was worried..."

"You did the right thing, Constable."

"I asked at the front gate of the factory if Birdie had arrived this morning, and she hadn't clocked in."

Delaney was already moving. "Phone the nearest station and get some uniforms around to Mrs Berkley's house. And get the car, Hunter. We'll meet them there."

Two police constables were on Mrs Berkley's doorstep when Delaney and Hunter arrived.

"No answer?" Delaney called to them as he hurried up the steps.

"No, sir. The blackout curtains are still up, so we can't see in," one officer said.

"Right. We're going in. You lad," Delaney gestured at the bigger of the two officers, "put your shoulder against that door. Quick as you like."

The officer obliged, and after two hefty blows at the front door, it gave way.

"Oh, dear Lord," Delaney breathed at the sight of Mrs Berkley's body crumpled on the floor in the hallway.

"You check on her, sir. We'll look for Birdie." Hunter was behind him as Delaney knelt beside Mrs Berkley's still body.

"Mrs Berkley? Diane?" Delaney used her given name for the first time in over twenty years, as he checked for any signs of life. He picked up her wrist and thought he felt a weak pulse.

"We need an ambulance. Get next door and see if they have a telephone."

One of the officers appeared. "Right you are, sir," he replied and hurried away.

"No sign of Birdie," Hunter said breathlessly, returning to Delaney's side. "Not in the house, anyway. I'll check the back garden and behind the house."

Delaney nodded and sat on the floor, with his back resting against the hallway wall, holding Mrs Berkley's hand and willing her to live.

Billy Hunter made his way through the kitchen to the back of the house. There were muddy footprints on the tiled floor, from work boots, he guessed. At least two pairs. There had been the same marks on the polished wood floors upstairs. But apart from the hallway where Mrs Berkley lay, there was no sign of any struggle.

On the kitchen table were two bowls with scrapings of dried porridge and empty teacups. One chair was lying on its side as if someone had pushed it over in a hurry.

Billy had first met Birdie when she'd just been abducted by Connor Byrne. She'd been shaken and upset, but she was no shrinking violet. He could tell that.

He doubted that she would have left this house without a fight. Maybe, he hoped, maybe she had run when she heard Mrs Berkley confront her attacker.

Mrs Berkley was a courageous woman. She'd have fought off fire-breathing dragons to protect Bernadette Carroll, Hunter was sure. She might have gained Birdie enough time to escape.

Billy went through the scullery to the back door. It led into a fenced, narrow garden with a path to a gate, which Billy guessed opened into an alleyway. He moved as quickly as he could to it, but it was bolted shut.

Strange, he thought. If Birdie had run through the gate, there was no way she could have bolted it behind her. And if her would-be attackers had chased her, then they wouldn't have come back and taken the time to lock the gate.

The fence was too high for anyone to climb over and there was nothing to stand on.

Billy turned and walked back into the house where he stood in the scullery. He could hear the ambulance sirens in the distance. What had he missed? Had Birdie left before the attackers arrived? Was there another reason she wasn't at work today? Could she have taken a day off and in a while, she would appear and wonder what all the fuss was about?

He shook his head and muttered to himself, "No chance. She loves that job."

He heard the ambulance arrive outside the house and Delaney's voice calling out. Then Billy thought he heard something else. A tapping sound? He stood still and listened carefully. Yes, he could hear a tapping or knocking sound coming from where? The walls?

"Birdie?" he shouted, hardly daring to hope. "Birdie, is that you? Where are you?"

And then he heard her muffled voice. "Down here. The coal cellar."

Billy saw the metal hatch in the corner. He rushed over and pulled it open.

Birdie's dirty face, streaked with tears and smeared with coal dust, peered out at him from the gloom.

"Birdie! It's alright, you're safe now."

Chapter 37

JUNE LANE, MIDHURST, WEST SUSSEX

The winter sun streamed through the window, casting a warm glow over Mrs Hazelton's living room. At the large oak desk in the corner, Patrick and James sat hunched over a piece of paper, their faces screwed up in concentration as they took turns dipping a quill into a small pot of ink.

"Careful, Jimmy," Patrick said as he watched his brother's hand hover over the page, his tongue poking out of the corner of his mouth in concentration. "Don't spill it."

They were not supposed to be in the living room. Mrs Hazelton was visiting a neighbour and had told them to play outside. But after a while, the boys were bored with playing hide and seek in the garden and trudged back into the house.

Mrs Hazelton allowed them into the living room for an hour before bedtime. She let them play with the tin soldiers and model tanks—especially the one that fired matchsticks—but they weren't supposed to be in there all alone.

"We're not alone," Patrick pointed to Baxter. The little dog had become a happy co-conspirator and was perched on Mrs Hazelton's favourite armchair, in equal defiance of the house rules.

For a while, the boys had played 'War' with the soldiers, emptying matchsticks on the rug and taking turns to attack each other with the tin tank. But they had quickly tired of that game and had looked around for something else to amuse them.

The desk fascinated them. They'd watched Mrs Hazelton sit at the desk and write a letter with the ink pen and had admired the way her hand swept over the page, producing curvy handwriting they'd never seen before.

They'd begged her to try, but she had shooed them away. "No, the ink can be very messy," she said. "I'll find you something else to draw with."

They had both stared at the desk and the pot of ink. Jimmy had succumbed to temptation first. He'd pulled open the drawer and found the pen and a piece of paper.

"I won't spill it," he said, sticking his tongue out at his brother and lowering the pen to the paper at the same time with exaggerated care. "I'm not like you, always making a mess."

Patrick opened his mouth to retort, but before he could speak, Jimmy's hand slipped, and the inkpot tipped over, sending a stream of black ink cascading across the desk and dripping down the wall and onto the carpet.

"Oh, no!" Patrick cried, jumping back from the desk in alarm.

For a moment, both boys stared at the ink pool, frozen in fear, their eyes wide. Then Jimmy said urgently, "Quick, Pat, help me clean it up before Mrs Hazelton sees."

The twins sprang into action, grabbing a stack of blank paper from the drawer and using it to mop up the spill. They worked quickly, their hands moving in a blur as they tried to soak up as much of the ink as possible.

So engrossed were they in their task that it took a while to notice that Baxter was standing on the chair, his ears pricked and his fur standing on end.

"What's the matter with him?" Jimmy asked, holding a bunch of ink-soaked paper in his hand, stopping to look at Baxter.

The dog was growling now, and his whole body was vibrating.

"Never mind," Patrick said. "We have to clean this up."

"Look, there's someone outside," Jimmy pointed at the window, and Baxter barked.

The twins froze. There was a man peering in. Baxter leapt off the chair and was on the floor, bouncing his small body up and down in front of the window, barking frantically.

The man disappeared.

Jimmy and Patrick ran to the window and saw the man hurrying down the path. Baxter calmed down and trotted back to the chair.

"Who was that?" Jimmy wondered.

"I hope he won't tell on us," Patrick whispered. "Come on, we need to clean this up."

In a few minutes, the boys surveyed their work. "That looks alright," Patrick said, jamming soggy paper into a wastepaper basket under the desk. "She won't notice a thing."

Jimmy agreed. "Let's go back outside." Baxter followed the boys back into the garden, and within minutes, they had forgotten the accident with the ink and the man at the window.

Chapter 38

MULGRAVE ROAD, SHREWSBURY COMMON.

Delaney hadn't liked the grim faces of the medics as they loaded Mrs Berkley into the back of the ambulance on a stretcher.

"Can you notify her family, sir?" one of them asked just before he slammed the door. "They should be at the hospital as soon as they can."

Delaney didn't have time to tell him that there was nobody. Just her work colleagues. But as he watched the vehicle speed away, he realised that Mrs Berkley was his family. And he'd failed her. It was a complete lack of judgment to allow Birdie to stay here. He should have insisted that the girl go with her brothers. He'd put both Birdie and Mrs Berkley in danger, and this was the result.

The significance of the events of the morning was dawning on him. Maggie's cover must be blown. Somehow, the gang had discovered where Birdie was staying. And now she was missing. God, Maggie would never forgive him.

"Sir! Sir!"

Delaney turned to see Constable Hunter and a dirty figure, black with dust from head to foot, leaning on his arm.

"Found her, sir. In the coal cellar."

"Oh, thank God." In a few steps, Delaney was beside them and he wrapped his arms around the shaking girl, holding her close as she sobbed into his chest.

"I thought I was followed on Friday night," she explained, her voice muffled by his coat. "On my way home from work. I told Mrs Berkley about it, and she said she was going to report it to you. But she never got the chance."

Delaney's heart sank. If Birdie had been followed, if someone had been watching her movements, then they were all in danger.

"Can you tell me what happened?" he asked, and he listened as Birdie told him.

"Where's Mrs Berkley?" she asked when she had finished. "Is she alright?"

Delaney shook his head. "I'm afraid not. She's on her way to the hospital. And that's where you need to go."

Birdie shook her head. "No, I'm not hurt. I'm just dirty. And besides, we need to tell my mother. She could be in danger. If those men knew where to find me, they might know about her."

Delaney knew she was right. "Let's get you back to the Yard," he said. "Get cleaned up while Constable Hunter and I question the neighbours, see if they saw anything that we help us. Then we'll get your mother out."

It wasn't difficult to find Mrs Berkley's neighbours. A white-haired lady from the house next door had appeared when the ambulance arrived. A small group of onlookers had watched in silence as it drove away and had murmured in shock as Birdie had appeared with Constable Hunter.

Delaney strode over to the group while Constable Hunter helped Birdie back into the house and then stood to attention at the doorway. Nobody gets in here, was the message his body language projected. The way Billy Hunter had gently comforted young Bernadette hadn't escaped Delany's notice.

He turned his attention to the curious group of neighbours.

"Is Mrs Berkley going to be alright?" the white-haired lady asked, as Delaney approached.

"We certainly hope so," he replied. "I'm afraid Mrs Berkley and her... er... niece, have been the victims of intruders. Did anyone see anything at all? We think the incident happened yesterday morning as early as seven o'clock."

"More like six thirty," a gentleman piped up. "I'm always up early, and I thought I heard banging. I live over there." He gestured with his head to the opposite side of the road. "I saw two gentlemen knocking on Mrs Berkley's door. Strange, I thought to myself, who would visit this early in the morning?"

"And you didn't think to raise the alarm?" Delaney asked, trying not to sound impatient.

"Course not," the man said. "When I saw who it was, I thought, well I never, I didn't know Mrs Berkley was one of them lot, but perhaps that's what they do? Anyway, I thought, none of my business. But if I'd known..." The man's voice trailed off and Delaney could see his eyes were glistening.

"Sir, I don't understand. What do you mean, 'one of them... I mean, those lot'?" Delaney was confused.

"You know, one of them Catholics."

Delaney blinked in confusion again before the light dawned. "You mean it was a priest knocking at the door? You saw a priest?"

"That's right. But he couldn't have been a priest, could he? Not if he hurt Mrs Berkley. A man of God couldn't have done that," the man said, pulling out a handkerchief and dabbing at his eyes. 'I should have..."

"You weren't to know, sir," Delaney tried to comfort him. "And you've been very helpful indeed. One of my constables will take a statement."

"I saw a priest hanging around here the other day," the white haired lady said suddenly. "I remember now. I thought he was visiting the lady down the road. Staunch Catholic, she is, never misses church on Sunday, but he did stop outside Mrs Berkley's house. I remember 'im because he had bright red 'air."

"Thank you all very much," Delaney said. "Here's my card. Please contact me if you think of anything else, and we will definitely be in touch soon."

It was late in the evening when Delaney, Hunter and Birdie arrived at Scotland Yard.

Constable Hunter helped Birdie to a chair and went to make her a cup of tea. The poor girl was exhausted and tearful and kept asking about her mother.

Delaney wanted Birdie to be somewhere safe where she could rest from her ordeal, but he also needed to ask her some questions.

"Birdie, I need you to think carefully. The neighbours said they saw a priest outside Mrs Berkley's house. He had red hair. Does that mean anything to you?"

Birdie composed herself and straightened up in the chair.

"Yes," she said slowly. "Ma told me about a priest who visited her. Just before the bomb. He left before I got home from work but Ma was worried about it." Birdie scrunched her face up and thought for a moment. "I think Ma said his name was Father Brennan."

"But why was he there?" Delaney knew Maggie was Catholic, of course, and priests often visited their congregation, but this was too strange.

"I didn't really know why," Birdie said. "We aren't regular churchgoers, but Ma said something about him wanting to pray with me and give me spiritual guidance. After the murders and when I... you know..." A tear ran down her cheek. "He'd seen a picture of me and you in the newspaper after you caught Conner Byrne. That's why he came to see us."

Then she looked at Delaney, a look of horror on her face. "A priest attacked Mrs Berkley. He knew I was there. And it's something to do with Connor Byrne."

"We don't know for sure," Delaney said, but everything was falling into place and Delaney felt he was tumbling into a dark abyss. He stood up, and for a split second, the room swam and he swayed. He gritted his teeth and gave his head a slight shake. He needed to focus.

"Are you alright, sir?" Hunter looked concerned.

"Yes, Billy. I'm fine." Delaney looked at his watch. "I need to catch Whaldon before he leaves the office. Billy, can you find somewhere for Birdie to stay tonight?"

"Yes, sir, I can take her to my Auntie Marge. She'd love the company."

"Excellent. Now listen, take her in the car. Not the bus. And make sure she's out of sight. And keep an eye out in case you are followed. If you think you have a tail, drive straight back here and stay with her in my office. Do you understand? I'm going to Whaldon's office."

"No need," came Whaldon's gruff voice. "I'm right here, Bob. What's going on here? I heard that Mrs Berkley has been injured. Is that true?"

"Yes, sir. I'll explain everything," Delaney said before he turned back to Birdie. "Birdie, don't worry. I'm sure your mother is fine. Just go with Constable Hunter and do everything he tells you."

He sounded confident and in charge, but Birdie stared at him in disbelief. "Those people came after me, and Ma is doing something dangerous for you. You need to get her home." Her voice rose slightly.

Delaney's face must have given his worry away, because Birdie started to cry.

"What's going on? Please tell me?"

"Birdie, please go with..." He stopped.

Delaney could hear the telephone from down the corridor, and he ran as fast as he could to grab the receiver before the ringing stopped. Birdie got up and followed him, with Hunter behind.

"Delaney," he barked and then listened to the voice on the other end, while Hunter and Birdie stood listening to his side of the conversation.

"What? Why am I hearing this only now? Oh, Oh I see. Are there officers on the way? Right... right, I'll get someone there as soon as I can."

Delaney replaced the receiver on the hook. This was a nightmare. For a moment, he was transported back to that terrible Sunday morning in 1920, when the military precision planning of evil men nearly took his own life. Maggie McVeigh had saved him. Now he needed to save her and her children.

"Constable, please take Miss Carroll to your Auntie Margie if you would be so kind," he said, not wanting to worry Birdie with the message he'd just received. "Then please report back here."

Constable Hunter took Birdie's arm, but she shook it off and looked Delaney in the eye. "That telephone call was about my mother, wasn't it?" she said quietly. "I want to know what's going on."

Delaney sighed. Birdie was just like her mother. It was no use lying to her.

"No, Birdie, the message wasn't about your mother. It was Special Branch. Mrs Hazelton, the agent assigned to look after your brothers, didn't check in tonight at the usual time."

"What happened?" Birdie's hand flew to her mouth, and the other gripped Hunter's arm as if to hold herself up.

"They don't know yet. Agents have been dispatched, but they haven't reported in yet with news..." His voice trailed off, and Delaney rubbed his face with his hands while he tried to get his thoughts in order.

This had all been planned. It had to be. First Maggie not showing up, the attack on Mrs Berkley, and now the boys. The gang must have known about Maggie for some time and—he clicked his fingers as something occurred to him.

"How did they know where the boys are?" He looked at Hunter. "Could they have followed us to the briefing.... no, no that makes little sense, we didn't know the address until we were there, so they couldn't have..."

"Oh," Birdie cried. "Oh, no..." She bent over as if she was going to collapse.

"Birdie, what is it? Tell me?" Delaney and Hunter helped her to a chair.

"I wrote a letter to my brothers," she said. "I left it in the hallway to post. They must have found it."

Delaney cursed inwardly. "It wasn't your fault," he told Birdie. "But now I need you to go with Constable Hunter and let us do our job."

Chapter 39

SCOTLAND YARD, LONDON.

"Let's go to your office, Bob. We'll sort this mess out," Whaldon commanded after Birdie and Hunter finally left.

"I don't understand," Delaney said, after explaining the events of the day to Whaldon. "Why would they go after the boys? Or Birdie? If Maggie's cover was compromised, why didn't they just kill her?"

One look at Whaldon's face reminded him that Maggie could already be dead.

"Sorry, ol' chap, it might be too late. We have to prepare for that possibility. And the boys and Birdie?" Whaldon shrugged. "In my experience, evil bastards don't need a good reason for anything they do, but if I had to guess, I'd say they were sending us a message, letting us know how clever they are, that sort of thing."

"So what do we do, sir? I think we need to get her out of there. If she's still... you know."

Chief Superintendent Whaldon pulled his pipe out from his inside pocket and put it in his mouth, chewing on it thoughtfully.

"Let's get the boarding house under surveillance, see if we can spot her, or at least put a tail on anyone coming or going. And let's get that fellow Knowles in custody. Make him sweat for a bit. Tell him we can connect him to Dowd's murder. Perhaps the thought of hanging from a rope might loosen his tongue."

"I can arrest him for his black market booze," Delaney said grimly, "and then lean on him a bit."

"Good man. Now, what about that information from the Hoxton boys about the warehouses on the Docks? Have they said anything else? If they are not holding her at the boarding house, they may have taken her there. Any progress on that front?"

Delaney shook his head. "Not much. I had Hunter going through all the owners of warehouses to see if we can find any connections, but we just don't have the manpower to watch them all. I'll try to contact Harry Coster. See if his men can dig around again.'

"Right you are then, Bob." Whaldon took the pipe out of his mouth and pointed it at Delaney. "Now, I know you are fond of our Mrs Carroll, and I understand why, but we can't lose sight of our mission." He paused and softened his tone. "Don't allow her good work to go to waste, Bob. It can't be in vain."

Don't let her die in vain, was what he was saying, Delaney realised.

Whaldon stood up. "I'll be in my office. Keep me updated, Bob."

As he turned to leave, there was a knock and the duty sergeant put his head around the door.

"Sorry to bother you, sir. There's a lady at reception. Says she needs to talk to you. She says it's urgent."

Delaney shook his head. "I'm too busy right now, sergeant. Take a message, please."

"Sir, I was going to do that, but the lady insisted. She said to tell you, it has something to do with a Mrs Carroll. She said you'd want to know."

"Please take a seat, Mrs... er?"

"Mrs Bernstein, officer."

Delaney offered the woman a chair, and she sat down, clasping her handbag in her lap. "I'm so sorry to bother you, Mr Delaney and I know it is terribly late, but I was so worried, and well, I know your name from all that nasty business last year, and how you helped poor Birdie. I saw your picture with that brave girl in the newspaper. Well, I worried and worried all day and last night I couldn't sleep at all, so tonight I knew I couldn't go to bed without doing something, so I got a taxi and came here. It's a relief you are still here."

Delaney smiled as reassuringly as he could. "It's perfectly alright Mrs Bernstein, please tell me what has worried you so much."

"It might be me imagining things, Mr Delaney, but I was so certain something was wrong as soon as I saw Mrs Carroll yesterday. Then I thought, no, maybe it's just me..."

"You've seen Mag.... I mean Mrs Carroll? Yesterday?" Delaney felt a rush of relief and adrenalin all at once. "Where was she?"

"That's the strange thing, Mr Delaney. She was in the market with a priest and a rough-looking fellow. Now, if it was just the priest, I wouldn't worry, but this other fellow... I didn't like the look of him at all..."

Delaney sat up straight at the mention of a priest. "Did you speak to Mrs Carroll at all?" he asked, trying to keep the impatience out of his voice.

"I am just coming to that part," Mrs Bernstein sniffed.

Delaney bit his lip and nodded, wishing that Mrs Bernstein would get to the point, but he could see she needed to tell the complete story.

"I said hello, but Mrs Carroll seemed to be in a hurry. She said the man was a handyman or something, and that made sense, but just as I was walking away, Mrs Carroll took my hand and said something very strange."

Mrs Berstein took a deep breath and recited, "She said to remember me to Mr Bernstein and to tell him, and these were her words; Until we meet again, may God hold you in the palm of his hand."

"What? I mean… pardon? Are you sure that's what she said?" Delaney asked, frowning.

"Yes, officer. Her exact words. I've been repeating them over and over, so I wouldn't forget."

Delaney stared at her. "And what made you think something was wrong with that, Mrs Bernstein?"

"Well, Mr Delaney, my husband died in the same bombing raid that buried Mrs Carroll and her children. And I told Mrs Carroll about that when I saw her the first time, just a day or so ago. She was very kind. I can't believe she would have forgotten."

Delaney nodded slowly. Maggie was trying to send him a message, he was sure.

Mrs Bernstein was still speaking. "I was so happy to see her the first time. I thought her and her family had died in the bombing. I even went to the Catholic Church to see if Father Thomas had seen or heard from her. But he hadn't. And when I saw her, well, she seemed distracted, which is understandable, of course, but I thought it very odd that she said her children were staying with relatives in the country. I know this about Mrs Carroll…" She leaned forward to emphasise her words. "She would never be parted from her children. Never."

Delaney closed his eyes, trying to make sense of what he'd just heard. Then something clicked in his mind. "The priest who was with her today, was it Father Thomas?"

"No, no, a younger man. With bright red hair. But he just left her with the other man when I was talking to her."

The priest. Mrs Berkley's neighbours had seen a priest with red hair. And now Mrs Bernstein had seen Maggie with a priest. Who was this damn priest? Then he remembered another mention of a priest.

"So I hope I've done the right thing, Mr Delaney? I do hope I'm not wasting your valuable time," Mrs Bernstein sounded worried.

"You are not wasting my time, Mrs Bernstein," Delaney reassured her. "You've done the right thing by telling me all this. Now, did Mrs Carroll mention the priest's name at all? Or the other man's name?"

"Not this time, Mr Delaney. But when I saw her the other day, she was surprised that I'd spoken to Father Thomas. She said another name. Now, what was it? Oh yes, Father Brennan. It might have been him. And she didn't say the other man's name at all. She just said that he was a handyman. But he didn't have any tools that I could see."

After Delaney reassured Mrs Bernstein that they would make sure Maggie was safe, he asked a constable to escort her out and call a taxi. Then he raced back to Whaldon's office.

It all made sense now.

"I've got a name," he announced. "Father Brennan. A priest. Connor Byrne's only visitor in prison has been a priest."

And he told Whaldon about Mrs Bernstein's meeting with Maggie earlier in the day.

Whaldon nodded. "Right, I'll get on to MI5. Anything else useful?"

Delaney rubbed his face with his hand. "Just something Maggie said to her. It sounded like a poem?"

He repeated Mrs Bernstein's words. "Until we meet again, may the Lord hold you in the palm of his hand."

"That's an Irish blessing, Bob. It actually goes, May the road rise up to meet you.

May the wind be always at your back.

May the sun shine warm upon your face;

the rains fall soft upon your fields and until we meet again,

may God hold you in the palm of His hand."

Delaney stared at him. Clever, clever Maggie.

"It must be a message to me, sir. And I think I know what it means."

Chapter 40

JUNE LANE, MIDHURST, WEST SUSSEX.

Audrey Hazleton stood in her back garden and watched the sun dip below the horizon and cast shadows over the fields. She waited while Baxter ran around, growling and chasing any rabbit that dared to hop among the rows of raspberry canes.

It was late afternoon and in a while, she'd go inside and make the boys some tea. Later, when they were tucked up in bed, Audrey would make her usual nighttime telephone call. "The babes are asleep in the woods". Just one short message to Special Branch. If she missed it, an agent would be dispatched to check on her and the boys.

She smiled as she thought of the twins. They were good boys, polite and intelligent. When they first arrived, they were quiet and withdrawn, suffering from the trauma of the bombing Audrey assumed. And they must miss their mother and sister.

She'd taken one look at their pale faces and knew they needed to play in fresh air, away from the worry of air raid sirens.

The twins were both fascinated with the old Cowdray Ruins. "Is it haunted?" Patrick had asked, his eyes wide.

"No, but legend has it that a monk once cursed the old castle," Audrey said solemnly.

"What's a monk?" the boys asked in unison, and then spent the next hour badgering Audrey with questions about the castle until she promised to take them to look at the ruins. "If you are good boys, and take Baxter for a walk every day, we'll go the first day it's not raining, when it's not too muddy."

They hadn't needed much persuasion to look after the little dog. They fought over who would feed Baxter and hold the lead when they walked him until Audrey had made them take turns.

The third day they'd been there, she kept her promise. It was a rare sunny afternoon in February, and Audrey thought it would do the boys good to be outside.

"We'll walk across the fields," she told them. "See that oak tree in the corner of the field? There's a path which runs nearly all the way to the ruins."

It had taken an hour to follow the trail until they reached the River Rother, which wound its way in front of Cowdray Ruins and the outskirts of the town.

The boys had been disappointed they couldn't get near the ruins and explore the tumbled-down turrets and moss-covered boulders.

"Why aren't we allowed?" Jimmy had asked.

"See those tents?" Audrey pointed to the rows and rows of green canvas tents that stretched behind the ruins. "Those are army tents. The military is using the land. The soldiers are training to fight in the war. Every one of them will fight so that we can be safe."

"Like Daddy?" Patrick asked.

"Yes, like your daddy and lots of other brave men."

"Mrs Grenfield said the stinking Irish are cowards," Patrick said matter-of-factly. "She was our neighbour. Once I kicked our ball into her garden and she called us dirty tinkers."

"Mrs Grenfield doesn't sound like a nice person," Audrey said.

"She wasn't. The bomb got her," Jimmy said.

"Well, nobody deserves that. Even if she said nasty things. And those things are untrue. There are plenty of brave Irishmen who are fighting the war. And you two are brave. You looked after your mother and sister when that bomb fell, didn't you? That was very brave."

Later on, Audrey noticed the twins scrapped their plates clean, and colour was returning to their cheeks. She noticed something else too, when she went into her living room.

Patrick and James both looked a little sheepish.

"Have you boys been playing in here?" she asked sternly.

They both shook their heads, but wouldn't look at her. The dog hair on the armchair and the toy bus left poking out from under the desk told a different story. Then Audrey noticed the stain on the carpet and the wastebasket full of her best stationery, soaked in black ink.

"Boys!" she said sternly. "You mustn't tell lies. Did you have an accident with my inkpot?"

The twins confessed. "We're sorry," Jimmy said. "We tried to clean it up."

She was about to send them upstairs to bed early, but Patrick raised his head and said, "There was a man in the garden."

Immediately, Audrey was on the alert, but she kept her voice calm. "Was there, dear? Did he say what he wanted?"

"We didn't ask him," James said. "We were cleaning the ink up." And he hung his head.

"It's alright boys," Audrey said. "Don't worry about the ink now. Tell me, did the man look in the window?"

They both nodded.

"Right. You are good boys to tell me. I expect the man was selling something. Nothing to worry about. Now, one of you brush the dog hair off my armchair, and the other one pick up the toys in the living room. Do you hear me?"

Obviously relieved to not have been punished for their transgressions, the twins hurried off to do as they were told, leaving Audrey deep in thought.

Audrey didn't want to worry the boys, so she let them play for a while in the living room. They didn't mention the man again, and finally, she chased them up the stairs to bed, making them giggle.

When the boys were sleeping soundly, she went into her bedroom and opened the wardrobe. She cleared out the shoes on the bottom and felt around the edge until she found a metal catch. When she pressed it, the false bottom of the wardrobe clicked open, and she lifted it out. Underneath in a metal box was the pistol and box of bullets issued to her by Special Branch. She took the pistol out and held it for the first time in many months. The Welrod pistol was small and it fit her hand nicely. The chamber held six rounds, and Audrey took out the box of bullets and fully loaded it. She hoped she was being overly cautious, but she wanted to be prepared for anything.

Then she carried the gun downstairs and went outside. Baxter trotted after her. As Audrey waited for her dog to finish snuffling around the garden, she knew she had to report the man to Special Branch, even if he turned out to be a travelling salesman. She couldn't take any chances. All she had been told was to protect the boys, as their mother was an asset to the British Intelligence Services. She didn't need to know any more to do her job.

Baxter ran over and wagged her tail. Audrey smiled down at her companion.

"Come on, Baxter, let's do a perimeter check."

In the dark, Audrey walked around the house, checking that the windows were secured. When she and Baxter went back into the house, she locked the front door behind her and secured the bolts, top and bottom. She set the gun down on the side table in the hallway and then went into the kitchen to lock the back door. Baxter followed.

Audrey stopped by the kitchen sink. She took a glass from a cupboard and turned the tap on, letting the water run for a moment. She filled the glass and took a sip.

Then she stopped. Had she heard something? It sounded like leaves rustling, but there wasn't any wind. Whatever it was, Baxter had heard it too, because the dog faced the kitchen door, his ears pricked, and his legs trembling.

Audrey heard it again. But it wasn't rustling. It was the soft thud of footsteps on cobbles and it was coming nearer. Baxter gave a soft, ominous growl, and Audrey let go of her glass and let it crash to the ground before lunging at the door to turn the key.

It was a split second too late. The door burst open and a man's silhouette filled the frame. Audrey turned to run. The man reached to grab her, but he didn't reckon on contending with an angry terrier who went for his calf and sunk his teeth through his trouser leg and into his flesh.

It gave Audrey enough time to run into the hallway to grab her gun. The man was quick, though. He'd yelped with pain as Baxter bit him, but he grabbed the dog by the neck, wrenched him off his leg, and flung the dog across the room.

As Audrey reached the hallway, she heard a thud and then a whimper from her brave companion.

Her hands closed around the gun. She cursed herself for her amateur mistake. She should have had the gun with her at all times. She had the gun in her hand as she wheeled around and pushed the bolt down to chamber a round, but before she could take aim and fire, the man was on top of her.

He grabbed her wrist and banged it with force against the wall, and she gasped with pain as the gun fell from her grip. She opened her mouth and screamed at the top of her lungs.. "Boys! Run, run..."

Instantly the man clasped one hand across her mouth and her nose, cutting off her air supply, and with the other arm pinned her against the wall.

He brought his face close to hers, and she could feel his warm breath against her face. "Now, darlin', we'll have none of that. I don't want to hurt yous, I just want the wee boys."

With her lungs burning, and knowing she wouldn't have much time before she passed out, Audrey drew her knee up and drove it with as much force as she could muster up between his legs.

"You... bitch..." The man screamed in pain and let her go momentarily. Audrey threw herself at the gun which lay on the floor and, for one joyous second, her fingers curled around it. She spun around and was sure she'd got a round off, but then, there was a crashing pain on the back of her head, and she found herself falling into a dark black void.

Chapter 41

JUNE LANE, MIDHURST, WEST SUSSEX.

"What was that?"

Patrick sat upright in his bed. "Jim, did you hear that?"

"What? Go to sleep," his brother said groggily. "It's nothing."

"I thought I heard Baxter bark."

"It's a rabbit in the garden. Baxter hates rabbits. Go back to sleep."

Then they both heard the crash of breaking glass, followed by heavy footsteps.

Both boys sprung out of bed and towards the bedroom door. Then they heard Mrs Hazelton scream.

For a moment, Jimmy and Patrick huddled together in the upstairs bedroom, their hearts pounding with fear. Downstairs, they could hear a struggle and the crash of furniture.

Patrick clutched at his brother's arm, his face pale and his eyes wide with terror. "What's happening?" he whispered, his voice trembling. "What do we do?"

Jimmy shook his head. "I don't know," he said, his own voice shaking. "But we have to get out of here. We have to escape."

Suddenly, there was a sharp cry from downstairs, followed by a heavy thud.

Patrick let out a whimper of fear, but James shushed him quickly. "We have to be quiet," he whispered, his mind racing as he tried to think of a plan. He pointed to a chair in the corner of the bedroom. "Help me," he said, and they pulled the chair over to the door and jammed it under the handle.

James' eyes darted around the room, searching for a way out or somewhere to hide. He could already hear footsteps on the stairs.

"The window," he whispered, tugging at his brother's arm. "We can climb out onto the porch roof, and then jump down into the garden."

Patrick's eyes widened with fear.

"Come on, Pat," Jimmy urged. "Mrs Hazelton said we are brave. Don't you remember?"

Patrick nodded. "Okay," he said, his voice small and scared. "Let's do it."

Moving as quickly and quietly as they could, the boys made their way to the window. James pushed it open, wincing at the creak of the old hinges, but there was no time to worry about that now.

James climbed out first, his heart pounding as he balanced precariously on the narrow ledge of the porch roof. Patrick followed close behind, his face white with terror.

For a moment, they crouched there, listening to the sound of the man moving through the house below. And then, gathering all their courage, they inched their way along the roof, towards the corner where the bushes grew underneath.

It was a perilous journey, the roof slick with damp and their hands shaking with fear. But somehow, miraculously, they made it to the edge and then dropped down into the bushes below.

The branches and twigs tore at their thin bedclothes and skin, but the boys barely noticed. They were too busy running, their hearts pounding and their lungs burning as they raced through the garden, towards the fields that stretched out beyond the fence.

Behind them, they could hear the shouts of the men, the thud of their footsteps growing closer. But the boys didn't look back, didn't stop to think about what would happen if they were caught.

They ran, their legs pumping and their chests heaving, across the muddy fields until the shouts faded into the distance. The shadows of the hedgerows rose up around them like a wall, and they collapsed to the ground, their bodies shaking with exhaustion and fear.

For a long moment, they lay there, gasping for breath and trying to make sense of what had happened.

"What do we do now?" Patrick asked. "Where do we go?"

Jimmy reached out and grabbed his brother's hand. "Come on," he said. "I have an idea."

Chapter 42

SCOTLAND YARD, LONDON.

"Palmer's Warehouse at the West India Docks," Delaney said to his Chief Superintendent an hour after Mrs Bernstein left Scotland Yard.

Constable Hunter had returned, and Delaney and he had spent the time pouring over a map of the London Docks, from the East End of London to the Isle of Dogs.

"You're certain, Bob?" Whaldon sounded skeptical. "How do you know?"

"That blessing," Delaney said firmly. "That time, in Dublin, when Maggie saved my life, the first line of the blessing was the last thing she said to me when we parted. 'May the road rise up to meet you', she said. And then again, a couple of days ago, she said that again before she went undercover. Maggie said that it was something that her Aunt Peggy always said to her. Then Byrne said it to me when I met him. I don't know if it was just a coincidence, but I am now certain that Byrne, McClary, and whoever else is involved in this group knows about Maggie and her past. But Maggie didn't quote the first line to Mrs Bernstein. She used the last line, 'May the Lord hold you in the palm of his hand until we meet again'."

"It wasn't quite accurate, either," Whaldon pointed out. "She said, Lord, rather than God."

"Exactly. I think she was sending me a message. She knew Mrs Bernstein would know something was up when Maggie sent her regards to her dead husband. I think Maggie was trying to tell me where the delivery is being made. And the only name that makes sense on this map is Palmer's Warehouse at the West India Docks. And maybe they are holding her there too."

Delaney hoped Maggie was there. He hoped she was still alive.

"Alright," Whaldon said. "Let's get the men together."

The inky blackness of the night enveloped the West India Docks, broken only by the faint glow of the moon occasionally peeking through scuttling clouds. The air was thick with the acrid smell of smoke and the lingering odour of rotting fish and other spilled cargo.

The docks were a maze of warehouses, some of them pockmarked with scars from previous bombings. The shattered windows gaped like soulless eyes, their jagged edges glinting in the moonlight. The eerie stillness was broken only by the gentle lapping of the water against the docks' edges and the creaking of the wooden pilings, as if the port were sighing under the weight of the war.

Palmer's Warehouse was intact. Vehicles were parked outside, but so far, they hadn't seen any men.

Delaney and his men had approached in silence. No sirens, he'd instructed. He wanted the element of surprise. A sergeant whispered to Delaney that nobody had located Bill Knowles. The Leinster Arms was closed. So Delaney had no intelligence to work with except his own hunches. It would have to be enough.

In the darkness, Delaney and the armed police and agents that Whaldon had gathered after a phone call to MI5 moved on foot to surround the warehouse. They spread out, and Delaney took a position near the entrance.

"We wait and watch for movement," he'd instructed. "Then I'll give the signal to raid the warehouse."

Delaney crouched as low as possible so he wouldn't cast a shadow. He thought he could hear the muffled sound of voices and edged nearer to the warehouse. He dropped to his knees to crawl a little further when he heard a rustling behind him. He turned his head, but a cold metal object was pressed behind his ear.

"Don't move," a raspy voice said. "Stay there, Detective Chief Inspector, on yer knees."

Maggie felt faint. Sunday morning was the last time she ate anything, and she calculated it must be near the end of Monday. Liam had held her head and poured some water into her mouth, but that had been hours ago, and now her lips were cracked and her throat was parched.

There had been lots of activity around her all day. Men were in and out of the warehouse. Occasionally, Sean would shout at them, "Careful with those bloody crates. Do ya want to blow us all sky high?"

Maggie thought about her children. It wasn't possible Father Brennan knew where they were, was it? She hoped that Mrs Hazelton would keep them safe. And Birdie? She missed her daughter so much.

The warehouse was now nearly empty of crates and the men were mostly silent, milling about as if waiting for something.

Sean came over to Maggie with the lantern. The light cast shadows over his face and gave him a monstrous appearance as he crouched down so their faces were level.

He was grinning.

"Maggie, it's a real shame we haven't had time to chat more. But as you can see, we've been busy. And now it's time to go. In a short while, it will all be over for you. They'll not find much of you, I'm afraid... after the warehouse blows."

He indicated to one crate that remained. "I saved that just for you."

Maggie spat in his face. "You'll get what's coming to you, Sean."

Sean chuckled and wiped his face with his hand. Then he straightened up. "Now, what was it you and Ma used to say to each other? Oh yes, I remember." He mimicked a woman's voice. "May the road rise to meet you," and then he laughed.

"Tommy, what the hell are you doing here?" Delaney demanded. The damn Hoxton Mob, they could mess up the whole operation.

"I could ask the same of you, Detective Chief Inspector," Tommy said, but he lowered his shotgun and allowed Delaney to stand. Then they both retreated back into the darkness, away from the warehouse.

"You've got men with you?" Delaney asked, ignoring Tommy's question.

"'Course I 'ave. You lot didn't see a thing. We've got this place surrounded." He jerked his head towards the warehouse.

"Tommy, you have to stand down," Delaney said urgently. "That warehouse could be full of explosives, and we possibly have an operative in there."

"Yeah, I know. A woman, right? We've bin watching all day. We 'ave to move soon."

"How did..." Delaney sighed, "Tommy, this is dangerous. Get your men out of here, and we'll say no more about it."

Tommy chuckled. "No can do. Mr Coster gave us orders. We 'ad a nice chat with our mutual friend Bill Knowles, and turns out, there's a nice lot of booze in there which is rightfully ours. Or it is now, anyway. So, we're going in. We'll get our booze and we'll warm 'em up for you. Then you can nick the Paddies after that."

"Tommy, no..." Delaney said, but Tommy was already moving away from him. Before Delaney could do or say anymore, he heard a loud whistle and men materialised from the shadows, running towards the warehouse.

Chapter 43

PALMER'S WAREHOUSE, EAST IN DOCKS, LONDON.

A loud crash drowned out Sean's laughter.

He swung around and dropped the lantern. It smashed on the floor and rolled, plunging the place into darkness. Maggie struggled against her restraints, terrified the crate of gelignite would explode at any moment.

There was shouting echoing around the warehouse and then the sound of a shotgun blast deafened Maggie and she closed her eyes, thinking that surely this was the end.

The smell of gunpowder hung in the air, but then a light appeared. A man with a toothy grin was standing, holding a lantern and a shotgun. He was with other men who were also armed, their guns pointed at Sean's gang.

Sean was clutching his shoulder, blood seeping through his fingers.

"Well, now," the man with the shotgun said, "you bog trotters 'ave been busy, 'aven't you?"

"This is nuthin' to do with you," Sean gasped. "Get out and leave us be."

The man walked forward and punched Sean in the face. Maggie winced when she heard the crack of Sean's teeth as he sank to the ground.

"That's better," the man declared before he kicked Sean, in his stomach who lay on the concrete floor, groaning.

The man walked over to Maggie. 'What 'ave we here? I don't think this is any way to treat a lady." He set the lantern down on the ground and untied her.

"Get outta here quick," he whispered in her ear. "A friend is outside waiting for ya."

Maggie stood and wobbled on her feet, but she forced her legs to move towards the entrance.

She heard the man behind her say, "All we want is our booze..."

Then Maggie felt the warehouse shake. A low rumbling sound was getting louder. She didn't stop to look back. Maggie ran out the door into the darkness.

"Get down!" Delaney shouted. "It's an air raid!"

He didn't follow his own instructions. This was the only chance he had to rescue Maggie. He started to run towards the warehouse, but then he heard a shrill screaming noise and the night sky over the docks was lit up.

The Luftwaffe had dropped a bomb on the other side of the Thames, but the ground shook underneath Delaney as the low-flying aircraft swooped down over the warehouse. The noise of air raid sirens filled the night.

Delaney's face was in the dirt, but he picked himself up and saw a figure running towards him. From the warehouse entrance, men were running in all directions. The figure stumbled and fell and cried out in pain.

"Maggie!"

Delaney grabbed Maggie's hand and pulled her to her feet. As he did, a blast rocked the docks again. Delaney felt heat on his face, and then there was debris raining down on him and Maggie.

"Explosives," she gasped. "In the warehouse and the vans."

Together, they ran from the flames until they felt the arms of other police officers guiding them to safety at last.

Chapter 44

JUNE LANE, MIDHURST, WEST SUSSEX.

"You should have gone to the hospital," Delaney admonished. He was sitting in the passenger seat of the police car. The driver was focused on the road as the car raced through the countryside. Delaney was swiveled around in his seat, looking at Maggie, concern in his eyes.

Maggie shook her head. "I'm fine." She felt the throb of the swelling around her left eye, where a piece of metal had hit her, but she didn't care. Not when the boys were in danger.

She clutched her hands tightly in her lap, her knuckles turning white as she silently prayed. The thought of them being hurt or worse was unbearable.

As soon as she was able to speak when she was huddled with Delaney on the docks, she'd said, "My boys. They're going for my boys."

Minutes after that, she and Delaney were in a car, weaving their way from the docks, avoiding the ambulances that were racing to the scene.

Delaney was still speaking.

"The local constabulary will be there, Maggie. They were dispatched as soon as we knew something was wrong."

Maggie nodded but didn't respond this time. She hoped Delaney was right, but she'd heard what Sean had said. The attacks were all planned. His anger at her had festered for two decades. He wanted to make sure she felt as much pain as he could inflict. Sean may have failed to kill her and Birdie, but his men in Midhurst were still steps ahead of the police.

Maggie clung on to the hope that Mrs Hazelton had been alerted to the danger and had moved the boys to safety, somewhere out of contact.

That would be it, Maggie hoped. They are all safe, they just couldn't telephone yet.

They reached Midhurst at the first light of dawn. The car roared through the cobbled North Street and swung right into June Lane.

Seconds later, the car slowed, and even before it came to a complete stop, Maggie opened the door and got out, running up the narrow path towards the line of terraced cottages.

"Maggie, wait," she heard Delaney call after her, but she ignored him.

Maggie's breath caught in her throat as she neared Mrs Hazleton's home. The front door stood ajar. She raced up the path, nearly tripping over a bicycle, which was lying on its side.

"Stop right there," a voice came from inside the house, but she kept moving.

Before she could get inside the house, a grey-haired man in a police uniform appeared and held his hands up.

"Stop there, Miss. You can't come in here,"

Maggie looked in horror at his hands. They were smeared with blood.

"My boys, my boys..." she choked out.

"What? There are no boys here, just a terrible..."

"Officer, move aside, please." Delaney was by Maggie's side, holding up his identification for the officer to see.

"Sir, it's bad in there. The doctor…"

Maggie pushed past the man, but the moment she stepped inside, her worst fears were confirmed. Mrs Hazelton's body lay crumpled in the hallway, her eyes closed. Her small dog, Baxter, was whimpering by her side.

Her heart ached for Mrs Hazelton, but she couldn't help her now. She had to find her boys. "Jimmy? Patrick?" Maggie shouted as she ran from room to room.

The boys' bedroom was empty.

"Where are they?" Maggie heard her voice coming from far away as if she were inside a nightmare and couldn't wake up.

"We'll find them."

Delaney had followed close behind. "It looks like Mrs Hazelton was shot. There's been a struggle. There would have been lots of noise, the dog would have been barking at an intruder. The boys are clever and resourceful, Maggie. Here, look…"

The bedroom curtains moved a little and Maggie felt a breeze.

"The window's open." Delaney moved forward, pulled the curtain and looked out. "Look," he said, pointing to the porch roof below. "A slate has been dislodged. They must have climbed out this way."

Maggie's heart leaped with a sudden surge of hope. If the boys had managed to escape, then perhaps they were still alive, still out there somewhere waiting to be found.

"Let's go," Delaney said. "Check the garden shed and the outhouse, and the neighbour's too. I'll get the officer to arrange a search party. We'll find them Maggie. We'll find them."

Maggie hurried down the stairs. A man wearing a coat over his pyjamas and slippers was in the hallway. He had a doctor's bag with him and was bending over Mrs Hazleton.

"She's alive," he was saying as Maggie ran out the front door. "But barely."

Maggie checked the outhouse and the garden shed. There was nowhere to hide in the garden. The trees and bushes had no foliage yet, so the boys couldn't have found shelter out here. She looked out over the fields behind the cottages and just saw ridges of ploughed dirt stretching into the horizon, broken only by farmer's tracks and the gathering of oak trees in the distance. Could the boys have got that far?

As Maggie stood in the garden, struggling to calm her frantic thoughts, a weak February sun climbed high enough to cast fingers of light through the clouds.

That's when Maggie spotted it. A small patch of blue material caught in the fence. She ran over and grabbed the fabric. It was from Jimmy's pyjamas. She'd sewed them herself.

"What is it?" Maggie turned to see Delaney hurrying towards her.

"Look," she said, holding up the material, "they must have gone over the fence into the fields."

"Maggie," Delaney said, pointing over the fence. There were large boot prints in the mud.

"Oh, no." Maggie's hand went to her mouth.

"But look again," Delaney urged. "The prints go back and forth, but I can't see them leading off anywhere."

He looked at Maggie and squeezed her arm. "It was dark. I bet the boys got over the fence and ran for it. Whoever attacked Mrs Hazelton must have been too late. He guessed they went over the fence, but it was too dark for him to chase them. They will hide somewhere, Maggie, I'm sure of it."

"I hope so," Maggie said.

"Mrs Hazelton has lost a lot of blood, but she's conscious. Let's see if she can tell us anything that can help."

They both raced back inside the house.

"Stay back, please,"

The doctor was still kneeling beside Mrs Hazelton. "This woman is going to the hospital. The ambulance is on the way. She's in no fit state to answer questions. You'll have to wait."

"Doctor, move aside. There are two boys missing. We must speak to Mrs Hazelton."

The doctor grunted his annoyance, but moved enough for Maggie to crouch down beside the injured woman.

"Mrs Hazelton, the boys are missing. We think they escaped, but we don't know where they might have gone. If you know anything, please help me."

Maggie heard Mrs Hazelton take a rasping breath, and she bent lower, so her ear was near Mrs Hazleton's lips. The one word she heard confused her.

Maggie repeated it back and took Mrs Hazelton's hand in hers. "Is that what you said? Please squeeze my hand if you can, if I've got it right."

Maggie felt a light pressure on her hand.

The doctor tapped Maggie on the shoulder. "The ambulance is here. We need to move her immediately."

Maggie stood up and two medics lifted Mrs Hazelton onto a gurney and went out through the door.

"What did she say?" Delaney was waiting. "Some neighbours are here. They want to help, and their local knowledge will be useful."

"She said 'castle'," Maggie replied. "I do not know what that means." She covered her face with her hands.

Delaney grasped her shoulder and said firmly, "Maggie. We will find them."

Then he turned to the police officer and group of neighbours who had gathered in the front garden.

"Can any of you tell me about a castle in the area? Or a Castle Road, or Street? Anything that comes to mind?"

"The nearest castle is Arundel Castle, but that's miles away," the police officer said.

"Anything that might look like a castle to two young boys?" Maggie asked, her voice cracking. "Please think. Anything at all?"

"I suppose the old ruins might look like a castle," one man said.

"That's it!" Maggie exclaimed. "The ruins. The boys were fascinated by them when we arrived here."

"I think Mrs Hazelton took them to the river just the other day," a lady said, who had shuffled up the path in her slippers. "Those two young'uns wanted proper bows and arrows so they could pretend they were knights, Mrs Hazelton told me. But the ruins are being used by the army, I think. Nobody is allowed in at the moment."

"That must be it," Maggie said. "Would they be able to get there across the fields?"

"'Course they could. The tracks take 'em right down to the River Rother, and then they would see the bridge. It's a fair walk mind."

Maggie and Delaney were already running to the car.

"It looks like a military training facility," Delaney said when their car came to a stop in front of the gate, which was locked with a chain.

They both got out of the car.

They could see a track beyond the gates leading up to the Ruins and rows of tents.

"What do we do now?" Maggie said. "How do we get in? Maybe the boys didn't get this far. We should search the fields. Maybe they found a hiding spot somewhere."

Or maybe Sean's men caught them. She pushed that thought away.

"Let's go. We could be wrong about this," Delaney agreed, and they turned to go back to the car.

"Hey! You there!"

A man in army uniform was running along the track towards them, on the other side of the gate.

"I'm Sergeant Haden. Who are you?" he said when he got near. "I'm expecting the police and an ambulance."

"I'm the police," Delaney said and pulled out his identification.

"Right, sir. We have the prisoner ready for you."

"Prisoner? No, you are mistaken," Maggie said. "We're looking for two young boys."

Sergeant Haden nodded gravely. "Then you had better come with me."

"Ma!"

Patrick and Jimmy both ran to Maggie and flung their arms around her waist. "We caught a robber," Patrick said. "He chased after us and we led him here, and then he tried to shoot us, and then…"

"Oh, my boys," Maggie cried as she hugged them tight.

"The soldiers gave us some tea," Jimmy said. "And they showed us their guns and everything."

"Well, that was very nice of them," Maggie replied, wiping tears off her cheeks. "I told you both that you'd have a grand adventure, didn't I?"

The sergeant had brought Maggie and Delaney to the Mess Hall, where the twins were being fed and entertained by a group of young trainee soldiers.

"You said something about a prisoner?" Delaney asked Sergeant Haden.

"Yes. We apprehended him when we heard the boys shouting for help, down at the gate," he explained. "We thought it was a prank, and we were about to send the boys on their way, and then a man came out of nowhere and started shooting. One of our men shot back and hit him in the leg. It's just a flesh wound. We've administered first aid and confiscated his weapon. But he refuses to say why he was shooting. He refuses to talk at all."

"I can explain everything, Sergeant, and I will send someone to escort the man to the hospital and then to London. But first, we need to get these boys home."

Maggie looked up, her arms still clutched around the twins. She smiled. "Home, Robert? I'd forgotten. We don't have one. But I don't care. We are all alive."

Chapter 45

SHREWSBURY COMMON, LONDON.

The sun was warm on Delaney's face as he stood with the mourners at Diane Berkley's funeral. She may not have had a family of her own, he thought, but many officers from the police force, past and present had filled the church and listened as Delaney gave the Eulogy.

"Every single day, she did her duty, as she saw it," he'd said. "Never complained, never shirked, always loyal. She never expected praise or sought glory, but in my mind, she was a war hero."

When he'd looked up at the congregation, he saw heads nodding and heard a murmur of agreement. At the back of the church, he caught the eye of Chief Superintendent Whaldon, who acknowledged him with an approving nod. Delaney hoped that Mrs Berkley would have been pleased with his words, although he suspected she would have not liked the 'fuss'.

After the funeral service, they all filed out to stand beside the grave as the vicar delivered the simple words of the graveside service as the coffin was lowered.

Maggie was there with Birdie and the boys. Constable Hunter stood behind Birdie, and Delaney noticed with a smile the protective way Billy patted the girl's shoulder.

Special Branch had been as good as their word, and Maggie and her family had been re-housed in a new pre-fab on the outskirts of Plumstead Common.

"I thought you wanted to be in the countryside. Why did you choose to stay?" Delaney had asked. Maggie shrugged and pointed to her boys. "They have had enough adventures in the countryside. Birdie refuses to give up her job, and me? Well, London is home. George will expect us to be here, waiting."

"I'm glad," Delaney had said. "It will be good to have my old friend nearby."

In line with Mrs Berkley's wishes, there was no gathering once the religious ceremonies were over. She considered wakes to be in poor taste, so Delaney was heading straight back to the office. He thought Mrs Berkley would approve of that arrangement.

Delaney thought he had already done his grieving at the funeral. When he arrived at the office and saw Mrs Berkley's neat desk and covered type-writer, it hit him hard for the first time that he would never again hear Mrs Berkley's brisk "Good morning," or look up from his work to see her delivering a cup of tea in the good china. He would miss her more than he'd ever imagined, and Delaney had to take a private moment alone in his office to compose himself.

Carrying on the work which Mrs Berkley had valued so highly was the best way to pay tribute to his loyal friend and employee, so Delaney pulled himself together to tackle the pile of files on his own cluttered desk.

"Connor Byrne," he muttered, grabbing the first one from the top of the pile. This file was closed. Byrne's execution date had been set. Under the Treason Act of 1940, he was sentenced to hanging. But appeals were still pending, and Delaney suspected Byrne would languish in prison for a long while.

Special Branch, with the help of Delaney and Maggie Carroll, had thwarted a major attack on England's defences against Germany, but the Prime Minister himself had expressed concerns about sentencing Sean McVeigh, and the surviving gang to death. Sean McVeigh had survived a gunshot wound and miraculously was found alive under fallen debris from the destroyed warehouse. McClary hadn't been so lucky.

"He's worried about repercussions," Whaldon told Delaney. "The deterioration of Anglo-Irish relations, if these men are hanged. More likely, they'll be deported," he'd said, taking a draw on his pipe. "Now, don't look so outraged, ol' chap. That's the way of it, I'm afraid."

Delaney had the satisfaction of charging Father Brennan with two murders, and if convicted, he would be swinging from the end of a rope. At least justice would be done for Patrick Dowd and Mrs Berkley. Delaney was sure that Brennan wasn't alone in the murders, but Dr Holberg's groundbreaking analysis of the fibres left on Dowd's body and Mrs Berkley could be matched exactly with the priest's cincture, the special rope which was part of the priest's vestments. Mrs Doyle had confirmed that Father Brennan was a frequent visitor to the boarding house and that the silver lapel pin, which Maggie had found, belonged to him. It was a satisfying amount of evidence against Brennan.

The Hoxton Mob had not lost any men, but all the booze was destroyed. Tommy was unhurt and grinned at Delaney when he visited the Regal Rooms.

"Wot a night," he laughed. "Never 'ad so much fun."

Harry Coster shook Delaney's hand. "There's a delivery for you at Vine Street Police Station," he said. "And now, Detective Chief Inspector, I believe our business is concluded. It's been a pleasure."

Delaney didn't agree, but he was pleasantly surprised to find a battered and beaten Bill Knowles at Vine Street. Coster's men had dumped him there.

Knowles would be charged with treason.

Delaney worked through his files, updating his notes and completing reports, until the light outside had dimmed enough for him to get up and arrange the blackout curtains.

Before he did, he stood at the window and gazed at the Embankment, the River Thames, and the glimpse of the Parliament buildings before the river bank swept left and out of his view. How long before the river boats were decorated with lights, and couples could walk along the river without the fear of air raid sirens?

The secret war against the IRA might be ended, for now at least, but how long would it take to defeat Hitler? He hoped for an answer soon.

PLUMSTEAD COMMON.

The white box kite dipped and curved and swooped like a giant bird above them.

Delaney squinted up at the blue sky and shouted instructions at Patrick and Jimmy, who were holding on for dear life to the wooden handles, as the kite caught the wind.

"Pull a bit more on your side, Jim... there she goes... and now your side Patrick... good, lads. See how she flies?"

Delaney moved as fast as he could to keep up with the boys, as they raced across Plumstead Common on the warmest day of the year so far.

Maggie and Birdie sat on a blanket they had laid out under a tree, and they laughed at the boys' and Delaney's antics while watching people strolling on the common, enjoying the sunshine.

This beautiful day in July was a blessing, Maggie thought. There was a time when nobody believed there would ever be an end to the relentless bombing. She watched the boys play with the kite and was glad they were all able to snatch a few brief hours of joy whenever they could, not knowing when the next reprieve would come. Hitler had indeed leashed his unmanned V-1 bombs, but thanks to the defences on the Dover coast, the impact had been far less catastrophic than feared.

The tide had turned, the newspapers were saying. A month ago, Churchill had rallied the country with his most rousing speech yet, and in a dangerous mission, with England's allies had launched their biggest offensive against the German army. The sheer daring and audacity of the invasion had lifted the morale of the entire country.

"We will never give in," Churchill had declared, and England now believed him.

People were walking the streets of London with their heads up, resolve and purpose in their demeanour.

Delaney had further case to celebrate.

"There was a knock at the door," Delaney had told Maggie earlier, with tears in his eyes, "and there he was."

Robert Jr. had been on leave for just a few days, but his brief visit had given Delaney a new vigour.

Maggie had wanted to visit Mrs Hazelton to thank her for saving her sons, but Special Branch had issued orders they were not to meet.

"They don't like agents fraternising outside of official business," Delaney explained when they met in his office. "It might compromise future missions."

"There'll be no future missions for me." Maggie was emphatic about that. "Please retire my file forever."

"Maybe no undercover missions," Delaney had suggested, "but what about a job?"

Looking at her confused face, he led her out of his office and down the corridor until they were standing in front of the empty desk, once occupied by Mrs Berkley.

"I have a vacancy," Delaney said, gesturing at the desk.

Maggie stared at him in amazement. "Robert, you can't be serious? I have never typed a word in my life. Sure, I can make a grand cup of tea..."

"I don't need you to type," Delaney told her. "In these times, a secretary is a luxury. I've been doing my own typing and filing and making tea ever since..." He took a breath. "Maggie, I need a team member. Somebody who can work alongside myself and Hunter to solve crimes."

"Robert, I don't know about a job," Maggie said. "What about the boys? There's no Mr. Larkham anymore to keep an eye on them." Her face clouded with sadness as she thought about the kindly gentleman who'd been so fond of her twins.

"Oh, we can work around that, I'm sure. I've already talked to Whaldon. He agrees, if you do?" Delaney had looked at her hopefully and when Maggie didn't respond, he said, "Think about it, at least, Maggie."

And Maggie was thinking about it, as she leaned against Birdie, and closed her eyes in the sun's warmth, letting the sound of her boy's laughter wash over her.

She must have dozed off, because the next thing she knew, Birdie was shaking her shoulder gently. "Ma, come on, the boys are getting hungry. We should go back and get their tea."

They all walked back to the small pre-fab house they now called home. Maggie missed the old Victorian terrace house on Patterson Road, but the pre-fab was less drafty, and it came with a new stove, and the height of luxury, a tiny inside privy. It was a fresh start, and Maggie reminded herself every day how lucky they were.

Delaney walked with them, carrying the kite, teasing Birdie gently about her new beau, Constable Billy Hunter.

The sun was in Maggie's eyes and all she could see was a silhouette of a figure when they neared their house.

"There's a man outside our house," Patrick said and Maggie shaded her eyes. "Is he waiting for us?" she wondered out loud.

Delaney put his hand on her shoulder. "Maggie, he is waiting for you." His voice was sad.

Maggie looked at Delaney's face and wondered why he looked so grave. It wasn't a man; it was a boy and he couldn't have been much older than the twins, Maggie thought. Then she saw he was holding an envelope in his hand.

"Mrs Carroll?" the boy said and held out the envelope. Maggie's heart lurched. "No," she whispered.

"Mrs Carroll?" the boy asked again. "It's a telegram for you."

Author's Note.

While writing this story, I discovered it is a delicate balance between keeping the plot as exciting as possible, without compromising too many historical facts.

For all the history buffs who have come to the end of my story, I ask for your forgiveness, for all the times I bent the facts to suit my purpose and for any mistakes I have made.

For those of you who are not history experts, let me sort out some facts from fiction.

The S-Plan or Sabotage Plan was a series of attacks on England by the IRA during 1939 and 1940. Many people were injured and at least five people were killed in coordinated bombing campaigns across the country.

The IRA abandoned the plan because of a lack of resources and enhanced security measures in England. Some perpetrators were apprehended and sentenced to hang.

As far as I am aware, there were no bombings or plans after 1940. That part of my story is entirely fiction.

Chief Superintendent Charles Whaldon is loosely based on Robert Fabian, a legendary police officer and detective between 1921 and 1949.

The Hoxton Mob existed, and Alfie Solomon was the leader for a short time before he was murdered. They were most active in the 1920s and 1930s. Harry Coster is a fictional character.

To my knowledge, MI5 did not use the King Edward VII Hospital in Midhurst during the war.

Audrey Hazleton was inspired by my Auntie Audrey Bilham, who lived in June Lane, Midhurst. She didn't work for MI5, but I bet she could have, if she'd wanted.

Last, Maggie McVeigh is, of course, a fictional character. She was based on my grandmother, Margaret Bilham (nee Carlon). My grandmother was born in Belfast but was sent to live with relatives in Dublin when her mother, Mary McVeigh, died. My grandmother left Ireland when she was a very young woman. We know very little about her life, except for small anecdotes (being thrown out of a Jewish household for cooking bacon was one!). We know she married my grandfather in 1926 and they had nine children.

In 1944, my grandfather was stationed in the Orkney Isles, and my grandmother lived in Plumstead with the family, a short walk from the gates of the Woolwich Arsenal.

A bomb hit their house, and my grandmother and her seven children were buried in their air raid shelter. Miraculously, they were all rescued, including the youngest, a six-month-old girl called Kathleen, who is also my mum.

I hope that my brother, my surviving aunts and uncles, and my cousins will not mind me taking liberties with our family history.

About the author

Jackie Sharp is the author of crime fiction novels.

When she was seven, she read her first Nancy Drew story and was hooked on mystery stories forever.

Until 2004, Jackie considered herself a true city girl, and then she emigrated to Canada and settled on Vancouver Island. She is now married to Bob, a commercial fisherman and accomplished storyteller – like most fishermen! Jackie got over the culture shock (eventually) and now, not one of her work colleagues in London would recognize her helping to clean fish and smoke fillets of salmon.

Her first crime series, (written as Jackie Elliott) was inspired by the small fishing communities on Vancouver Island and features the fictional town of Coffin Cove. Hell's Half Acre, the second in the series was shortlisted for a Crime Writer's of Canada Award of Excellence in 2022, in The Whodunit Award for Best Traditional Mystery. The series is published by Joffe Books.

She also loves to write warm cozy mystery or historical crime stories, the kind you can read with a large mug of tea and a slice of cake on a rainy afternoon.

Jackie is passionate about local history, and her ideas are often prompted by an afternoon browsing around a museum, or by digging back into her own family history.

When she is not writing or reading, you'll find Jackie waging war with the weeds in her garden, hanging out at the beach, or volunteering for the local Maritime Society.

You can stay in touch with Jackie by visiting her website: www.jackiesharpauthor.com

Also by Jackie Sharp

Also By Jackie Sharp.

Murder at the Marina

Death on the Dock

Writing as Jackie Elliott

Coffin Cove

Hell's Half Acre

Hope Island

The Vile Narrows

House of Lies (2025)